Life for a Life

A Pact Novel

D. Brumbley

Other works by D. Brumbley

The Eleusis Cycle
The Initiative
The Rebels
The Fugitives
The New World

The Ironborn Cycle
The Ironborn Claim
The Heartborn Mate
The Lightborn Queen

The Broken Isles
Rise with the Tide
Run with the Wind*

Pact
Life for a Life
Love for a Memory
Live for Today*

*forthcoming in 2026

To Krista
for being the first and best
of all possible advance readers.

CONTENTS

ONE

Before

Rocking back and forth on her feet, all Molly could feel was anxiety. Chewing on her bottom lip, she pushed her thick-rimmed glasses higher on the bridge of her freckled nose as she peered into the bar from the outside. The evening was chilly, but still she hesitated, even though she knew her boyfriend was inside waiting for her.

He said he would have a drink while he waited, and then they could grab food and head out, since he knew she didn't particularly care for crowds. While she watched she saw a waitress in a tight t-shirt laugh at something Tony said, and his charming smile encouraged a brief graze across his elbow when she walked away. He didn't look anxious, or fazed, and he didn't even seem to notice when the waitress walked back to a friend and pointed him out with a smile behind the bar.

But Molly noticed.

Tony was too good for her. Too charming, too smart, too hot with his hipster glasses and arms that proved his strength and muscles underneath. The waitress was out of her league as well. How she had managed to snag Tony, she still wasn't sure. Her wavy, mousy brown hair was almost always a mess, and she never could figure out makeup, other than the occasional lip gloss. Often she spent her time in jeans, an oversized t-shirt, and converse shoes.

A lot of her time was spent in a dark room developing photos, and in the red glow, it didn't matter what she wore or how much makeup she had on. All that mattered was the black and white art floating in the dektol that eventually made it into a picture frame. She wasn't that smart, she wasn't a conversationalist, but she found her home in photographs.

Every moment frozen in time was re-imagined by whoever gazed upon it, and that, to Molly, was magic.

Well. Until she met Tony.

Magic had taken on a new meaning recently.

After building her resolve to head into the crowded bar, she pulled her hair back and walked in, making a beeline for her boyfriend. "Hey." She mumbled when she was close enough, even though it was loud. "Sorry I'm late."

"Hey, no, you're alright." Tony slid off his stool to pull her in when she got to him, giving her a quick kiss as he hung onto her at the hip. He was grinning as he took a handful of her oversized shirt, quietly possessive of her while also teasing her for what he had referred to before as her 'uniform'. "Did you have to wait a while for a ride on the way over here?"

She shook her head but melted into him easily when he pulled her in, all too happy to have him as a human shield from everything and everyone. Tony was the first real friend she'd had in a long time, and when they became something more, he became her everything. Her parents were all too glad to be rid of her when she went off to college, the accident that she was in the first place. The last holiday season she had spent with Tony instead of her own parents. "Rideshare was a little behind, but nothing crazy."

"I don't have anything for that, I'm sorry to say. Being on time has never mattered to me enough to try and . . . you know." He took his seat on the stool again and reached a hand up to scratch his arm just under his sleeve. There was the faintest glimpse of a tattoo below his sleeve, the lower few spokes of a stylized wheel with flames surrounding it.

Molly's gaze snagged on the glimpse of the tattoo but she eventually cleared her throat and reached for his drink. Even though she hated beer, she took a gulp anyway. "I'm not worried about . . . that." She remained at his side, grateful that he was still holding on to her when the waitress came back.

"Ready to order, hot stuff?" The waitress had strawberry blonde hair and a figure that had the attention of every man around them, women too. "Looks like your friend finally made it." Even the waitress' smile was perfect, almost blindingly white.

"You heard her, hot stuff, what're you hungry for?" Tony turned it back on Molly with a smile, pointedly not looking at the waitress. "I just need some potato skins, I think. And some water. We may be here a while."

"A club sandwich and some fries." Molly responded afterward as she eyed the waitress, who clearly had eyes for her boyfriend. Before the beautiful snake could slither away, Molly leaned into Tony's ear. "I thought we could get the food to go?"

"Oh, yeah, sure." He got out his wallet and started counting out cash. "You're right, walking and talking would probably be better."

She watched the waitress disappear to put in their order to go, and she relaxed again. She had an undeniable pull to women and men, but Tony was hers, and she didn't need anyone vying for his attention. Molly felt bolder around women, safer, but just barely. Anxiety and self-consciousness kept her from saying much to anyone at all. "Everywhere you go. I bet she thought I was your sister at first."

"I don't have a sister. And if I did, I wouldn't have the fantasies about her that I have about you." He kept his voice down to keep the conversation between them private, but he couldn't help the smirk on his face. Getting a blush from his intensely-shy girlfriend was too much fun for him to pass up.

As her cheeks burned with both embarrassment and desire, she leaned in to kiss him gently. "I still don't understand you. But I . . ." Molly pressed her forehead to his. "I love you." The noise around them fell away for just a moment, but she knew it wouldn't last. Anxiety was always a breath away, even in the special moments. It wasn't the first time that "I love you" came from her mouth, but usually she was too afraid to say the words very often. She didn't want to scare him off.

"I love you too, Molly." His hand tightened its grip on her shirt, as if to keep her from running away. He always seemed nervous about that, for reasons he had never explained. "I hope you still feel the same way after you know . . . a little more about where I came from." His look went down to his sleeve again, nervous as always about the mysterious tattoo hiding beneath it.

Molly had seen too many strange things happening around him, and he finally promised he would explain everything to her, as well as he could. But he was clearly just as nervous about the conversation to come as she was about everything else in life.

"Whatever you have to say won't change how I feel." Molly wasn't confident about much, but she was confident that Tony was her person. She didn't want to lose him. If there was a way she could be sure she would never lose him, she wished she could find it.

It wasn't long before the waitress returned, this time with their food in a bag and without a smile. Tony left cash on the receipt and they shared the rest of his beer to finish it off before they headed out of the bar. He had a car, at least, while she walked everywhere around campus and lived on student loans that would eventually drown her. He lived right off campus in a studio, but she lived in the dorms. Molly clung to his arm as they walked toward his car. "Your place or mine?"

"Up to you. Mine has a bigger bed." He grinned, doing his best not to be nervous about the conversation to come. "And fewer roommates. Though my neighbors have been a pain in the ass lately. All kinds of loud all night and day. Guy can't get much sleep."

Molly kissed his cheek before they walked up to his car, holding onto the food as he unlocked the door and opened it for her. "Your place. And stop looking so nervous. It makes *me* nervous."

He stood beside her door as she slid past him to get into it, shaking his head. "As much time as I spend telling you not to worry about things? This is . . . this, is something worth being nervous about. Anybody who isn't nervous about this thing is . . . doing something very, very wrong with their lives."

He closed the door for her and went around to his side, starting the car and pulling away from the bar to get back to campus. As he settled in, taking deep breaths, he put a hand down on her thigh to hold onto her as he drove with one hand, eyes on the road but thoughts clearly swirling.

She glanced over at his expressions a few times as they drove, but they didn't talk on the short drive back to his place. After silently climbing up the stairs into his studio apartment, Molly left her converse by the door and plated their food before she set it down on his tiny table. She grabbed a previously-opened bottle of wine and poured a glass for them both. "We can talk about it over food and wine, right? Food and wine makes everything better."

"They do, that's true." He went to the table with her and took a seat while she poured the wine, though he was looking more at her than he was at the food. He met her eyes as she finished pouring, then put out a hand to gesture at the kitchen drawers across the room.

One of the drawers slid open as his fingers beckoned to it, and a handful of forks and knives bundled themselves together, floating in a jumble across the room as she watched. They drifted down onto the table as if set into their proper placement by some unseen waiter. It was one of the first times he had ever done anything so openly around her, but he was clearly trying to remind himself that he had promised openness and full disclosure for the evening.

"That one," he began tentatively, "is . . . actually one of the easier ones to balance out, so long as I don't try and push around anything too extreme. I just can't move from wherever I am for a while if I use it. Mobility for mobility." He balanced the statement by swishing his wine from one side of his glass to the other before taking a sip of it.

It was amazing that Molly only managed to spill a few drops of wine on the faux-wood table, but she grabbed a paper napkin to wipe it up once she wasn't worried about being impaled by floating silverware. Her breaths were shallow, and she couldn't respond at first when she took her seat at the table. "I might need you to pinch me so that I know this is real." Molly's hand trembled a little as she grabbed her glass of wine. "Other than real weird."

Antony just grinned and flicked one finger, at which her fork picked itself up and poked her arm gently before it drifted back on the table beside her plate. "It's both. Real *and* real weird. Even to me, and I've been living with weird for a long while now."

Her initial reaction was to freeze when a floating fork poked her in the arm, but she reached for a french fry once the fork was still again. "A long while? So . . . you're experienced with this . . . I mean, is it magic? Do you call it that?"

"People call it a lot of things. I personally try not to call it anything if I don't have to. Magic doesn't feel quite right, but it's as good a word as any." He almost reached for his wine again, but settled for one of his potato skins instead. "All it is, at the end of the day, is balance. There's lots of people like me who would come down hard on me for oversimplifying it like that, but it's true. I don't have a magic wand, I didn't study it in some kind of school, and I wasn't born with it. It's given, from one person to another. It's a little more like measles that way than magic."

"Measles." She wrinkled her nose but cleared her throat and pushed up her glasses again as she stared down at her food momentarily. When she looked across the table at him again, she studied him carefully. "So, it's not . . . good or bad, it just . . . is? Like air? It just exists?"

"It just exists." He confirmed with a nod. "And it . . . I don't even know how to say this in a way that's really going to say it all . . . it . . . it does not *care*." He met her eyes, his arm moving a little away from his body as if he could distance himself from the tattoo under his sleeve. "It doesn't care about me, or you, or right, or wrong, or good or hurt, none of it. It does not care. It will do whatever you ask it to, so long as you have some way of paying for the balance of it. It doesn't care what it takes or what you ask. I've known a lot of people who've destroyed themselves that way."

Molly still didn't know where she stood as far as religion or believing in God, with any certainty, though she knew she believed in *something*. Was this that *something*? "Not God, then. People always describe Him, Her, It, as something that dictates morality. This is just a . . . thing?" She chewed on her lip slowly before she took a gulp of wine. "Are you scared of it?"

"Like nothing else in the universe." He answered immediately, then seemed to think better of it. "And at the same time . . . not really? It's not . . . it's not really *active*, if that makes any sense. It's never harmed me in a way I didn't consent to beforehand." He thought for a beat. "That came out sounding kinkier than I think I meant it."

A nervous laugh escaped her chest and she followed it up with gulping down the rest of her wine. Instead of refilling her glass, she abandoned her food and moved her chair so that she could sit closer to Tony. "This isn't like a weird cult, right? I mean . . . are there a ton of people who are in on this and I'm in the minority? Like when you read these fantasy novels and vampires and werewolves were always living there, lurking, and humans were the prey all along?"

He shook his head, holding her hand as he leaned back to do more talking than eating. "There's some groups that make it into something like that. There's people who make it into a lot of things. Some are more like churches. Some are like . . . packs." He took a deep breath, and needed a sip of wine before he went on. "I don't really know how many people have it, though. It's not a unified group. Most of the time, when I see someone else with it, one or the other of us just nods and moves on as quickly as we can."

She gripped his hand with both of hers and stared down at their joined hands. "And you're trusting me with this information? I mean . . . you don't owe me anything, I just . . . does this mean that I'm part of it now or something?"

He shook his head, squeezing her hand as he looked her over. "It's not like that. Just because you know about it doesn't . . . bind you to it." He gestured up at his sleeve, which drew itself up over his shoulder to show the tattoo on his bicep. "This binds you to it."

The tattoo was a five-pointed star inside a circle, and looked, for all that Molly could see, like nothing more than a plain tattoo. The flames around it had clearly been added later, but the star itself still appeared dark and fresh, its lines clean and crisp the way an old tattoo never would have been. "I was . . . really young when I got this. I wasn't ready for it. But I've managed to not get myself destroyed by it so far. Mostly."

Molly leaned in closer and she hovered her hand over it until he gave her nod. Once she had his permission, she ran her fingers along the lines slowly. "It doesn't look very scary. Especially on your sexy arm."

Her opinion just made him laugh, but he didn't stop her examination. "It doesn't look like much to you, but to anyone else who has it, and to me, it . . . glows a little. Like . . ." he looked up and pointed at one of her photographs in his kitchenette, framed in a place where it was easily visible.

It was a work she had done with a long exposure and some light painting, creating a blaze of fire surrounding a still shot of the moon through some trees. It was one of his favorites she had ever done. "A bit like that, actually. Not quite as bright as your work, but enough for someone to see if they're looking for it."

"Really? So it's like a . . . living thing?" Her eyes widened before she looked up into his eyes. Molly could easily get lost in his eyes, and had, so many times. She realized she should feel more nervous, but with Tony, she didn't. All she wanted to do was kiss him.

"It feels alive sometimes. I don't know if it properly is or not." Being a medical student, he certainly should have known, but he had no idea. "The thing behind it . . . speaks. Some people just call it the Voice. But it doesn't feel exactly alive. Maybe it is. I don't know."

Going with the newfound curiosity instead of fear, she kissed his cheek gently. Tony was her safe place. "What other magic can you do?"

He turned his head into the kiss, and pulled her in for a fuller one afterward, his lips warm against hers in spite of his nervousness in the conversation. "The rest of what I do, I try very hard not to do lately. It all comes with a cost I'm not interested in paying right now. So I stick to moving things around without touching them."

"Okay." Molly moved from her seat and slid into his lap as she straddled him and wrapped her arms around his neck. "So if you want to acquire new magic, you just ask?" She kissed him after the question, trading questions for kisses.

"You . . . negotiate." He admitted finally, between slow kisses. "Sometimes it just takes a few minutes, sometimes it takes hours or days to work out all the specifics. I've heard some crazy stories. Sometimes it will tell you what it will accept in balance, sometimes you have to find a way yourself. It all depends on what you want and what you're willing to offer in exchange."

"Anything? You can ask for *anything*?" She was hung up

on imagining what she would ask for without caring much about what it would cost. If she could have anything, what would she even ask for? She didn't really wait for his answer before she asked another. "If I . . . are you telling me all of this because you want to share it with me? Or . . . are we getting even more serious and you just want me to know? We've been together a year . . ."

"A little over, I think. Hopefully just the first of many." He watched the look in her eyes, smiling at it quietly, since he knew it too well. "I want you to know, and if you want me to share it with you . . . you need to know that's a choice you can never go back from. I think that's part of the reason why I want you to know about it. Because it's not something I can change, or walk away from. Once it's a part of you, or once you're a part of it, I'm not really sure which way is more accurate, then that's it. You can never be rid of it. Even if you choose never to use anything it gives you ever again, it's still with you. It's not a decision to be made lightly."

"It sounds . . . well . . . not as scary as I thought?" Kissing him was easier than stopping to think too hard about what he was telling her. The idea that she could be or do anything had her fantasizing as though she would be the next billion-dollar lottery winner. Hell, with his magic, she could have a billion dollars if she wanted it. "I don't want you to change, Tony. I would never want you to change. This isn't so bad."

"I certainly don't think so." His hands moved up her sides as she clung to him, enjoying her grip. "I don't know if there's any way to take something like this and *not* change, though. I know I certainly would have been . . . someone very different without it."

"Some changes aren't bad." She suggested as she took off her glasses by example. "I can't even afford contacts. Or Lasik. What if I could be rid of my glasses forever? You're already so sexy but I . . . pale next to you."

"I like you in glasses. They're very you." He teased as he kissed her. "Of course, I also like you out of them, but mostly because that means you're either in bed or headed that direction."

Molly laughed softly, but she thought back to the strawberry blonde waitress at the bar. The woman was stunning, undeniably attractive. "I just . . . I'm just saying that maybe some changes wouldn't be bad. *If* I had the power to make some improvements." She put her glasses behind her on the table, even though her vision was poor and everything around her turned into a blur except for Tony's face in front of her. "I think logically I know I should be scared of whatever you're telling me, but it sounds like winning the lottery to me."

"It's not the lottery if you have to pay for it." He smiled at her excitement, since he could understand it. "And the first one is especially a pain. Nothing I say would be enough to really prepare you for it. It gets . . . very insistent . . . when you first receive it. It's loud and urgent until you agree to your first deal. So it's good to know what you want going in, and what you're willing to give up to get it."

"You're giving me some sound advice there. Does this mean you'll consider . . . sharing it with me?" She kissed him several more times, though she didn't know what to think or even what to expect.

"If it's something you think you want as a part of you. Like I said, there's no getting out of it once you're in it. It's for life." His tone was hesitant as he wrapped his arms around her back. "It's been a long time since I gave it to anyone. It's not something I even consider lightly. It's usually better for people not to have access to that kind of . . . possibility."

"I see. I guess the bedroom isn't the only place you like to be bossy." She smirked and buried her face into his shoulder. "Are you less nervous now that I'm not running for the hills?"

"I don't know." He laughed against her neck, strong fingers moving over her back in a slow massage. "A sane person should probably be terrified of anything that looks like magic, but I probably should've known better than to think you qualify." He teased with a chuckle and another kiss down her shoulder.

"I'm not sane. I also trust you more than I trust anyone else on this planet." Chills ran down her spine with every single one of his kisses against her skin. "I'm lucky that somehow you decided being friends wasn't enough. I don't deserve you."

"And I don't deserve you. Even if I know you're not gonna take that the way I mean it." He drew back to look her in the eye. "I've done a lot of things with the Mark I'm not proud of. I've stepped away from a lot of it, but like I said, it's all still there. I can't get rid of it completely. I just want you to know enough about what it can do that you don't end up with that kind of . . . regret hanging around."

"I understand." Molly ignored everything else to press her lips to his, and when the kiss broke, she was breathless. "What about sex magic? Have you been using sex magic on me?"

"I have not." He claimed innocence with a grin that was anything but. "Seriously, I have not. But I've heard from plenty of people who work deals like that. I've just never tried anything like that myself. Kinda feels like a cheat, I would think? Like to be amazing one time you'd have to be absolutely terrible the next time, something like that. I don't know, I haven't done any negotiating for it."

"Yeah, that doesn't sound like a good tradeoff. No bad sex is worth it." She tugged on his shirt as she leaned backwards toward the table, still straddling his lap. "I think I could eat this food later . . . what do you think?"

"I don't think it's going anywhere. And neither are you, any time soon." He lifted his arms to allow her to pull off his shirt, then got to work on hers, though she had more layers on than he did.

Molly glanced around at the bright lights before she finally slid off of his lap and grabbed his hand to tug him out of his seat. "The bed is more comfy." She leaned in and kissed his bare chest. "You are so hot."

"I admit I can't fully take credit for that. There's some magic involved there. But I'm still glad you think so." He let her pull him along, and only paused to gesture at the blinds in his room, which pulled themselves closed as if tugged into place by an unseen hand.

It was weird to see him use magic so . . . openly and freely, but she was grateful that he felt comfortable enough to do so after spilling his secret. Molly discarded clothes once the blinds were closed, but her body was nothing to write home about. Small perky breasts and lots of freckles, and only straight lines instead of curves she wished she had. Curves she had both envied and admired on so many other women. "I'm glad you trust me. I won't tell anyone, Tony."

He walked her backward toward the simple bed across the room, his hands on her jeans to unbutton them one playful step at a time. "Honestly, one of the best parts about magic? Everyone thinks you're lying even if you say outright that you have it. And even if someone sees you do something, they think they're being pranked or it's a trick. That assumption's gotten me out of more than a few tight scrapes." He grinned as he slid her jeans down over her hips. "I trust you, Molly. With this and everything else."

By the time they made it back to his bed, their clothes were a trail behind him, and she easily fell into his comforter, though it was clear she wasn't confident in her skin. She never was. Molly forced a smile past the vulnerability she felt. "I trust you too. I love you."

"I love you too." He leaned himself against her completely, his well-defined muscles bunched above her as he held himself over her. He wasn't a big man, but he was built lean and solid, and he easily eclipsed her against the sheets. "Should I try some magic on you, then?" He grinned as his kisses moved down to her neck. "I never have before, but it could be fun."

Molly whimpered softly with every kiss, loving each one. "I'm up for a *magical* adventure." She mumbled as she looked up at him, as always, enraptured by him. "Let's do it.”

TWO

Seven days of questions later, and Molly felt like a month had passed. She spent all of her free time with Tony under usual circumstances, but they spent even more time tangled together after he told her about "the Mark". She hadn't even gone back to her own dorm room in a week except to get clothes.

Still wrapped up in his embrace, Molly decided she would skip her classes and call out of work, even though he told her not to. She hadn't missed either in a long time, so she didn't care about missing it now.

She tenderly ran her index finger along the lines of his tattoo, his "Mark", before she trailed her fingers down his body and south of his waist while he slept. It was early in the morning, but time didn't exist in their own little world. All she wanted to do was touch him and learn every secret detail about him.

He had always talked in his sleep, ever since she had started spending the night at his place, but he almost always spoke in Spanish. She teased him before about keeping secrets even in his sleep, even if he assured her that wasn't his intention. There were a few phrases she had picked up over the nights she'd spent with him, though. *"Lo siento"* was an easy one she remembered from high school introductory classes, but it didn't come with any context of what Tony was sorry for, or who his subconscious seemed to think was owed an apology.

He flinched in his sleep, but felt her there next to him and instinctively gathered her closer as he took in a deep, sleepy breath. "Mmmm, you looking for something down there?" He didn't stop her explorations, just arched his back to get more comfortable as he put his other arm behind his head.

"Maybe." She teased as she ran her hand along his length before she kissed him. "I'm skipping my classes and work. I don't care what you say. I want to stay here with you." They talked extensively the night before about the Mark, and Molly wanted Tony to give it to her. He still hadn't decided when they fell asleep, but she hoped he would still consider sharing that part of his life with her. "I love our little world together."

"So do I." He kissed her lazily, holding himself back on account of his morning breath, but grinding his hips under her touch regardless. "I can't remember the last time I took a decent vacation. Not that this counts as decent, I guess, but I like this way better." He took another deep breath and attempted to open his eyes. "Breakfast. Breakfast is required."

"Breakfast." She agreed, before she slid down his body slowly. "Let me say good morning first, then I'll make something." Some of her brown hair fell into her face while she smirked, but she disappeared beneath the covers afterward with clear intent.

He knew her smirk before she even started moving, and he had no interest in stopping her. Every aspect of sex with Molly had always been amazing, though nothing he said had ever seemed to convince her he was being truthful when he said so. He wondered, as she moved beneath the sheet, if anything he said or did would ever make her believe she had nothing to prove to him. The thought was banished as soon as her mouth wrapped around him.

After enjoying her pre-breakfast, Molly showered, dressed in shorts and a t-shirt, since she was in no way confident enough to sit and eat breakfast fully naked. She made a couple of omelets and plated them with some buttered toast. As he took a seat, she poured some orange juice for both of them. "So, um, is it too early to talk about it?"

His torso was still steaming from the shower, but he had thrown on a pair of boxers on his way out to the table, his hair still a damp mess of black slicked away from his face. "Probably, but why should that stop us?" He smiled and took her hand when she dropped off his omelet, spinning her around once. "Have you thought about where you want it? No moving it after that happens, so it's a good thing to figure out in advance."

Instinctively she looked down at herself, but her thin frame drowned in her oversized t-shirt. "Probably somewhere easy to hide, right? You said having it out in the open can be dangerous." She gave a one-shouldered shrug before she took his grasped hand and placed it on her breast, even buried in her t-shirt. "Here?"

"Well, hopefully you won't want to keep those hidden *all* the time?" He teased her with a few caresses over her shirt, tugging her in closer with the loose fabric. "But that's a strategy. I've seen a lot of them on people's ribs or near their crotch. Knew one guy who actually had his on his ass. I always meant to ask him if the Voice seemed offended by that, but I never got around to it."

"I could go with my ribs." Molly countered after a snort at the ass comment, and she stared into his gorgeous eyes, her smile tentative. "So that means yes? You're definitely going to give it to me?"

"If you're sure that you want it." He was clearly hesitant about it, but there was nothing hesitant about the way he was holding her. "I don't want it to be something you regret being a part of. It can do amazing things, but it's also . . . hard. Your life will never again not be complicated."

"I don't see myself regretting it." She leaned in for a kiss as he held her in place, more eager than anything. "I'm sure. We've discussed it at length by now, right?"

"We have." He confirmed, sounding somewhat more resigned than enthusiastic, even if he was still smiling. He reached over to the table to push his plate aside, then lifted her easily to set her ass on the table in front of him as though he intended to finish her for breakfast instead. "Are you sure about the ribs?"

Molly's eyes widened as he perched her on the table, since she was stunned that he was moving forward. She didn't have words for several seconds. "Y . . . yeah. I, um, I don't have a lot of cleavage anyway . . ." she stumbled over her words and cleared her throat. "I want you to be sure too, Tony. Don't do this if you feel like I'm forcing you."

"I don't feel forced." He stood up to lean against her, laying her back on the table slowly to stretch her out beneath him. "I want to give you everything, Molly. I want to share everything with you. I've met a lot of people, but no one else I can say that about except you. Just . . . be careful about what you agree to give away. We can do amazing things. Together."

Her words were again caught in her throat, and her vision blurred with unshed tears as she looked up at him. She would do anything and everything for this man. She would sacrifice the world to deserve him. "I would do anything for you, Tony."

He took her in a heated kiss that arched her back beneath him, then laid a hand against her ribs as he took her breath away. "It doesn't hurt, but it's going to feel very, very strange. Close your eyes, and don't try to get up or move until you've got your bearings." He left one more gentle kiss on her lips as if to seal his instructions, then his touch moved over her ribs along her right side, and the world began to go dark.

There was a kind of tingling rush of sensation under Tony's touch, as if that part of her abdomen had fallen asleep like an arm she had slept on too long. Her vision blurred and went dark before she could even glance down for a visual. The ambient sounds of the apartment complex around them disappeared, the light of the soft lamps in his kitchenette, down to the gentle draft from his air conditioning from the ceiling vent. Everything about the world turned dark, and somehow empty without being cold, though she felt the sudden lack of Tony's warmth against her as her senses faded out.

But just as one moment she felt too little, her mind on the verge of crying out to the void in panic at being abandoned, suddenly her senses filled too fully, golden light and heat and prickling caresses of sensation drowning every nerve in her body. There was a kind of blissful agony to the overwhelming tumult, as if she had suddenly been plunged into the core of an icy comet as it dove into the heart of a star.

Both extremes slowly began to merge and meld and shift in her senses, tendrils of shadow dancing with ghosts of the light, weaving and binding to themselves and others as the world of her perceptions became more complicated than either extremity.

And somewhere, out in the maelstrom, was a presence.

She couldn't see it, couldn't hear it, couldn't taste or touch it, but she knew it was there just as surely as she knew her own name. Every part of her knew it, down to the depths of her soul, if indeed she had one.

And whatever it was, it was, as of that moment, aware of her as well.

The feeling of the presence in her mind, her thoughts, as if someone was waiting on bated breath for her to speak, had her crying out in a panic. The natural reaction was fear, but she could now feel Tony's hands on her body, even though her head buzzed with a headache and her ears hummed with noise though she couldn't tell if it was real or imagined. She didn't open her eyes as her heart pummeled her rib cage painfully with her fear.

You can hear me, can't you? I knew his magic was real, but this . . .

The voice that answered her explained immediately why Tony had referred to it as nothing more than The Voice. It had no tone, no particular inflection or personality, just a response in her mind that seemed to reverberate from her hair down through the tips of her toes.

You are heard.

Molly wanted to scream, but the scream burned in her throat and remained silent, frozen by her fear.

What do you desire?

The question was already insistent in her mind, but it felt like a missed meal, a small gnaw of hunger that was easily ignored. At least for now. She opened her eyes in defiance of answering the question and looked up at Tony as he hovered over her. "I'm okay?"

He gave her a reassuring nod and moved his hand to take hers, steadying her as he felt her breathing heavily. He knew that kind of panic. "It's a lot, the first few times. Don't try and fight it, it won't hurt you. Did you make a deal to start off with?"

"No?" Her voice came out squeaky and cracked. "It's in my brain and it's *unsettling*." She knew she didn't have to describe it to him but she knew *it* was listening. She could feel it, like watching a cat assess its surroundings, but coiled for action. Her breath was shaky. "I don't know what I was expecting."

He gave her a reassuring nod, clearly familiar with the sensation, and squeezed her hand tighter. "It gets a lot less . . . present, once you've made your first deal with it. It's always there, but it keeps its distance a bit more after that, unless you reach out to say hello first."

Molly launched herself into his chest from off the table and buried her face into his neck. She didn't feel like crying but her whole body was trembling with the unknown. She gripped him so hard that her fingers hurt from clenching. "I . . ."

Molly thought she had a plan, she thought she was prepared, but all she wanted to do was avoid it. She did lift up her shirt slowly to look, and there was a 'Mark' just like Tony's, except it was glowing. Shining. Glittering. It looked like it was alive along her ribs.

"Yeah, that takes some getting used to." He agreed, letting her have all the time she wanted to inspect the new addition to her skin. Eventually he moved so she could see the one on his arm, no longer just a plain star surrounded by flames, but glowing like hers, subtle undulations of shadows and gold moving over the surface of his skin like a living thing.

She stared at his Mark in stunned silence for a moment before she looked into his eyes with tears in her own eyes. "I, um . . ." Molly leaned in and kissed him gently, since she didn't know what to say, and she was still scared. "At least I have you."

"Of course you do. Nothing's changed since five minutes ago." He nodded down to her ribs. "I mean, a few things have, but nothing between us. You're still you, I'm still me, and we're still here. Of course you still have me."

Molly wrapped her arms around his neck and just held onto him in silence for several minutes. She waited until her pulse evened out before she pulled her face away from his neck and the scent of his body wash. "Let's eat." She knew the suggestion was abrupt, but she didn't want to think about what just happened or what she needed to do. Not yet.

What do you desire? The Voice persisted in the back of her mind, a quiet ache that reminded her, in every quiet moment, that it required her attention.

* * * * *

Breakfast went smoothly enough as they talked about

some of Tony's first experiences with the Voice, but he was clearly more worried about her through the rest of the morning than he was interested in talking over the finer details of his past. He described dozens of different people he had known, always in fairly vague terms, and the nature of their arrangements with the Voice.

Pacts, he called them.

He didn't know if people had taken the term from the Marked and misunderstood it to mean a deal with the devil, or if the Marked in centuries past had decided to use the name being thrown at the source of their abilities. He was in school to study medicine, not history.

Every time he described someone he'd known and what they could do, he looked at her expectantly, watching the anxiety of the Voice's presence rising in her and hoping that one or another would spark some idea for her to set the Voice, and therefore herself, at ease.

Even by evening, Molly hadn't made a decision, and the Coice was almost relentless as she sat on the couch against him. They were trying to watch a movie, but everything seemed like white noise around her in comparison to the Voice.

"I talked about my eyesight. What about fixing my eyes and getting rid of my glasses?" She questioned abruptly, though she knew he had to be aware of her distraction, even if he couldn't hear the war in her head.

"That's a fairly common one, actually. I'm sorry I didn't mention that before. Probably because I like your glasses." He grinned over at her as she sat fidgeting, though his expression was still concerned. "You'll probably lose some kind of sharpness in another respect as a trade-off. Some people prefer to do that kind of arrangement permanently, maybe your sense of smell or taste isn't as good, maybe your balance could use some work, that kind of thing. Other people decide to do those arrangements in short bursts. Give themselves the ability to see with eagle-eye vision for brief minutes or seconds in exchange for being blind for an equal time later. It depends on what you want out of it."

"I just don't want to have to wear glasses to see. Or contacts. I want 20/20 vision." She could feel some relief after announcing out loud that she was considering an option, at least, but she looked toward Tony. "Should I just do it?"

"It sounds like a good start to me, but it's up to you. I can get an eye exam chart ready for you while you're negotiating." He gave her a quick kiss before he leaned against the side of the couch they sat on. He put a hand up to manipulate some papers and markers across the room.

Molly watched him use his magic and closed her eyes, even though she didn't have to. It felt more . . . appropriate for her to close her eyes. It felt like . . . praying? Once she closed her eyes, she cleared her throat.

Okay, stop harassing me. I want to have 20/20 vision. What is that going to cost?

She could feel the alleviation of urgency from the Voice immediately once she made her desire explicit, but its presence loomed around her more heavily, banishing the sensations of the room around her.

Many forms of balance exist. All are choices to be made. A form of color blindness would be one acceptable price. Alternatively, the loss of most of your sense of smell, or sensation in one limb, a drastic reduction in your tolerance for spicy foods . . .

Those . . . Molly wrinkled her nose in distaste. She didn't like the options being presented to her, but she also didn't know what the hell she was doing either. *I don't know what I think about that.* She also felt insane talking to a voice inside her head, but she was attempting to suspend logic. Molly tried to think about all her senses and something she could live without, but the spicy foods suggestion was about all she could consider. *With 20/20 vision, I suppose I could sacrifice my considerable tolerance for spicy foods.*

Was she imagining the lights and the darkness spinning quickly around her? Pulsing with richer brightness and deeper shadows? Was that her anxiety or was it a sign of the

Voice's enthusiasm to make the deal? Could it even be enthusiastic as a disembodied thing?

The balance is acceptable as it has been stated. Do you agree to the terms?

Molly could feel her anxiety ramping up again but she didn't want to think about trying to negotiate any other terms at the moment. *I agree.*

The motion around her swirled to a crescendo that thrilled through her, like an exultation of light and movement even though she could distantly feel that she was still stationary on the couch. There was a tingling that moved through her face, as if an unseen hand had grasped her by the eyes and the chin and taken something from her. The sensation only lasted a moment before it passed, the Voice's presence withdrawing, silent at last, to its tiny corner of her mind.

She let out a noise of relief and her body relaxed at the feeling of the Voice receding, but it took a minute before she felt brave enough to open her eyes. When she did, she felt like it didn't work, since her vision was blurry. She sat up before she realized she still had her glasses on, so she pulled them off slowly. "Okay, it's over . . . I think."

Tony grinned beside her and took her glasses from her to set them aside on his coffee table. "Seems quicker than laser eye surgery. Hopefully it was also cheaper?"

"No more wasabi with my sushi for the foreseeable future. Goodbye sriracha." She looked over at Tony with perfect clarity, and the sight of him actually made her smile. He looked perfect as usual, and she couldn't help but lean in and kiss him. "Now when we're naked, you won't be blurry."

"Aw, no more sriracha is a sad day. But that's a pretty good trade-off, actually. That's your first deal done, babe. Does it feel better?" He gathered her into his lap as she kissed him, tucking her hair away from her eyes so that she could see the rest of his apartment more clearly than before.

"I feel less . . . crazy." She curled into him as she looked around, and she didn't have to worry about her glasses bumping into his chest. "It's . . . weird to be able to see. Clearly. Perfectly."

"If that's the weirdest sensation that comes out of making a deal with an impersonal, disembodied voice suffused with magic, I think you're probably doing it wrong." Tony spread his arms against the back of the couch to either side, letting her get settled.

Molly kissed along his jaw before she said anything else. "I . . . maybe I was overreacting? It really doesn't feel so bad now."

"You were coming into contact with the source of all magic in the universe, as far as I'm aware of it. I'm not sure it's possible to overreact. But I'm glad it feels more comfortable for you now." A shiver went through her body as he ran his hands up her sides, his thumb brushing the Mark he'd given her. It was as if it recognized him, the magic bound into her purring at the touch of the one who had given it to her.

After feeling the shiver and the response to his touch, she watched his hands trace the lines on her ribs. "Are we always connected by this now? It feels . . . you feel familiar. When you touch it."

He shuddered at that thought for some reason, glancing at his own, but he shrugged as he thought about it. "Maybe someone who knows more about it would know, but I . . . I mean, for the sake of being connected to you? That would be great. Being connected to the one who gave it to me . . . not so much."

Molly searched his eyes for a moment before she kissed away whatever memory momentarily haunted him. He didn't seem eager to share, so she didn't pry. Once the kiss broke, she pressed her forehead against his. "I'm so tired now. I've had anxiety about this all day, and I just want to go to sleep."

"Sleep is one thing I never mess with, when it comes to the Mark. That way I've always got dreams to fall back on when reality gets too strange." He hugged her tightly and stood up with her still in his arms, carrying her through the house with her legs wrapped around his waist.

He tossed her back onto the bed and she reached up to remove her glasses, only to be reminded again that her glasses were gone. She chuckled to herself as she tossed off her clothes and crawled up the covers to slide into his comforter. She looked at him as he stripped, and smiled through a yawn. "I wonder what else I could do to look a little better next to you."

"Don't get carried away." He chided as he stripped off his shirt, clearly on his way to join her whether he was tired or not. "You look great, next to me or anyone else."

Molly snorted in her disagreement, but she was quickly too tired to argue. She pulled the pillows closer, surrounded by his smell since it was his bed, and she gladly sunk down into the comfort of it all. The world was definitely different . . . what could she do next?

Your options are not presently limited.

The Voice in her mind didn't push like it had before. It didn't even feel as though it was exactly tempting her. Her mind was tempting itself, the Voice seemed to be merely inclined to help remind her of her options.

She winced momentarily at the sound of the voice in her head, but as soon as Tony was in the bed, she snuggled into him. Molly kept her eyes closed.

Later. She would worry about it later.

* * * * *

Within a week, Molly had made two more significant changes, but the price for her beautiful breasts was random sharp back pain. Between sneezing with new allergies for her fixed nose and random back pain, she was frowning as she looked at her reflection in Tony's bathroom mirror. After drowning herself in huge clothes to hide the change in her breasts during class, she rushed back to Tony's apartment, stripped down and showered, hoping the steam would clear up her stuffy nose. Molly liked the changes to her physical appearance, but the ache in her back really made her wonder.

After drying her hair (still brown, though she had plans for it too), she slipped on a new nightgown that complemented her new, full breasts. A week of changes had her appreciating what the Voice could do, but she didn't think she could overhaul herself and live with all the costs that came with it.

She heard the door open softly, and she continued to stare at her reflection. "Tony?"

"Yeah, it's me." He sounded tired, but he'd been out shadowing at the city hospital for the last twelve hours. Some fatigue was expected. "Everything alright? I thought you had pictures to develop tonight on campus."

Molly grabbed a robe and wrapped it securely around herself before she exited the bathroom. "These allergies and random back pains are going to take some getting used to. I'm fine." She gave him a reassuring smile as she walked up to give him a kiss. "You look ragged. I can draw you a nice warm bath."

"Mmmm. Bath would be good right now, actually. As long as you'll be joining me. Might help your back too. Win win?" He put his arms around her to hold her, the impressive sources of her back problems pressed between them inside the robe.

She gladly held onto Tony, though it felt strange to have actual breasts between them, since her size difference was significant. "Win win." She agreed as she kissed his jaw. "I missed you."

"I missed you too. And you two." He leaned her back to kiss down her collarbone onto the slope of her breasts with a low chuckle, hoping to get a smile out of her with the touch.

Molly smirked and ran a hand through his hair before she yanked on the strands gently. "I'm still glad you like them. Much better than before, right?"

"I like that *you* like them. And you look hot in the new stuff you started picking up, that's a good time." The robe was only one of several new additions to her wardrobe, as she tried out different styles that she'd never been accustomed to wearing before.

She tugged the robe open so that he could see the skimpy negligee underneath. "I could listen to you say that all day. 'You look hot.'" It wasn't as though Tony didn't compliment her before, but it didn't seem sincere to her most of the time. She believed it now, because she made it happen.

"Well, my next day off, that's exactly what you're gonna hear. Until you start getting tired of it." His fingertips moved over the sheer fabric of the negligee, exploring her over the new texture as he quickly forgot about the stress of his shift.

Molly's cheeks flushed with his touch before she stepped back out of his hold and discarded her robe at his feet. "Let's draw that bath." Her voice dropped into breathlessness as she quickly headed for the bathroom but stripped along the short distance.

The tub of the apartment was in no way built for two people, but they had made it work before, and they made it work that night. It was deep enough to mostly cover them both as long as she was lying on top of him, which was all Tony needed or wanted out of life for the time being.

By the time they had gotten into the warmth and settled against each other, he had his arms wrapped around her back, her arms folded and her elbows up on his shoulders to kiss him. Beneath the water, his hands never stopped moving, every caress followed by the whispers of the hot water.

"I can hear you thinking about it." He eventually said as she got a distant look in her eyes. "Not actually hear you, I haven't figured out a way to read minds that I'm alright with yet, but still. You are scheming very loudly."

"Thinking seems to cause a lot of trouble lately." She did

seem distant, but mostly because she was in a constant state of wondering what she could, should, would do next. "I need to stop thinking."

"I can help with that for a while." His voice and his touch both promised distraction, made all the more binding by her body's perfect knowledge of just how well he could deliver on it. "But not permanently. It takes time to not be always wrapped up in the possibilities all the time. I know what that feels like."

"I definitely don't want to stack up on the costs of all of these things. I just want . . ." She sighed and met his eyes. "Do you ever feel satisfied?"

"I don't know if satisfied is the right word for it. Contented isn't quite right either. You just . . . at some point, at least for me, I got to a point where I felt like I could handle the price, on the one hand, and the reward had made my life into what I wanted it to be. At least, at the time. Things change, but the possibilities never go away. So when things change, you can change with them. You just have to find the space where your life looks the way you want it for the time being."

"Hm. I guess I'll get there." Molly ran her hands along his body and gave him a small smile. "Let's get you all clean and into bed so that you can relax after your long day. There's no reason to worry about me. I'm worried about *you*."

"You don't need to be worried about me. All I need is a night's sleep." He rubbed her back as she rested against him, a little worried about that particular aspect of her most recent pact. "How're you feeling? Still comes and goes?"

"Comes and goes." Molly rested her face against his chest and listened to his steady heartbeat. "I hate thinking about all the what-ifs. I hate wondering if I'll always be chasing. It'll get better, right? It's only been a week."

"It'll get better. You'll settle into what you can do, decide that you've paid enough for the time being, and life will become . . ." he paused, looking up at the ceiling briefly before he went on, "well, I was going to say 'normal', but that doesn't really apply, so . . . something approximating normal?"

"Approximating normal. Isn't that just all of us?" Molly kissed him several more times before she sloshed in the tub on top of him. "Okay, let's get washed up and into bed, this isn't nearly as comfortable as I hoped."

He smiled as they got out, but there was some concern on his face at the same time, since he could tell she wasn't finding the results of her pacts quite as fun as he had hoped. "I thought once or twice about doing something with dreams, like being able to control them or choose to remember them. I could just never figure out anything that felt worth giving up to pay for it."

"That's something I didn't really expect." She dried off and grabbed a fluffy robe this time. "It's . . . difficult to negotiate with parts of yourself you always took for granted."

"It's an easy way to lose parts of yourself along the way, it seems to me." He shook his head as he got out to dry off himself, though unlike her, he didn't bother getting dressed again afterward. "But the good thing is, the Voice has never seemed to care much about direct trades. What it accepts doesn't always have to be the obvious thing to us. Like I read once about this one guy years and years ago who wanted to be better at talking to people. He sort of wanted to know what to say and when to say it, and he made himself selectively colorblind to do it." He shrugged as he hung the towel back in place. "Its idea of balance is . . . beyond what I'm willing to spend my time trying to understand."

"It's mind boggling." She agreed as she watched him dry off with all the admiration she always had for her boyfriend. In the last week, she was amazed to discover that nothing about his body was altered by a pact. She cursed her bad genetics for leaving her with not much to work with. By the time he was dried off, she was on him and kissing the breath out of his lungs.

"Mmmm. Yes, please. All of that." His hands tugged the hem of her bathrobe up so he could hold her against him with his hands on her ass directly, chuckling under the vehemence of her attack. He stepped her backward and picked her up to sit her on the edge of the counter next to his sink. The roughness of it and the moaning from him set Antony's neighbor to banging on the thin walls from the other unit, but he just laughed and kept kissing her anyway.

Molly laughed softly against his lips after the neighborly intervention, but she kissed him a few more times before she rested her hand against his cheek and whispered against his lips her love and devotion before he carried her back to his bed. Her insecurities could be ignored. For now.

* * * * *

Hours into the night and a few orgasms later, Molly was awake and staring at the dark ceiling of Tony's bedroom. Insomnia was a constant companion over the last week, since her mind wouldn't stop obsessing over the power lingering at her literal beck and call.

She glanced over at Tony's sleeping form a few times, at the perfect slope of his nose and face, at the lips she longed to kiss all the time. He was going to become a doctor, probably a prestigious surgeon, and she was . . . what?

She had her photography, and she was proud of her art, but that was all she was proud of in her life, except for her relationship with Tony. What was she going to be for him? Not an intellectual equal. Not a trophy wife, if he even wanted to actually marry her. The spiral quickly took her down into an accustomed kind of panic.

I wish I could be the woman of his dreams. She ached a little too openly, but her mind went back to the strawberry blonde waitress from what felt like a lifetime ago. She knew that prior to Molly, Tony's exes were beautiful women. Social media made it impossible for all of his past to be erased, not that she thought he should. Molly was a shadow of a woman in comparison, except for her now magically bestowed rack. Which, amazingly, had garnered her more outside attention than anything ever had.

You do not presently have access to view the dreams of others. The Voice, ever on alert for her wishes and desires, clarified her unspoken wish. *However, a complete alteration and realignment of the self is possible. Such a transformation would supersede the balance you have already created.*

A whole body transformation? Molly moved a little on the bed but closed her eyes so she wasn't just creepily staring at Tony while having a conversation in her head. *You mean, I can change everything and get rid of the allergies, the back pain, everything?*

The price would be altered in light of the comprehensive nature of the transformation. That is correct.

I don't want any more body pain. I just . . . I want to be beautiful, stunning, redheaded . . . a model standard, but curvy.

As she described her ideal, the image of her imagination came into focus in front of her, visible as a floating, spinning form in the midst of the swirling gold and shadows of the Voice's presence. Her idea of beauty, the precise shade of red in her dreams, the exact proportions that she desired. The figure wasn't making any sound as it spun in open space, but Molly could already hear what kind of voice the person would have. *What else do you desire?*

Molly stared at the potential of what she could look like in her mind's eye, so she indulged the fantasy by asking for beautiful light blue eyes and creamy, porcelain skin, a butt that was perfectly rounded and grabbable . . . the fantasy she was sure would make Tony proud to have her at his side as a prestigious doctor. *Okay. That. What would it take?*

This is a representation of a complete transformation. Enacting such a transformation would involve the creation of an entirely new identity. In order to preserve balance, such an act of creation will require you to leave behind your current identity entirely.

Leave behind her identity? Molly opened her eyes again and looked at Tony. She ran her fingers across his arm and stared at him, since he was the only thing that was truly important to her, and she wanted to be worthy of him. She wanted to be worthy of being at his side.

Everything else in her life . . . was unsatisfactory. Her parents rarely even checked in with her, happy that she was out on her own and no longer their problem. She didn't really have friends, she just had some classmates she had coffee with from time to time. Her one ex was a secret girlfriend from high school, someone who hadn't wanted anyone to even know that she and Molly were dating. Her college career was just her going through the motions, and she really didn't know what she wanted to do with her life.

All she wanted was to be good enough for Tony. He loved her for her personality and not her appearance, so even if she left her identity behind, he would still love her. Right?

What does that mean?

The Voice was impassive as it held the possibility of her future self in front of her, letting her contemplate the future that self could have. *You will cease to be yourself. All possessions, relationships, personal identification, and ability to identify yourself under your current identity. The price of a new self is the loss of that which came before.*

Ability to identify myself. What if someone who knows me figures it out? She looked at Tony again and chewed at her bottom lip. *I can't control that.*

No, you cannot. Such an event will be rendered impossible, insomuch that any you meet following your transformation will regard you as a different person entirely, such that your relationships with those people will be different than they have been prior.

Different. Well, she would *look* entirely different. So Tony could still fall in love with her as someone else, with her personality intact. Someone beautiful. On the inside, she would still be herself. And if her previous pacts could be nullified to create this one, then she could always find a way back, right? If she wanted to. There was always a way. As far as she understood the Voice, literally nothing was impossible, and everything had a price.

Molly slid closer to Tony and planted a gentle kiss on his lips as he slept facing her. "I love you." She whispered against his cheek, wanting desperately to be the woman in her mind's eye and to be his match.

He mumbled an "I love you" in his sleep and she kissed him once more before she moved away. They were meant to be. She would find a way back to him, even altered, and she would be better for him. *Okay, what do I need to do?*

The light and darkness in the back of her mind swirled quicker, the intangible landscape itself eager at her commitment. *This manner of transformation requires distance from that which is familiar. Only in such a place can you be remade without ties to your former self.*

Molly trembled as she slowly slid out of Tony's bed. She shook as she looked at him sleeping peacefully, but she stopped on her way out of his apartment to leave him a note.

I made a pact that means some distance for now, but true love always finds its way back. I need to do this for us, I need to feel worthy of belonging to you before we can take any further steps in our relationship. Look for me and I'll be waiting.

She took a deep breath in the middle and finished the note.

I love you so much. I promise to be worthy of you.
-Always yours,
Molly

She kissed the letter and grabbed her keys and her phone before she made her way out. She wasn't eager to jog back to campus in the middle of the night, but terrified or not, the Voice in her mind was scarier.

The path back to campus from the apartment complex

passed through a park, which in daylight was a pleasant and well-maintained landscape. In the dark, there was something malicious about even the open, manicured field. It was quicker to cut across the field directly rather than take the jogging trails, and in the moonlight, the streaks of asphalt around the field seemed more like flattened walls than safe passages.

As she ran, she felt her phone fall from her pocket, though she could have sworn it had been secure there a moment before. Her keys followed a few steps later, jingling to the ground before she could even stop to go back for her phone. With each impact, the presence in her mind swirled faster.

She looked around for her phone, but it was long gone, though she didn't understand why. *You can't take them from me while I'm still me. That's not fair!* She scrambled for her keys so that she could get into her dorm room. *Are you going to make me do this in the middle of a field?*

Your former possessions, including your place of residence, are part of the balance. If you desire to see this transformation fulfilled, all must be left behind.

Where am I supposed to go?! Molly was on her knees in Tony's shirt and her jeans, though at least she wasn't naked. Yet. She was almost certain that she would lose the clothes on her back after all was said and done.

When she looked around, she could see the campus library lit up in the distance. It was next to the workout facility, both of them open twenty four hours. She got up and ran toward them, desperate for someplace to go where she wouldn't end up naked outdoors in the night.

There were people outside between the two buildings, a few nocturnal groups goofing off in the glow of the campus lighting. No one outside either building looked familiar, even though she had used both a hundred times. Her approach was apparently beneath the notice of anyone outside, either absorbed in their own books and devices or too wrapped up in the group conversation. Molly herself was beneath their notice. Nothing new about that.

Even though the pull of the Voice was making it more and more difficult for her to focus, she waited until someone opened a door to the rec center and made it inside without her card. The smell of chlorine and sweat made her nauseous, but she wandered her way into the girls' locker room.

She found a privacy stall with a bench and locked herself inside, barely holding back from throwing up. *This feels like torture! Just get on with it already! No one here knows me. You took everything already.*

As soon as she gave her consent to go forward, it was like the world around her caught fire in the brilliance and darkness of the Voice's power. The vision of her idealized self turned toward her in her mind, formed from nothing. A vision of her current self's limbs turned and shifted until the porcelain redhead was in the same pose she was. The distance between them closed as a kind of numbing fire swept through her body.

The pact is made.

THREE

Before

Molly didn't think there would be so much pain. Her body felt like it was stretched and burned at some points, which had her crying out, but the late night was on her side. There was likely no one else in the area of the locker room to hear her, even if it sounded from time to time like she was being abused. All she could see were the Voice's gold and shadows, and the pain was incomprehensible.

By the time it started to abate, the first thing she could feel was cold tile beneath her back, pressed against her bare skin. She barely remembered being clothed prior, but the chill seeping in now said otherwise.

The silence of the locker room was intense, but there were sounds that she had never heard before. Had her hearing been a problem too, and she never knew it? She could tell the pitch of the fan operating across the room, hear the quiet sloshing of water in the swimming pool past the locker rooms. Both were a calm counterpoint to her own racing heartbeat and ragged breaths.

Outside the changing room, she could hear the splashing suddenly get much louder, as a group came into the locker room from the pool doors, dripping everywhere as they walked past her room.

"Well, whoever they are, they must've finished. Sounded like somebody was getting railed in here." One soprano voice echoed through the locker room, leaving wet, bare footprints behind it as it went.

"Right? Made me a little jealous." The voice's apparent friend was laughing about the same thing. Lockers began to open as the laughter continued.

She was glad at that particular moment she was at least in a private stall, even though she could still hear everything in the locker room around her. When she finally moved her sore muscles enough to sit up, she glanced down at her body only to feel panic at the unfamiliarity of what she saw.

She was flawless. Her only unchanged feature was the Mark, exactly where Tony placed it. She reached down to touch it along her ribs, and perfectly manicured fingers ran along her skin. With a groan she wobbled to a mirror in the private stall, and she whimpered when she saw her own reflection.

It was unreal. She was unreal. *Who . . . who am I? This . . . my name?* She still had her memories, but she could already feel that some of them were blurry or out of reach. Her home address. Her phone number. Social security number. Everything. *If I traded my identity, you must have one to give me.*

You may choose your name and other demographic details if you wish. Records of your existence will come to be accordingly.

She reached her hand up to her face and pinched it in several places to help reality sink in, but she was still amazed by the reflection looking back at her. "It's all so different. Top to bottom. A to Z." She ran a finger down her own perfect nose. "A to Z. Aimee Zimmerman." It was the first name to pop into her head, and she figured it was as good as any.

So it will be. A plain clutch appeared beside her in the changing stall, formed from the Voice's presence made manifest in the physical world. Looking inside, she found a driver's license (apparently she was still twenty, though her birthday had been reset to the present date), a birth certificate, an immunization record, and a social security card.

"Couldn't give me a credit card or some clothes?" She growled as she looked down at her new identification, but then she glanced at her reflection again. The woman she was now was gorgeous. Perfect. Once she figured out a way to reconnect with Tony, they would be happy together.

Except now she wasn't a student, and she didn't have a job. She didn't have anything.

On sore legs she grabbed a nearby fresh towel and held it in front of her body as she peered out, voices still lingering. Did some kind of team have weird, late night practices? "Anyone out there?"

Hushed voices came back from elsewhere in the echoing locker room.

"Is she talking to us?"

"Who just yells that in the middle of the night in the gym?"

Mol . . . Aimee was more self-conscious by the second, but she remained mostly obscured by the door and the pathetic towel. "Could I get some help?"

One of the girls came back around the corner of a few lockers, still in her swimsuit but with a wrap and a t-shirt barely covering her. She looked like she might be considering joining a contest, with the way the shirt was clinging to her. "What's wrong, hotness?"

Hotness? She was taken aback for a moment before she processed what to say, but it was still strange that even the voice in her head sounded different. "I, uh, hi. So I came in with a friend . . ." first lie of her new life, but lying was all she had at the moment. "Now my clothes are gone. Do you . . . is there anyone who can help me?"

The look on the blonde's face went from confusion to amusement in a matter of seconds, and she actually burst out laughing as she strutted closer. "Ohoho baby, baby, hazing is a *bitch*! Come on, come on, I got you. I mean, I ain't your size or anything, but come on. Michelle!" She shouted for a friend of hers, who luckily hadn't gotten dressed yet and was more Mol . . . Aimee's new size. "I mean, it sounded like it was a good time while it lasted at least, right?"

"It was something." She muttered as she shook her head. "Thanks, I, um, I didn't want to run out of here naked. Especially with people lingering outside."

"Yeah, for sure. You gonna be good getting home? We're heading back to the dorms, we could walk you?"

Aimee hesitated again before she let out a sigh. "I got kicked out of the dorms. I don't really have anywhere to go. I can figure it out, the clothes are great. Thanks." She gave a smile to Michelle and the other woman just shrugged. "The library has some soft couches. They stay open all night, though I never understood why."

"Well you don't want to just go sleep in the *library*, do you?" The blonde sounded like she was having a vocal allergic reaction to the idea. "What did you get kicked out of the dorms for? Girls a couple doors down have a cam girl account together and nobody's said shit to them. Can't imagine what you'd have to do to actually have somebody do something."

"It's a long story." She didn't want to come up with a story, but she realized quickly that her whole life now would be one big lie . . . every part of it fabricated. Aimee took a deep breath. "My roommate accused me of trying to steal her girlfriend and things went downhill from there. She made up a lot of things and I got kicked out. I was staying with my boyfriend but then that ended recently . . ." Aimee winced in real pain when she thought of Tony, but it wasn't over. She refused to think that. This was for him, for them, to be together.

"Oh, girl, you got *drama*." The blonde pulled her into a hug with a delighted squeal. "Alright, here's the deal. I let you sleep on my floor, and you don't tell campus police about the bottle of schnapps you're gonna help me drink until we pass out. Deal?"

Just at the mention of making a deal of any kind, Aimee could hear the Voice in the back of her head, excited by just the theme under discussion. She opened her mouth and closed it a few times, speechless at first. "Why, um, you're being so nice to me . . . that's . . . I don't . . ."

Apparently confidence didn't come free with her new looks, though she didn't hesitate to dress and talk, once the clothes were handed over. She had a skirt that was dangerously short and a t-shirt that wasn't equipped for her breasts, but she was dressed. Flip flops would have to get her across campus.

"Oh come on, don't gimme that shit. Some asshole dumps you without clothes . . . ooh! Maybe him and his boys are outside thinking they're gonna get to watch you streak across campus naked. Can't have that."

"Definitely not." She agreed wholeheartedly. "Sleeping on the floor is no problem. If you really don't mind."

"I've had a lot uglier than you on my floor for a lot worse reasons. And in the bed. Or were you really *not* trying to steal the girlfriend?" She looked as though she might be disappointed if the answer was no.

Aimee's cheeks flushed, since she wasn't at all used to the attention, even though it both intimidated her and excited her. The stranger was beautiful and sexy, but Tony was still her boyfriend, as far as she was concerned. "I'm not one to steal anything from anyone." She tugged nervously at the borrowed clothes, her clutch and only possession tucked at her side. It was late and she was exhausted. "I really appreciate it."

On her way out through the small groups loitering in the dark, she could see her new friends watching for anyone who was playing some kind of prank on her. The only people outside were those who had been there when her old self had come through. But instead of ignoring her and going about their conversations, most of those she could see turned to get a better look at her as she made her way across

41

campus.

The new attention was both enjoyable and nerve wracking all over again, and she walked close to her new friends. She thought about asking to borrow a cell phone, but try as she might, she couldn't remember Tony's phone number. Or his address. Maybe she could see him on campus in the morning.

* * * * *

"Oh my god, yes, I *need* that in my life right now!" Her primary rescuer (whose name, she had learned, was Viv) was about halfway through her makeup, yelling out of the shared dorm bathroom at the others scattered down the hall. Aimee was keenly aware of all the annoyed looks some of the other girls on the floor were giving them as they went about getting ready for the day, but Viv and company never seemed to notice. "We need to go this weekend. Just grab a bus! My aunt knows somebody who rents those out, we could all totally go!"

Aimee watched as Viv applied her makeup, but not being very skilled with it, she opted out of trying to paint her own face. They were talking about going to Vegas, which had Aimee's eyes wide with curiosity. She had spent the last week stalking Tony's favorite coffee spot to no avail, but she didn't have anything better to do with her time anymore. She pretended to go to classes to convince Viv and the others, but she was a ship loose in the sea. Soon she would need to get a job, but Viv had hooked her up with a meal card for now. "Vegas? I've never been there."

Every head in the vicinity jerked in her direction, every set of eyes giving her a once-over as they took in her appearance from head to toe. "Oh my god! That's it, we're going. We are gonna pop this cherry's Vegas cherry!"

"Sounds scandalous." Aimee teased gently as all eyes remained on her. There was no way to get used to the attention, and she found it both a curse and a blessing.

Exactly the way the Voice wanted. She wasn't going to acknowledge the Voice again, at least not for a long time. It didn't feel like a game she could reasonably play anymore, especially with every passing day of never being able to find Tony.

"Oh it will be. That's a promise." Viv was already dancing in her chair as she worked on the rest of her makeup. "How the *hell* have you never been to Vegas? You'd make a killing. Maybe do some dancing, work at one of the casino bars? I'd bet you a nipple piercing you could walk into one of the casinos on a Friday and leave on Monday morning with three sugar daddies. Minimum."

"I've just never traveled much." She tried to act like it wasn't a big deal but the surprise of the others made her want to hide from their attention. "Nipple piercing? I'm not . . . nope."

"Oh come on, they're fun! Michelle just got hers done a couple weeks ago." Viv tossed back into the hallway.

"And they're still healing! That part, not so fun." Michelle, still adjusting her shirt for the day (carefully) popped into the bathroom to share a mirror.

Aimee glanced down at her own shirt and shook her head again. She wasn't going to risk her now-perfect breasts with piercings. She was already paying a steep price. "I'll . . . I mean, Vegas sounds like fun. Maybe it'll be good to get away for a weekend or something. A sugar daddy . . . feels a little soon after my boyfriend."

"Oh come on, no man is worth holding yourself back like that." Viv rolled her entire head back to glare at her. "Especially one that's making himself as hard to even find as your guy. You've been out every day for a week after that asshole. If he's not where you can find him, then he isn't who you thought he was. We need to get you moved on, like, yesterday."

"It's complicated." She looked and felt defeated, but she didn't want to give up. Her biggest worry was that the Voice had done something to Tony, and she had no way of knowing. Any time she considered asking about him, the Voice refused to give her any information. Her best bet was the coffee shop, and it looked bleak. "I've only ever slept with people I'm dating."

"Well that's fine. Vegas is a great place for dates that last for days. I knew a girl who went on a date with her boyfriend and they decided to be married for the weekend. Crazy bitch." She focused on her eyelashes as she reminisced.

Aimee didn't have anything to say about that, but she watched as Viv did her makeup perfectly. "You're so good at your makeup. I'm terrible at it."

"Well you probably never had much reason to practice, hotness." Viv pulled her in and plopped her down in the seat next to her, dragging Aimee closer by a razor-tipped grip on her thighs. "You're about as punched-up as it gets, but I've got a lip look that would look *amazing* on you right now."

She smiled at Viv and again felt fortunate that she was in the right place to find a rescuer like her. She would have been lost without Viv and Michelle. Even if they were a bit much at times. "You're one of the nicest people I've ever met, you know." Aimee didn't know if her new appearance was entirely the reason for her new friends, but she was grateful regardless.

Viv returned the bright smile as she worked on Aimee's makeup. "Well that's just because you haven't seen my bad side yet. Much less been on it. I'm a vindictive bitch when I set my mind to it. Usually only to my exes, though, so you should be safe. Until you decide to fall madly in love with me, anyway."

"I'm glad for the warning. I will not get on your bad side." Aimee sat patiently and when Viv was finished, she gasped softly at her own reflection in the mirror. Now her beauty was unreal. Between magic and makeup, she was something else. "I, um, I think I will go to Vegas with you, but there are a couple of classes I can't miss before we go." She had to check campus a few more times before they left, but she knew she would be back to stalking as soon as they returned.

"Okay, do your thing, girl. Just make sure you have room in your schedule for a long, *long* weekend. Oh, I'm gonna call my aunt on lunch, oh and I know this one girl who lives in Reno, she'll come down and ride with us, she's got all the ins and outs. Oh I already love this idea! I need this. Need! In my soul. My soul needs this."

"Long, long weekend." Aimee laughed softly and gave her newfound friend a nod as she got up and went to get her shoes by Viv's door. After two nights on the floor, Viv felt bad, so they shared her bed for the rest of the week. Spooning with a stranger wasn't so bad, especially because Viv was an expert snuggler.

She tugged her shoes on and gave Viv a wave before she grabbed her bag and headed to campus. Once she reported being robbed, the school was nice enough to help her with some aid and some supplies, though she was certain that if she still looked like her old self, no one would have batted an eye. She wondered if anyone would have helped her at all.

Campus was busy by the time she was released by her new friends to her own devices, the spring days finally starting to get warmer after a long winter, and people were out in force to make up for lost time. There was a particular set of steps where she and Antony had hung out multiple times, but there was no sign of him. A set of trees and benches outside of one particular classroom building held similar memories, but similarly, no sign of Antony.

Aimee wandered for an hour and ended up back at his favorite coffee shop, though she expected to find nothing. Today, though, the heavens opened and she saw him. Sitting alone inside, tucked away, and she found herself running toward the shop.

Aimee burst inside and went directly toward his table, trying to find a way to stay calm. She couldn't reveal herself, but actually seeing him again gave her hope that this could be salvaged. "Hey. Um. Hi."

She had seen him before after pulling several consecutive shifts at the hospital, but as bedraggled as he had been on those occasions, he had always found a way to get home, get cleaned up, and catch at least a little rest. The version of him sitting at that table, though, had bags of fatigue under his eyes and a much taller cup of coffee than he typically got for himself. She could see a slight glow from the Mark on his arm as it barely showed beneath his sleeve, but his head was in his hand. Maybe that was what she looked like when she was negotiating with the Voice? There, but not there?

He looked up when she spoke to him, but it took his eyes a moment to focus on her completely. She could have sworn there were tendrils of gold and shadows in his eyes still retreating as she looked down into them. "Hm? What? I . . . can I help you?" His voice sounded ragged and his eyes were red.

She desperately wanted to reach out, touch him, comfort him, kiss him, but all she did was sit down across from him. Wasn't she the woman of his dreams? Wouldn't he be fascinated with her in front of him? "You look like you're having a hard day. Like someone who could . . . use a friend."

He attempted to give her a smile, but it didn't get very far in lifting the corners of his mouth. "I . . . it's been a bad few days. Some of the worst, honestly. But that's nobody's fault but mine. I appreciate the sentiment, but I'll . . . manage. Whatever that looks like."

"I'm sure it's not entirely your fault." She tried to assure him, since *none* of it was his fault. Aimee felt pained, not being able to say anything. "My, um, my name is Aimee." She took a deep breath and let it out slowly. "Is there anything I can do to help you?"

"I'm Antony." He introduced himself as if it was a name he was giving up on. "I, um, probably not, but I'm . . . kind of asking anybody who'll listen." He reached into the bag he had on a chair beside him and took out a photograph she herself had taken of him and her former self from months before, framed in a window with a snowy world behind them. "My girlfriend disappeared a week ago. They found her keys and wallet in Almsford Park just off campus. Is there any chance you've seen her?"

Aimee looked at the picture of the two of them and her hand actually trembled when she tried to reach out. She couldn't touch it. Some unseen force wouldn't let her. "I'm sorry." Her apology stopped abruptly and she swallowed hard, as the Voice wouldn't let her compromise her current identity. "I haven't seen her. You . . . do they . . . any signs of violence?"

He shook his head, looking at the picture rather than at her. "No, none. Her phone just shuts off in that park and hasn't been picked up since, there's no cameras in the area for them to pull from, there's just . . . nothing."

Aimee actually convinced herself to reach out and touch his hand, and she felt like her heart was shattering as she watched him. He didn't care who was sitting in front of him, he just cared that Molly was gone. "I'm sorry. Maybe there was a reason."

"Yeah, I'm sure there was." He shook his head and put away the photograph without returning her touch. "I'm sorry, I've just . . . been asking around, hoping someone saw something."

"I wish . . . I had something to tell you." She stared at him and felt like she was on the verge of a panic attack.

This was a mistake. Even though she enjoyed the attention of her new self, it was nothing compared to Tony and what they had between them. She thought she was doing it for him, for them, but he looked so broken. He wasn't even looking at her, and she was there waiting for him to discover her. How could she possibly get him to see?

"If, um, if I see her or something is there some way to reach you?"

"I . . . yeah, that's . . . very kind. I'm . . . I'm enrolled at the med school, I work with Dr. Price up there a lot, she's my attending. I might end up running around more looking for Molly, but Dr. Price will know how to get in touch with me."

Aimee opened her mouth to try to get his number again, but he still wasn't looking at her. She felt nauseous. "I'm sorry." She whispered as her eyes filled with tears that she hurried to blink away.

She got up from her seat slowly. "No one deserves to have their heart broken like this." She chewed on her bottom lip, a habit that even a new body couldn't change. There had to be a way to reverse what she did, but it would take time to work out a deal. Would he even forgive her if Molly came back? What if she changed herself back and he didn't want her anymore? Then where would she be?

"Sorry to be a downer, Aimee." He sniffed as she got up, and attempted to give her a quick look and a nod. "Thank you. For . . . caring."

"More than you know." She felt even more nauseous as she took a few steps back. "I'm sorry." She repeated as she stared at him a moment longer and forced herself away.

As soon as she was outside of the shop she was gulping for fresh air, and panicked. *Can I go back? What if I want my old life back?*

The pact is made. The Voice reiterated, its hazy life moving slowly, contentedly, within her consciousness. *It cannot be unmade.*

Can't be unmade? She stumbled her way to a nearby bench and fell into it. *There's always a way! What would be the cost? I can go back, there's always a way!*

The balance, once attained, is not to be diminished, though it may be expanded. The price of your new life was all that you once were. It will not be undone.

Aimee looked back at the coffee shop and felt like her chest was going to explode with pain. *I did this for him! For us! He didn't even look at me, what good are you if you can't fix this?!* She buried her face into her hands as her whole body trembled. There was no way back. She didn't have anything to offer, nothing to create a counter-balance to get her old life back. *I love him.*

The Voice had no response to her protests, or to her declaration of love. Maybe, as far as the Voice was concerned, love was irrelevant. Or at most, just one more thing to balance.

Behind her, Antony left the cafe, coffee in hand, heading back to campus. If he saw her as he passed by on the other side of the street, he gave no indication of noticing.

It was later than she planned to be by the time she made it back to Viv's, but it wasn't as though she had much to pack. Between an unused duffel that used to belong to one of Viv's exes, and a backpack that Michelle had given her secondhand, she was all packed up for Vegas.

After sobbing in the library for almost the entire day, then showering in the rec center, she was already exhausted and depressed, but she made a decision. If she couldn't be with Tony, she wasn't going to torture herself by being near him. He wouldn't stop looking for Molly, but she could tell that the Voice would prevent her from giving him any kernel of truth. She wondered if it would go so far as preventing her from finding him again, even if they crossed paths.

She was going to Vegas and she was going to stay there, as much as it tore her soul to do it. "Viv, I'm all ready to go. I'm leaving my emotional baggage here too. No more ex drama."

The look on Viv's face was sympathetic as she stepped in to take her strange, taller friend in a tight hug. "Oh, honey, whoever he was, he wasn't worth ruining that mascara." She held Aimee and rubbed her back under the sharp points of her manicured nails for a while. "What happens outside of Vegas, stays out of Vegas. Fuck him. I mean, not actually fuck him, but fuck him. You know? We're gonna have fun. It's gonna be great."

Tony was worth it. He was worth it all, but she had already gambled too much and lost. Going to Vegas wouldn't break her, she had nothing left to lose. The cold reality of a deal too costly that couldn't be unmade sat like a boulder in her stomach.

"It'll be great." Her voice shook as she attempted to agree, but she wasn't sure anything would ever be great again. "Let's hit the road."

FOUR

After

Aimee strutted her way off the stage covered in sweat and glitter when Joe touched her on the arm just as she made it through the curtain. She looked up at the tall, muscled body guard and quirked an eyebrow, but she shook her head. Usually he only talked to someone at the curtain if a special request had been made, and she felt way too tired to do a private dance.

"Oh come on, Joe, it's the end of my shift." She pleaded as she looked at him doe-eyed, though topless and in a thin black thong. From college dropout to stripper, she was at least making more money now than she ever thought possible. "I'm so tired. Can't you get rid of whoever it is?"

"Sorry, babe, can't do it. But this one you can actually get wrapped up for, if you're of a mind to. Fella says he doesn't want a dance, just to talk." He nodded out through the curtain at a man sitting by himself at a table near the back of the room, with a full spread of plates nearly covering the table in front of him. He was paying a great deal more attention to the food than the entertainment.

She looked confused as she looked out, but she heaved a sigh. "Fine. I'm gonna do a quick rinse. This glitter is not traveling anywhere I'm gonna regret." Aimee gave him her traditional kiss on his cheek before she hustled away in her heels, a talent she had developed after too many months of sprained ankles.

It'd been nearly a year since she arrived in Vegas, and Viv still came to visit from time to time. Mostly because Aimee had all the hookups now. She never had asked many questions about where Aimee had come from in the first place. Free drinks and VIP room access helped with that.

After a quick rinse, a pat dry, a few swipes of makeup and a dress tossed over her head, she slipped her feet into some flats and headed out to have a chat with a stranger. It was a norm by now, but she still wasn't thrilled about it.

She had acquired a knack for reading the kind of person she was dealing with on her way to any given customer. Tourists were most of their business, given the club's location, and they came in all flavors. The man who had asked after her was clearly no tourist. Or if he was, he was a very hungry one.

Blond, spiky hair tipped with a few waves of icy blue formed a kind of crown on top of a perpetually smiling face, the man's features stretched into a broad grin that seemed like his default expression. He was writing in a notebook as she approached, his pen racing over the page in hurried lines that couldn't possibly result in more than gibberish at his pace.

He wore a blue suit with gold stripes, his torso hugged by the vest, with no tie to be seen. In spite of how much food it appeared he consumed, judging by the empty plates, either he'd just had four of his closest friends having dinner with him in a strip club, or the man had downed enough buffet food for two Thanksgivings, and was still snacking on potato wedges every few lines of scribbling.

As she got closer, he looked up like a squirrel that was alarmed by a passing lawnmower, his stretched expression turning to curiosity briefly before breaking apart in a brilliant smile all over again. "Ruby! Delighted to meet you. Please,

please, join me. Are you hungry?" He stood quickly to pull out a chair for her across a corner from his own, and was back in his seat before she'd even taken a breath to answer.

Aimee looked at the chair before she sat down but she didn't decline any food. The one thing she discovered early on was a perk of her magical perfect body . . . she couldn't gain or lose more than ten pounds either way. Although overeating or undereating made her sick really easily, so the balance was still maintained, apparently.

She grabbed a mozzarella stick and took a bite. "Ruby is what we'll stick with for now. I'm not really hungry but I *am* exhausted."

"A ruby indeed. A bit on the nose, but I'm not really one to talk. I'm Casey, and yes, I used to be a case worker. So." He shrugged with a giggle and ate another potato wedge, closing up his notebook. "And you have every right to be exhausted. Ugh. The *work* you all put in up there, I get tired just watching you, hand to the gods. Did you come off with a good night, at least? I hope?"

Aimee looked even more confused. "You're asking me if I made good money?" She looked around to see if someone was filming her secretly or something. "I pay taxes, this place is legal. I checked."

He looked at her inquisitively for a few heartbeats before he burst out in another fit of giggling. "Oh nonononononono no, I could not possibly give fewer shits about that than I already do. Are you kidding me? No no, I want to know if this place is doing alright for you. Paying the bills, keeping the nail polish on, all the whistles and bells. I've got a bad habit of buying out places if I find out they're treating their workers like trash or they're not turning as much profit as they should be, and this place oughta be turning up like lost luggage. I just want to make sure you're doing well here. Are you?" Did the man have to breathe? If he did, it seemed someone had forgotten to give his lungs the memo.

She still wasn't entirely convinced that she wasn't being filmed for some kind of trap. But apparently the man was rich, with a bad habit like that. "It pays the bills. I'm not wealthy by any means, but I don't have to work on the side if you know what I mean. Just strip." She finished off the mozzarella stick and grabbed another. "I'm not sure I'm your type, since you haven't looked down at my tits once. Why, um, why did you ask for me if you're not here to catch me doing something illegal or ask for a dance?"

"Well, people are allowed to be interested in you for other things besides what gets them off, aren't they, sweetheart?" He did look down at her tits when asked, and shook his head. "But you're right. They are two truly marvelous pieces of work, as is the rest of you, but no, you are not at all my type. My boss thought it would be unwise to send a straight man for this particular conversation, and I wholeheartedly agree. My husband might like you, but I locked him down years ago, so even that will be all look and no lick. Can I get you a drink?"

Her nervous habit kicked in and she chewed on her bottom lip. His boss? Oh god, was he with the mob? Was the mob real? "Do I need a drink?"

"I mean, I don't really think so? There's not going to be anything unfriendly about this conversation. Or particularly stressful. At least, I would rather it wasn't. I manage enough people and deal with enough bullshit for my job, this part doesn't need to be all high-intensity and stressful, I don't think. I'm having one, though. Helps slow me down a little. Or so I'm told. Can I get a mojito, please?" He flagged down one of the waitresses passing by, then pointed to Aimee. "And a . . . what're you drinking?"

"Just a glass of red wine is fine. I don't have a car so I'll be taking a cab home anyway." She munched on the food a little more. "You do seem pretty high strung. Did you order this food only for yourself?

"Yup! I was just a little peckish. I had dinner earlier at one of my bars." He gave her a broad grin, but he didn't seem to be joking. "You'd be surprised how many calories you burn when you're running just shy of Mach One through this city's streets. The worst is making sure you avoid all the pedestrians, you know? I mean, not like anybody can actually *see* you when you're moving that fast, so it's not like anybody's gonna ID me off of it, but just all the wiggle and bob and weave to get out of their way, it's *killer*, especially on the calves."

He piled up a few empty plates to make a little more room between them, absent-mindedly pre-busing the table a bit to make life easier on the waitstaff. "Oh, I forgot about these. I shouldn't have to tell you, since you work here, but if you haven't, you should try the meatballs. They're amazing. And just a touch ironic considering the venue, which I respect."

"Running . . ." Aimee cleared her throat and sat up a little straighter. She actually itched at her side as though she could feel her Mark burning her skin, but it had to be imagined anxiety. "You . . . ran? All the way . . . ?"

"Cheaper than a cab and it beats fighting traffic." He spoke succinctly for once, watching her reaction with an intense look that eventually turned into a quieter smile than his usual. "Not your preferred flavor of magic, though, I'd guess. Wouldn't really help to be all high-strung and hyperactive doing everything you do up on that pole. Good way to fall off and break a neck."

Her eyes widened as soon as he said the word magic. It felt like ice water was dumped on top of her, and her heartbeat took off. "I've never met . . ." the only other magical person she had ever known was Tony, and she hadn't seen him since the day she found him in the coffee shop. "How did you find me?"

"Well it's not like you're in witness protection, sweetie." His eyes did flick down, but not toward her breasts. They lingered lower, on her ribs that were presently covered up by her dress. "A guy in my covenant saw you dance here a couple nights ago, sent the information up the chain. I'm actually either terrified or deeply disappointed in some of my organization's security measures that you've been working here for what, better part of a year? And this is the first we've heard of you? You're either very good at keeping yourself below the radar or we just don't get out to this side of town as often as we should, I'm not sure which."

"There's a chain?" As soon as the drinks arrived, she started gulping her wine. "I usually find a way to cover it up." She clarified after drinking half the glass. "I'm not perfect at it, but I . . . it's kind of a toxic relationship, me and the disembodied asshole. I only 'commune' when it feels absolutely necessary."

"The disembodied asshole!" He leaned his head back and roared with laughter, coughing into his arm afterward. "Oh gods I needed that. That is *spot* fucking on. I love it. And yes, toxic is a very nice word for what it can be sometimes." He sipped at his own drink rather than guzzling it, but he was still talking around mouthfuls of what little food remained on his table. "Did you come into town from another covenant and just never bothered to meet the locals? Where'd you come in from?"

"Another what? Covenant?" Aimee felt weird talking about things out in the open, but it was late and there weren't a lot of people around anymore anyway. The closer to sunrise, the more people went back to their homes. "I'm from . . ." She sighed and rubbed at the back of her neck, since she didn't always know when a limitation would kick in. "Out of state. I can't really talk about my past. It's a condition. My name is really Aimee, by the way."

"Zimmerman, I know. We try our best to do the homework and the reading before showing up to class." He shrugged and lifted his drink, clearly not about to apologize for checking up on her. "Moved three times since you got into town, best we could find for your point of origin was a shot of a party bus on your way in from the west side almost a year ago. A little late for the spring break crowd, maybe, but it's bikini o'clock somewhere."

His tone was even and casual, clearly not judging her or threatening her with any of the information he was rattling off. "You just planning on drifting, then? Most of the time floaters don't stick around for a full ring around the rosie ball of death in the sky if they plan on moving on someplace else."

"This is my life now, I don't intend on going anywhere else." She was uncomfortable with their investigation, but she knew they wouldn't find anything beyond what they already found. Her past self was erased. Gone. Even *she* couldn't resurrect her own past. "I don't have family or friends, beyond the other girls here. No roommates, not even a cat. This was the easiest way to make money without risk of STDs."

"I mean . . . that's a fair point. Though this job is a *lot* harder than a lot of other jobs I know of. You're really good, though, I can see why you'd stick to it. And I know the money can be good." He looked at her quietly a while longer, considering some of her answers. "So you don't . . . have any ties? At all? Even to the one who gave it to you? I'm not trying to say you're a liar or anything, but you've gotta understand, people like us . . . we tend to stack up connections, good or bad, along the way. Hearing you say you don't have any is more than a little weird. And, you know, that's someone like us, calling something weird. So that bar starts a lot higher."

"Why would I have any reason to lie about being alone? You sought *me* out, not the other way around." She looked into her wine glass and swirled the liquid a little before she drank the rest. "I paid a high price to look like this. It cost me everything. More than I realized at the time. The love of my life. So this is just easier. Less collateral damage."

Understanding passed over Casey's face like a shadow as his lips parted, and sympathy immediately replaced the laser focus in his eyes. "Oh, sweetie, we are gonna need a lot more wine." He tipped back the rest of his mojito with an appreciative smack of his lips and stood up, grabbing his suit jacket from a chair nearby. "You're done here for the night, right? Because I've got a shift I need to check on at sunrise and we've got half a dozen people you need to meet before then. That is, if you meant what you said about sticking around."

"I meant what I said." She stood up even though she was exhausted and sore, but she also didn't know what other options she had. This Casey person knew her biggest secret, and she didn't want to run. She had a home in Vegas. A job. Stability, as much as she could have it. "I'm done here."

She looked around and gave Joe a nod when they made eye contact, since Joe was one of her favorite protectors. No way would he let her out of his sight without a nod of reassurance. Joe looked a little nervous on her behalf, since she didn't usually leave with customers, but with her reassurance, he went back to his usual spot near the stage and let her be.

The quick interaction had caught Casey's notice, and he was smiling when she looked back at him. "I'm glad they look after you. That's not an easy thing to find sometimes." He stopped a waitress and paid his bill, with what was clearly a hefty tip, given the woman's reaction. When he led her out into the relative chill of the early desert morning, he guided her over to a motorcycle parked up against the building. "You might want to try and get a handle on that dress. I'll try and mostly obey the posted speed limits, but even those won't save you from the laws of aerodynamics."

"Maybe it will air out some glitter." She knotted her dress at the side to tighten it around her thighs and shrugged as she kept her purse close. "Best I can do. It's not like I'm hiding my kitty on stage, the Vegas air can handle her."

"Oh, I forgot about the glitter . . ." he looked her over in concern and heaved a dramatic sigh as he threw a leg over the bike. "Oh well. It's not like it's the first time I've been doused in the stuff, and it won't be the last." Once she settled onto the bike behind him, he revved them into motion and tore off through the Vegas streets at speeds that registered as poorly advised, at best.

Traffic, in spite of his earlier complaint, seemed not to

be an issue while Casey was driving. It was possible he was just that good at weaving through it, but the complete lack of red lights along their path suggested it was more than that.

The breakneck pace took them a few blocks west of the highway, past a strip mall and into a complex of subdued three-story apartments that were built in horseshoe pockets, as if to put their collective backs to the hubbub of the city and securely enclose all the residents. The muted shades of faded blues and red-tiled roofs washed out the appearance of the complex against the desert morning.

There was a gatehouse with no gate at the complex entrance, and Aimee could see what looked like a pair of brothers inside, watching Casey's approach. One of them leaned out the window with a curious look as her new fast-talking friend finally slowed his pace on approach. "You good?"

"Yeah, we're good, William. No worries. Is the boss up at his place?" Casey put one foot down to stabilize the bike as he slowed.

"Last I checked. We'll call up and let him know you're bringing her in." The man gave her a friendly nod of her own as Casey got moving again. The other brother inside the gatehouse was already moving to a phone on the wall inside.

Aimee didn't loosen her grip for fear of her life, but the man she was clinging to was also the cause. She looked at the guards monetarily and gave them a small smile. "Cute guards."

"They're both single, in case you're in the market." Casey's voice was much easier to hear at the sedate pace he kept on the way through the complex. He turned in at the second pocket of units, where the central tower of the building seemed a bit more built out than the others.

He hopped his bike up onto the sidewalk beside the entrance to let her off, setting the kickstand in some spilled mulch. "You don't have any mind-blocking or thought-altering pacts, do you? They're not a problem, exactly, but the boss gets annoyed with those."

"No. I only have two. One for my appearance and one for luck." She shrugged after that, since she knew it was probably weird that she didn't have many. "Like I said, I have a toxic relationship with the disembodied asshole."

"Some of us do, for sure." He walked ahead of her at a pace that blurred a little in her vision before he consciously slowed himself down to walk with her toward the entrance. "We've got a variety of outlooks in the covenant. There's some here who have it just as a family thing, kind of an inheritance, some actually revere it like the closest thing they're going to find to god. Most of us, myself included, are a lot like you. We're just what the cat dragged in. We collect a lot of transients and people with a diversity of talents. Our bosses don't care much where you came from or what you believe, so long as you're willing to be a part of things and be helpful when you're called upon to help."

"The mob, then. Got it." She looked around at the design of the complex on the way in, making a small world for itself. Garages and cars, apartments, a couple pools and lounging. Vending machines here and there, a laundry facility. "Just don't tell me it's a cult where someone expects me to be the stripper sister wife."

"I mean, if that's what you're into, I'm sure I could find you somebody. We've got all kinds, like I said." He opened and held the door for her as he laughed. "But no, it's not a requirement for entry. No blood sacrifices or ritual orgies either, though you might have a headache after your meeting. We all do. It doesn't last too long."

"A headache? Who am I meeting, exactly?" She walked through the door cautiously. "Do I get any more warning than that?"

"No, sorry. If I could tell you more, I would. Most of us don't bite, don't worry, you're not in any kind of trouble." The building was clearly not laid out much like an apartment building, leading initially to a foyer with what looked like a grand ballroom beyond it and a staircase nearby leading up directly to the third floor, which Casey was already taking two stairs at a time. "Right up here, sorry about the steps."

"I dance in heels. I'm fine. These legs are made of steel even when I'm tired." Aimee hustled after Casey, though she did wish she was in her own bed. "Mostly fine. It *is* late. Early. Something."

"Something something five o'clock something something . . ." Casey muttered as they got up to the landing. There was a lavish hallway at the top of the stairs that looked down on the foyer below, with a door at the other end that looked like it could be either an apartment or a maintenance closet, it was hard to tell which. The overlook had an internal hallway coming off it at a T, cutting the building in half down the center, with two doors at the end to the right and left and a final door at the end. Casey led her to the door on the left, which opened before he could even lift his hand to knock on it.

"That never stops being weird, you know that, right?" Casey joked with whoever was on the other side.

"Anticipating people's needs is my specialty, Mr. Nielsen, just like you have yours." A polite and heavily-accented voice came from the other side of the door. "He is on a phone call at the moment, but he asked that I see you both seated with refreshments. Please, come in."

"Thanks, Jacob. Jacob, Aimee Zimmerman, Aimee, Jacob. The boss's butler. Sort of." Casey made the introductions as quickly as he did everything else, gesturing between Aimee and the tall, mediterranean man on the other side of the door. "I'm not actually sure what the official title is, to be honest."

"That's because there isn't one." Jacob's snark was dry enough it could have been British. "Pleased to meet you, Ms. Zimmerman."

"Uh, sure." She held out her hand but she wasn't sure if she should. "I'm not entirely sold on how pleased I should be, but you seem nice enough. Also, I think 'personal assistant' sounds better than butler."

"That . . . would not be an inaccurate title." His tone was as reserved as the smile and the handshake he gave her, not quite fully agreeing or disagreeing as he closed the door behind them. He showed them to a couch across from an absurdly large television flattened into the wall above a fireplace, where a pair of drinks were already waiting for them.

The unit was apparently a single enormous open floor plan that clearly took up its half of the floor, with only two visible doors, one of which was open to show a guest bathroom on one end of the space. Every surface shone in black and white marble with silver accents, punctuated in a dozen places by strange flowers in elegant monochrome pots. Some of the windows looked out on the empty lot under construction just outside the complex, while the others looked inward at the parking lot where Casey had parked a few minutes before.

They could hear a man's voice from the closed door of what must have been the bedroom, but Aimee couldn't understand what language the man was speaking, let alone what was being said.

"You're definitely a part of the magic mob." She finally reached out for the drink after looking around carefully. "I don't know what you all want with a stripper who has an occasional lucky streak."

"Like I said, we take all kinds." Casey reached for his own drink and sipped at it quickly, then reached out to tap the bottom of hers. "Yeah, you're gonna want all of that. Down the hatch. It'll help with the headache, backwards as that might seem."

She raised her eyebrow but went ahead and gulped the drink. "If it turns out you drugged me or something, I'll come after you." She wasn't exactly the threatening type, but she also wasn't going to be a pushover either. "Does he usually make people wait to talk to him after sending someone to stalk them?"

"To be fair, most of the time when we find someone Marked in our territory, there's a bit of chasing involved. He probably didn't expect us until a little later." Casey shrugged and gulped his own drink, but there was a rather heavy silence from the other room. The boss's phone call was clearly over.

Out from the bedroom stepped a man that was well over six feet tall, slightly darker in complexion than Jacob, with short black hair and maybe a week's worth of stubble covering his cheeks and chin. The suit he was wearing looked both tailored and expensive, but he wore no jewelry that she could see as he approached the sitting area. He looked like a man in his late thirties or early forties, but there was a depth to his dark eyes that made her question any assumptions she had made about him based on the rest of his appearance.

"Ms. Zimmerman. Thank you for coming, and for your patience. That bit of business just now was . . . unscheduled. I hope Casey has made a good impression on you so far, though I believe I heard the word 'mob' used a moment ago. Hopefully by the end of this conversation you won't feel that entirely applies." He held out a hand and Jacob immediately filled it with a bottle of water without needing to be asked.

She pointed a finger and motioned up and down his suit and nodded toward his drink. "Sure quacks like the mob." Aimee gave him a one shouldered shrug. "I don't think I'm normally this snippy or sarcastic, but I'm exhausted, so can we . . . what are we doing, exactly? If you looked into me, you know I'm not a prostitute. You're good looking, though. I'll give you that."

The man actually smiled as he set aside the bottle. "I'll be brief, then." He held out a hand for hers, sitting in a chair across a corner of the coffee table from her. "I'm called Darius. My sister Sofia and I are the overseers of this covenant, which includes several hundred members living both in this complex and throughout the greater Vegas area, with a branch up in Reno and Tahoe as well."

He took a sip of his water as he sat back to give the rest of the apparently-abbreviated pitch. "We serve each other's interests, work together when necessary, and protect each other when threats inevitably present themselves. We are bound together, all of us, by a pact that permits us to know when one of our number has been injured, so as to facilitate that common defense. The same pact allows us to heal quickly, as all within the covenant heal every wound as a whole."

Darius smiled at the description of the pact's design, clearly rather proud of the system by which his people lived in harmony. "Being a peaceful stranger we have found to be living in our territory and bearing the Mark, you have two options. First, you are free to depart as a friend with our best wishes and relocate yourself wherever you see fit outside of our territory. Second, you may choose to stay, and participate in this collective effort to build a safe community here in Vegas. The choice is entirely yours."

"Several hundred?" She was stuck on that number for a minute before the rest registered in her head. "Wait, what? You're recruiting me or I have to get out? I haven't done anything wrong. Vegas is my home now, I don't have anywhere else to go."

"You asked for the condensed version." Darius didn't seem apologetic in the slightest. "The ultimatum is not meant to be punitive. You've been living on our territory for some time without us noticing and without you apparently having any knowledge of us. It's not as though we are tossing you out of your apartment this morning and insisting you catch the first bus out of town. If Vegas is indeed your home, as I said, you are welcome to stay, but to do so, we require that you do so as a member of our community."

Aimee frowned and looked him up and down again, clearly considering her words carefully. "I've spent the last year avoiding attachments of any kind. The Voice cost me everything. I'm not really eager to . . . it's messy. Why do I have to leave if I'm no threat to you?"

He actually nodded sympathetically at her mention of the Voice causing a mess, seeming unsurprised. "That is a valid question. Let me answer it with an example." He looked away at Jacob. "What year was it, nineteen . . . I want to say seventy-six?"

"Seventy-four, Sir." Jacob supplied easily.

"Nineteen seventy-four, yes." Darius turned his attention back to Aimee. "That was the last year we permitted transients to establish themselves permanently inside our territory. Two months after doing so, they had been approached, corrupted, coerced, and compelled to act against the interests and well-being of the people of this covenant. Fifty-seven people died." He did not look to Jacob for confirmation of that number. He apparently knew that one perfectly. "So you could say that as you've come to be less than eager about the idea of magical attachments, we have, on the other hand, learned the prudence of insisting on having them."

"I've been here a year." She countered, though she didn't want to seem callous about their losses, she didn't want to be manipulated either. "No one has approached me or coerced me or done anything of the like. Until tonight." She crossed her arms under her perfect breasts out of habit. "Listen, if you're going to mandate this, then I guess I have no choice, since I'm not leaving. But this is bullshit. And your excuse is bullshit. If you have hundreds of magical people at your disposal who can do a million different things, I'm no threat to you. Casey over there can run faster than I can blink, and I'm the scary one? That's absurd."

"You are quite right. You are no threat to us." Darius agreed easily, clearly not bothered by her complaints.

"Listen, Aimee, if I may call you that?" Casey chimed in on her other side, setting down his drink. "You . . . it sounds like you got a rough start with the Mark. I don't need details, and nobody here is gonna force any of them out of you. But you seem like one way or another, you got left high and dry and out in the cold someplace after you got it, and that's a lot of shit to deal with. But it also means you don't . . . really know the world you belong to now. And whether that's your fault or not, it's still the one you've gotta live in as long as you've got that star on your skin. You go out to the West Coast, they've got the same practices, you're just answering to different people."

"You go up to Canada and you've got a bunch of warring factions that jump all over the border like they're pulling weeds. You go to pretty much any major city in the Midwest and you're gonna find two or three local covenants fighting for power, not to mention climbing over each other trying to be the first to call Hunters out on each other. And don't even get me started on the east coast. Bunch of biker gangs and all-purpose assholes. My point is, everywhere you go, you're gonna have a conversation like this to look forward to. That's not something many of us can avoid. It's just a matter of which deal you end up taking, and speaking for myself, this one's pretty great."

"I don't know what you are talking about with covenants and Hunters and . . ." She shook her head again and let out a sigh. "I already said I'm not leaving. So I guess that means I'm making whatever deal this devil is offering." She looked away from Casey and back at Darius. "You both have the advantage of spinning whatever story you want and you know I don't know the difference. So what part of my soul are you demanding, exactly?"

Darius regarded her silently for an uncomfortable space, apparently unbothered at the notion of being called a devil, but contemplating her answer in the space offered by the quiet. Eventually, he sighed, and shook his head without looking away from her. "I will not have someone bound to this covenant who feels they've been forced in under duress. And as you said, it's been a long night for you, and you're already tired. Take a week to decide, and come to see me when you've made up your mind whether to stay with us or find your way elsewhere. We have a spare unit available already, I believe, yes?"

"We do, Sir." Jacob's voice came from behind the couch somewhere, attentive as always without intruding on the conversation.

"Good." He turned his attention back to Casey. "Get her fixed up and see about supplementing her education with whoever's available."

"Sure thing, Boss." Casey quickly agreed, with a note in his voice of . . . not exactly fear, but a vested interest in making sure Darius knew he was a team player.

Aimee looked between them again but she was beyond done with the conversation. She worked her ass off, literally, to survive in Vegas on her own. Now they were telling her to bend the knee or get out? It wasn't exactly friendly. "So I'm expected to stay here until I decide? I work across . . ." She remembered that he probably knew where exactly she worked but he didn't seem to give a damn about much of anything.

"Of course not. You are not a prisoner." Darius clarified, not rising to her alarm.

Casey leaned in closer. "The unit comes with a car. And a house out in the suburbs. I think we're actually cleaning the one that goes along with the one I'm thinking of right now, but I'd have to check with Zeke to be sure, he might be switching things around."

Aimee's shoulders slacked a little and she rubbed at her eyes, forgetting momentarily about her makeup. Even a year later she wasn't used to wearing makeup. "I just want to get some sleep. In the bed that I earned." She took a deep breath and let it out slowly. "There's a lot of details I couldn't give anyone even if I wanted to, okay? I've been watching out for myself for a year."

"I understand." Darius gave her a nod, dark eyes still mostly unreadable, but not precisely cold. Something in his voice told her he meant it. "Better than you may think. Mr. Nielsen will see you home. Get some rest. I look forward to hearing from you before the week is out."

She stared a moment longer and headed out without saying anything else, she didn't have anything else to say or do. She didn't know how her mind would be changed, she felt forced regardless, and she didn't want to leave. There was no way for her to outpace Casey, but she didn't know her way around this side of the city anyway. "I agreed to join. I don't know how the forced part is avoidable, you told me to get in or get out."

Casey clearly had no trouble keeping pace with her as she descended the stairs and headed back to his motorcycle. "The forced part is avoidable in that you getting out is still an option on the table." He kept the statement mostly under his breath as they exited, moving to get his bike started as she got herself settled on the back.

"If you don't want to take the deal, I know a guy who runs a club in Dallas I could probably hook you up with. Nice place, good bouncers, stays busy, guy who runs it does a good job making sure the dancers are treated fair. He also doesn't know a damn thing about magic, at least not from me. I don't know what kind of factions are active down there, or if they're as all-or-nothing as we tend to be around here. I can look into it for you and let you know."

Aimee took a few measured breaths as she sat on the back of his bike. "I don't want to go to Texas. I want to stay here."

"Well, you've got a week to decide if you're sure about that." He revved the bike into motion and took them out of the complex, past the two cute security guards on duty at the gate, and east across the city into the sunrise. He didn't even have to stop to ask directions to her apartment. Apparently he already knew where she lived. Because of course he did.

When she got off his bike at her complex, she chewed on her bottom lip, since fear had settled in on the quiet ride. She was scared to lose everything she had worked for and be completely lost all over again. She looked down at her feet when she spoke. "What should I expect next?"

"Um . . . well, sleep would probably be a good start? You know where the complex is, so if you want to come and visit, meet some other folks in the covenant, you're welcome any time. The guys at the gate will get you set up. I've got work the next . . . I don't know, thirty-six hours or so, but if you need anything, here's my number." He handed her a card from a pocket of his suit jacket. "If you're free on Tuesday, we can go hit the Bellagio and have kind of a walk-and-talk education day. It's kind of like you said back with the boss, you don't really know what you don't know. There's a lot I can help fill you in on. Plus they make great margaritas."

"Sure. Tuesday." She eventually looked up from her feet and gave Casey a weak nod. "I'll see you later." Aimee took another deep breath and started walking away as the feeling of fear sunk in. She didn't know what she was going to do, and this time she hadn't done anything wrong. Once again, having the Mark was fucking up her life.

FIVE

Aimee wasn't looking forward to Tuesday, but she took the night off, much to the shock of her employer. She never took nights off.

Not wanting to look as nervous as she felt, she wore a low-cut top and distressed jeans that hugged all of her curves. Aimee thought about heels but went with black converse instead, hoping to remain as comfortable as possible. She arranged a ride to the Bellagio so that she wouldn't have to depend on Casey for transportation and met him on the casino floor. "Hello again."

Walking through any of the major casinos of the city was always an overwhelming experience by design, but her fast-talking new acquaintance seemed right at home among all the brilliant lights and extravagant decor. He had a messenger bag slung across his chest and had ditched the suit he'd worn at their first meeting in favor of running shoes and shorts, topped off by a button-up shirt that hugged his torso.

"Hey, you didn't flee the country! I take that as a win." He was clearly in a good mood (was he ever not?) and seemed genuinely happy to see her. "Have you been here much while you've lived here? I've got the magic keycard, let me show you around."

"I've been here once. Just to see what it was all about." She was clearly quieter today, but she also wasn't exhausted and irritated like she had been the last time. "Oddly, I'm not much of a gambler."

"That is a little odd. I thought you said you had some kind of a luck pact? I would think you'd be throwing that thing around all over the place around here?" He led her through a hall filled with slot machines, people moving in small groups either to find a pod of them they liked best or just passing through on their way to some of the hotel's other wonders.

They passed beneath an art installation of thousands of flowers and butterflies formed from colored blown glass, but Casey barely seemed to notice. He was clearly familiar with the place. "We've run into a lot of new folks like that, people who get the Mark and then come to Vegas thinking they can beat the system with magic. It usually works, until it doesn't."

"I have a luck pact," she affirmed with a nod, but as they passed more slot machines, she decided to make a show of it. One man she passed, she paused, wished him luck with a smile, and a few steps away, he won $500.

He shouted gratitude her way, but she just waved, nodded, and kept walking until she heard a waiter crash into a woman who was showing off some new heels. Heels now dripping with wine. Aimee winced and looked back at Casey. "I can control where it starts, but not where the price of the luck lands."

Casey sucked in a hissing breath at the sight of the crash, clearly impressed. "Yowza. That's . . . you are a dangerous person, I like you." He watched to make sure the waiter had the situation under control, but kept moving along with her, though there was no way anyone in the vicinity could have tied either event to Aimee. "Got Lady Luck on speed-dial over here."

"Depends. I am also Lady Misfortune." She continued

to take in her surroundings as they hustled through, since clearly Casey had an objective in mind.

"Well, Lady Luck is also allowed to be a bitch occasionally. Wouldn't be luck if it only ever swung one way." He chuckled as he led her along, heading for one of the elevators away from the gambling floor. "I thought we'd start with whatever questions you have on your mind after meeting Darius the other day and we can go from there. Hopefully work's been alright since?"

"Yeah. Everything's been alright." She ran a hand through her hair, clearly displaying her nervousness. "I'm really not that much of a bitch. Not usually, anyway. Like I told him, I don't like the idea of depending on anyone or being attached to anyone. I logically realize that maybe I *should* want to know more about the Voice and whatever this is all about, but to me the Voice feels like an enemy that lives in my head. I don't want to feel closer to it."

Casey pushed a button for the 35th floor, leaning back against one of the walls as the doors closed on them. "That's never been my experience with the Voice, but I've known some folks who feel that way. It's possible to Mark someone against their will, which . . . sounds to me like one of the worst things one person could do to another, honestly. Getting shoved into something like that without getting a chance to prepare for it. I don't need to know if that's what happened to you or anything, that's your business and not mine, I just . . . I've known folks who had that happen to them before, and for them it almost always feels like the enemy."

He shrugged and continued, hands clasped over the strap of the bag he wore. "The good news, though, is when it comes to covenant membership, there's no need for you to get any deeper into things than you already are. In fact, some folks prefer that, sort of like you said. You'd be woven into the pact we all share that protects us, yeah, but the covenant will never, ever, *ever* force you or even ask you to make any more deals than you already have. No one's going to force you to learn any more about the Voice than you want to."

Knowing that she wouldn't be forced into much else did seem to relax her a little, but clearly she was still standoffish. "It wasn't forced on me." Aimee clarified quickly. "I asked for it. He was hesitant to give it to me, *I* made a deal that was too steep. I'd only had the Mark a short amount of time and he had only explained basic inter-workings because it hadn't been long. None of this is his fault."

"I'm still sorry. That's . . . not ideal. But hey, it's a good sign that you're still here, at least. You didn't give away so much that you completely ceased to exist. Or wound up in constant . . . yeah, I've seen some weird shit. But that gets more into knowing more about the Voice, so I'll stay away from that if you'd rather." The elevator was still rising, but they were getting into the high 20s.

"For the covenant, the way our pact works is like Darius said the other day, we all participate, and if one of us gets injured, everyone's body works kind of as a collective to heal it. Works as kind of a double system, we all know how each other's doing and if somebody's in trouble, and we all help each other stay alive. I've been a part of it for . . . twelve, no, wait, thirteen? Thirteen years now. I have to say, it's pretty great. Unless we have a neighborhood party and everybody is hung over all at once. Never doing that again."

Aimee chuckled a little at the thought. "I drink occasionally, but this body comes with a lot of . . . well, when I asked for perfection, I got it. I don't gain weight more than is within my weight range because I get sick if I try to consistently eat too much. Same with eating too little. It happens with any kind of indulgence. I can get drunk, but not wasted. High, but not blackout. Anything too far beyond equilibrium is not allowed."

"Wow. That's a hell of a package deal you got there." Casey laughed as he looked her over, clearly impressed. "You definitely are, though I'm sure you're pretty thoroughly aware of that by now. Flawless. I heard no end of it from the Porter twins at the gate the other night, asking when I was gonna head out and bring you back. Like I said, they're both single."

"That might get complicated if I'm living there. Hookups are fun. Not much else." She looked down at herself and sighed. "Yeah, it's flawless. Better be, for the fucking price I paid." She looked over at Casey with a sad expression. "You know how people always say that the flaws make the person? Sometimes I miss them. I miss a lot of things."

"Well, missing things is maybe a good reason to add on some new ones. That way you don't have to miss the old ones as much?" He gave her an unapologetically salesman smile as the elevator chimed their destination. Rather than letting the doors open, though, Casey's hand moved supernaturally fast, and swiped his access card across a part of the plating, closing the doors again.

The elevator rose just a few more feet before the doors opened again, this time on a corridor that clearly didn't belong to the rest of the hotel. The hallway was plainer than the others, with carpet that was done in sandy desert colors and floor-to-ceiling glass windows looking out over the Vegas skyline. It was a breathtaking view. Rather than numbers, each of the doors bore names. Darius. Sofia. Jacob. Zeke. Amber. The list went on in both directions until the hallway vanished with the subtle curve of the hotel's wings.

"We call these panic rooms. Not somewhere you necessarily want to live, though you can if you want to. All the leadership has one of their own, and the rest of us have the rest of the floor that we can cycle into if we need a place to lie low for a while. Nobody can bother you in a place that isn't supposed to exist."

"I didn't know places like this were necessary. Once I was hired at the club, I signed up for self-defense. I've been around too many aggressive men on the floor, but they do a good job of kicking them out. I did get followed home once, but I called Joe and he came right away. Slept on my couch like my hero and his wife brought us both breakfast. After that I bought a gun and I go practice at a range every now and again. I'm no sharpshooter but at least I don't cry when I pull the trigger anymore."

"Oh I can't handle guns, you're a better person than I am. Unless I'm trying to outrun them. Which I can't . . . most of the time. Clothes catch on fire from the friction." He shrugged as if his clothes being on fire was no big deal. "You can think of the whole covenant sort of like a bouncer that way, if it makes it easier. The person you call when you're in trouble, who you know is going to take care of you, who also lives partly off your tips. It's actually not a bad analogy, it's just not one I've ever thought to use before when making these pitches."

"So . . . you all take care of me and I turn in my paycheck?" She didn't know how she felt about that, but she did know that extra protection for someone who looked like her couldn't hurt. She had no interest in being attacked or . . . worse. "I can't lie and say that having more people have my back isn't tempting."

He snorted at the mention of her paycheck. "Oh hell no, you keep your paycheck. The covenant doesn't need it, believe me. We all get called upon from time to time to help out as other people need it. For instance, and I'm just brainstorming here, if we've got a new girl who's looking for a job, maybe you can put in a good word with your boss to bring her in and get her working. If we've got a guy we need some information from, they might ask you to get him in a chair and see how much you can get him talking. If we need an extra set of eyes or hands someplace, you might get called up for that. Hell, if you know how to handle a gun, maybe they'll ask you to take a shift on guard duty at the complex. Or escorting covenant property. There's all kinds of odd jobs people need done. And if they end up being illegal, then I can at least promise you the only reason will be to help sustain the covenant and maintain secrecy, not because we need to go ripping off bank tellers."

Aimee looked down the hall again at all the various rooms and she chewed on her lip in consideration. "So you own the Bellagio?"

"No, the covenant owns a hefty share of the groups that control . . . most of the casinos in the city. The Bellagio's just my favorite. I'm a sucker for the fountains." Casey's grin was incorrigible. "Like I said, we're not after you for your paycheck, I pinky-promise."

"Well. Shit. I'm surprised you don't own the club I work in." She shook her head slowly but she was glad they had the privacy of the exclusive floor. "I desperately wanted to do an internet search on 'Hunters' but something told me that I should probably just ask what that was all about. Individual panic rooms and Hunters?"

"Internet wouldn't have done you much good with them, but it was still a good idea not to. I don't know how closely they monitor people going searching for them, but I try to know as little about Hunters as I can." He sighed, leaning against the glass.

"The Hunters are an order of assholes who believe the Mark shouldn't exist. So they take whatever measures they can to ensure that it doesn't. Which means killing everyone they can find who has it." Casey shook his head. "That's an oversimplification, but that's the quick version. They're all over the world, always looking for evidence of one of us to go after, and they're not what I'd call reasonable people. They're zealots. And not my favorite people."

"It would have been nice to know about them before now." Aimee felt her panic rising all over again. "Between regular non-magical assholes and murdering zealots . . . I suppose I'm screwed if I try to keep to myself." She covered her eyes with her hand. "One of these floors has a bar, right?"

"Most of them do, honestly. But my favorite is actually down by the blackjack pits. They like showing off, and I'm a sucker for flair bartending. Come on." He led her back to the elevator, past the strange and peaceful skyline observatory deck. It was comforting, in a way, that such a sanctuary seemed empty at the moment.

They were quiet on the elevator for a while, but she eventually looked back at Casey. "And you're really happy here? No bullshit?"

"No bullshit." Casey gave her a smile. "I mean, the place has its ups and downs just like any other job and any other bunch of assholes all shoved into the same place. I like some folks in the covenant better than others, but it's . . . a good place. When Darius says we're here to have each other's backs, he means it. Once you're in and you're known to people, really settled into the covenant, it's . . . home. There's not much I wouldn't do for this place."

Aimee nodded slowly, but she was grateful when they were able to get off the elevator and into a bar. She needed a few drinks as she reconsidered her life. "I don't want to get attached and lose anything again." She reiterated as she fidgeted nervously. "But . . . could I get a different job? Here?"

"Oh, sure! You bartend? Or would you need to get set up with somebody to teach you?" She could see him giving a brief smile and a wave to various employees as they passed through the casino, clearly a known face.

"Not really. But I could be one of these waitresses, I bet they get decent tips here while keeping their clothes on." She gave a shrug, since she wasn't against stripping, but she didn't want to spend her life doing it. She also didn't know how or if she would age, which was a concern of hers. "And maybe it's not as exhausting."

"Sure you could. And if you've been dancing almost a year, you've already got the most important skill set you'd need for tending bar. Turning down customers who want your number more than a drink." He winked at her as they headed into one where he knew the woman who was making drinks.

When they sat down at the bar, the woman looked up

and smiled immediately as she saw Casey. She walked from one end to where they were seated. "You caught me right as I'm leaving. What can I get you and your friend, Case?"

"Mojito for me, thanks, Tam. I don't know what our potential new neighbor is drinking, but it's on me, whatever it is." He took a seat and adjusted his bag so that it would rest between him and the bar, leaning back against it to look out at the casino behind them.

"Rum and Coke, please." Aimee gave the woman a small smile and looked out as well, but she wasn't really capable of relaxing. "I do have a question about your boss."

"If I know the answer, you're welcome to it. I don't promise to have all of them where he's concerned." Casey visibly looked a bit cautious about Darius, but given the man's imposing nature, that was hardly surprising.

"If I . . . have questions about my own pact, would he have a way of helping me navigate it? He seems like the ominous mob-boss type who knows everything."

"Sofia's actually really good at those kinds of questions, helping people negotiate the Voice and all, but Darius could help too. We had a guy on the rolls a few years ago who was sort of the fixer for everyone, he specialized in that kind of negotiation. But Darius can probably help you with it if you want, sure."

"Good to know." She cleared her throat and looked up as someone approached with their drinks, although it wasn't Casey's friend. Aimee met a lot of men in her career, but the one in front of her with his sleeves rolled up and his muscular arms on display? Gorgeous.

"Mojito for the boss, good to see you around, Mr. Nielsen," the arms delivered Casey's mojito smoothly and then turned to Aimee. He bounced up the tray holding her rum and coke, then yanked the tray out from under it as it fell, and caught the glass by its base to hand it over to her. "And if you're here interviewing, let me be the first to say I really, *really* hope you get the job."

The man was built more like a linebacker than a

bartender, the formal suit jacket of his uniform struggling to contain the bulk of his shoulders. Clean-shaven and square-jawed, either his smile was practiced and professional or he really was just that friendly. It was hard to tell which.

Aimee couldn't help but admire the man, all his muscles required her undivided attention. She took the glass from him slowly as she tried not to gape. "I'm not sure about a job. Maybe." She eventually answered before she took a drink. "I, um, I'm Aimee."

He put out the same hand to take hers after she'd had a drink. "Pleasure to meet you, I'm Cody. I'm normally either working security or cleaning up in the back, but there was a bachelorette party in here a little while ago and Tom decided it was in the best interests of the hotel for me to serve some drinks." He laughed as Casey rolled his eyes. "I'm fairly sure they drank more than they otherwise would have, but I couldn't swear to it."

She smiled genuinely at his laughter. "I'm sure they did." Aimee held up her own drink before she took a gulp. "If the hotel knew what they were doing, they'd always have you front and center."

"Oh hell no, I don't think anybody wants that. I'm better off in the background until somebody needs to be reminded to have some manners." He nodded out at the rest of the casino floor, but couldn't keep his eyes off Aimee for very long. "What else can I get for you? You staying around for dinner?"

"I . . . don't know, actually." She realized she was still with Casey and she looked over at him briefly before she looked back at Cody. "I took the night off, I don't usually have a night off. I'm . . ." Normally she didn't really hesitate over her profession since this was Vegas, after all. "I'm a dancer at Club G."

"Oh hey, a friend of mine works over there, I've just never gotten over to that side of town. Which is clearly my loss." He looked her over with an appreciative smile. "You know Joe Beauchamp?"

She relaxed a little when he didn't flinch, and even moreso when he mentioned Joe. "Yes, I know Joe. He's saved my ass on more than one occasion. And his wife is the best cook I know."

"Macy's great. Especially when it comes to taking in strays like me. There was a while about two years back where I survived mostly on that woman's spaghetti. Good times." He grinned down at her, but another group was on their way into the club to be seated, so he moved past her with a hand on her shoulder to scoot by. "Tell Joe I said hi the next time you see him, it's been a while since we were in the same spot."

"Uh yeah. I will." Aimee watched him walk away and turned her attention back to her drink. "Seriously, if I can't get the phone number of someone like that, what am I even doing? He's gorgeous." She gulped down her drink feeling dismissed, but she quickly reminded herself that she shouldn't be chasing anyone anyway. Hadn't she just explained to Casey her need to avoid attachments? That meant no phone numbers, no chasing.

Casey had watched the entire interaction with a grin on his face as he sipped at his drink. "Oh, you wanted his number? I've heard a good way of getting one of those is asking for it." He chuckled at her and turned to look over his shoulder at Cody as Cody attended the new customers. "You've got good taste. I'd ask him myself, but I'm pretty sure I'm not his type. Plus, you know, the whole 'married' thing." He shrugged and kept watching the well-built waiter anyway.

She laughed softly at Casey's reaction to Cody. "He told me to tell his friend 'hello' and walked off. If he was interested, he would have mentioned paying a visit or, well, anything else." Aimee shrugged and finished off her drink. "Everyone has a type and no matter what you look like, you don't fit everyone's type." She looked contemplative as she stared into her now-empty glass, remembering how her appearance didn't even catch the attention of the one she changed it for. "When, um, about my question from earlier, do you think I could schedule a time to talk to your boss about my question? About getting help negotiating with you-know-who?"

By the time she was finished asking the question, Casey was staring at her as if she had suddenly switched to speaking Mandarin mid-sentence. "You . . . are serious right now. *How* are you serious right now? You really think . . . you *really* think . . . oh no. This, I will not abide." He took another sip of his drink and got up, clearly heading in Cody's direction to intercept the man on his way back to get drinks for the newcomers.

"What are you doing?" She tried to reach out for Casey but trying to stop the man from anything was impossible when it came to speed. Apparently. "He's working! What . . .!"

"He might be working, but I'm not and neither are you. You want his number, I'm gonna make sure you get it." He crossed the club to catch up with Cody on his way back into the kitchen, and held him up for a quick conversation that Aimee couldn't hear. Cody did, however, look back her direction at something Casey said, and then grabbed a pen out of his vest to write with, mouthing 'hell yes' as the only part of the conversation Aimee could pick up on at a distance.

Aimee's cheeks were burning as soon as Casey returned, and she wanted to make a run for it. She was wearing jeans and converse, she could make it out really quick. "Oh my god, I cannot stay here now." Her breath was shaky and small as she barely glanced at Casey but she was off her stool already. "Why did you do that?!"

"What do you mean, you can't stay here? He's hot!" He went back to his stool next to the one she vacated, picking up his drink as he handed her a coaster with Cody's number on it. "Plus, you had to see the guy's face. Like reverse Christmas morning. Never seen somebody so happy to be giving something away before." He sat back on his stool and sipped at his drink, clearly happy with a job well done.

She looked at the coaster in her hands and at the masculine scrawl before she looked at Cody again. He was talking to someone else by now, but her cheeks were still on fire. "That doesn't make any sense." She muttered as she kept a firm hold on the coaster.

As much as she liked to play indifference, when she actually cared about something, she was still a timid, insecure woman trapped in a body that said she should be otherwise. "He didn't try to chat me up or anything." Aimee was used to men at her club, women too, who were not at all shy about trying to monopolize her time. Cody was sweet, smiled at her, and then went on his way.

"My last boyfriend was . . . well, it took time before we started dating. And other than a few hookups with women here in Vegas . . . I haven't been with a man since. Or on a date with one either." Women were safer, kinder, sweeter. Never had she been threatened by a beautiful woman. No woman had tried to stalk her or cling to her. As she developed a reputation around Club G that she spent her off-time with women, the men were less likely to push so hard. Beautiful women were just as fun as sexy men.

"You made a deal for all this and you haven't taken it out for a full test drive yet?" He gestured to her from head to toe with an incredulous open-mouthed look. "Okay, I was not apologetic a second ago, but I am super not apologetic now. You need to call this man as soon as possible, and start getting your money's worth."

"I've had a few one-night-stands with women. Just not men." She looked at Cody again and her cheeks were heated for an entirely different reason. "He's gorgeous."

Casey leaned back on the bar and lifted his glass in a silent toast, shaking back his hair with a self-satisfied grin. "My matchmaking fee is modest, all I ask is a middle name of at least one child dedicated to me and an invitation to drink free at the open bar you'll have at your wedding."

Aimee snorted and actually laughed a little too loud,

based on the people looking their way. She covered her mouth with her hand and shook her head. "I'm never getting married." Aimee whispered afterward. "Are you insane? I can't risk loving another person. Bringing a child into this."

"Isaac and I are thinking of adopting sometime next year, thanks for asking." His grin still didn't deflate, but he did lean into her a little more closely. "What's the risk? I mean, aside from the usual hazards of getting your heart broken and crushing betrayal as a gateway to hard drugs. You know, the usual. Did you have to give up everything for your whole life? All of it?"

"A life for a life." Her laughter deflated even if his smile did not. Despite herself, Aimee still held tightly to the coaster. She didn't want to take the risk, but she also really wanted to go on a date with Cody. "I lost everything. Literally everything."

Casey just stared at her as she talked about it, then put his drink aside and reached out tentatively to take one of her hands. They hadn't known each other long at all, or very well yet, but he knew how long she had been dealing with things on her own. No one deserved that.

"If it took your life from you to give you a new one, then it gave you a new one. I'm not a master negotiator or as knowledgeable about what you've agreed to as Darius will be, but to me, that means whatever you were capable of having before, you're capable of having now. It wouldn't be a balance otherwise."

Aimee looked down at his hand holding hers and before she could really stop it, her eyes burned with tears. Logically what he said made sense, but she was still terrified of loss.

"I tried to undo it." She whimpered as she fought to hold back her tears. Before Casey, she hadn't ever spoken to anyone about the Voice, so her pain had been bottled up for so long. Tony was the one other person she knew that knew about magic and the devil behind the Mark. Who else could she talk to without sounding insane? "I regret it. How can I enjoy this life when I regret this so much?"

Casey shook his head. "I don't know how to answer that. But I know there's never any going back. It never gives up what it's been given. But you're still here. So you've still got life to be lived. Maybe that could be a life with us. We know how to party, I can promise you that."

Her shoulders slumped as she thought about Tony, and how she missed so much between them throughout the last year. He had probably moved on without her, but she didn't know if she could. "It's hard to mend a heart I broke myself." She met Casey's eyes with her tear-filled eyes. "This is going to sound really weird, but can I hug you?"

"That . . . is not weird. That's only weird because you said it was weird. Hugs are not weird. Hugs are human." He turned toward her on his stool and pulled her into a tight hug, lean arms gripping tight around her back. He clearly wasn't the strongest person she'd ever been hugged by, and she could feel the way his muscles seemed to be in constant twitchy motion even at rest, but he swayed a little as he held her, as if rocking her would help in any way.

A few tears slipped silently down her cheeks as she held onto the relative stranger in front of her, though he knew more of her truth than anyone else in the world did. She cleared her throat after a few long minutes and released him slowly. "Do you live in the complex? I know you're married, but it would be nice to live near someone I . . . could trust."

"Oh we all live wherever is convenient at the time. We've got an apartment in the complex along with everybody else, but Isaac likes the quiet, so our house is way, way out on the east side right up against the mountains. But we're always back and forth. And it's not like it takes me long to get from one place to the other. If I'm really pushing myself and not wearing particularly flammable pants, I can make it across the city in about two minutes."

"Okay." She took a few deep breaths as she decided to take another risk. "I want to stay."

Casey nodded as he squeezed her tight one more time.

"Yay! This is going to be so great, you'll see. I'll call Darius and let him know you want to meet up with him again. He's got final stuff to go over with you for the actual admission and all that."

Aimee tried to avoid another panic attack as she looked down at Cody's number. She wanted to say something to him, but when she looked for him, he was gone. "Will you take me for another tour? Trying not to freak out. Also this is my first day off in a long time."

He returned to his drink, but narrowed his eyes comically at her over the rim of it before breaking into another of his grins. "I'm going to go out on a limb and guess you've never shot craps. Is that a fair assumption?"

"Other than the stripping . . . I'm not really a risk-taker. Even that was totally a dare by one of my college friends, Viv, and it ended up turning into something bigger. She likes to gamble when she comes to visit but it's always on my dime." She laughed softly as she tucked the coaster into her back pocket. "I'll see him again, right?" She definitely had an ocean of self-doubt about a lot of things, but only because Casey had cracked her surface was she willing to voice it out loud.

"Only if you call that number. Which you'd better. Also, he works here, so I can just steal his information from personnel files and totally stalk him until you run into each other again." He finished off his drink and handed it off to Tam with a grateful smile before he grabbed Aimee's hand and headed away. "Come on, you're learning how to shoot craps. Call it a rite of passage."

Aimee gladly stumbled after Casey as he led her out, and she happened to catch sight of Cody on the way out. He was across the room but she paused long enough to smile and give him a wave before she let Casey lead her away.

* * * * *

There were no clocks inside the casino to tell them how

long they spent around the craps table, but by the time they stepped away, they'd had a good run. Casey had gotten a call from the complex that Darius was on his way back from an appointment and would have time to meet with Aimee sooner than later. They caught a ride back to the complex with Tam, who had just gotten off her shift.

Aimee was nervous all over again as they pulled into the complex, but Casey was a burst of reassurance when she looked at him. "You must sleep like the dead to pay for all your energy."

"Funny you should mention that, I actually do." He laughed and cracked his neck, as if sitting in the car for ten minutes to get across town to the complex was too long to be so confined. "So if you ever ask after me and somebody says I'm in a coma, just . . . realize they're not being serious, they just mean I'm in payment mode. My longest stretch so far is two weeks. That was a weird year."

"Two weeks?!" She knew that magic shouldn't surprise her so much, but in all fairness, she hadn't really seen that much magic. "You must have an amazing husband. And he's probably gorgeous too, huh?"

Casey melted into the seat. "Oh my gods, he's so hot. But like . . . not your-guy hot, more like librarian hot? But with a beard? Like, he somehow managed to sidestep professor energy, which would *not* have worked for me, and slid right into librarian energy and just set up shop. I could just . . . mmmm, but yes, he's the best. Though he's kind of a homebody type? So if I'm down for the count a while, he's fine with it because it just means the house is quieter and he can work on his research. It's amazing."

Aimee relaxed a little bit with Casey going on about his hot husband, and she took a calming deep breath. "I think I want you to be my best friend."

He grinned as he came out of his own head and back to the conversation, taking her hand again. "I think that'd be fun. I go fast, though. You better keep up."

Casey was kind enough to escort her to Darius yet again,

except this time she figured she could handle having a conversation with him on her own. She gave Casey a hug as they waited for Darius' summons, then she was on her own.

Jacob was there at the door to escort her in, as he had been the first time, but this time there was no waiting to see the man. He was getting up from a desk across the room where he had some paperwork under review, and set down the pen in his hand before turning back to her with a polite smile. "Ms. Zimmerman. I'm glad to see you back. I hope this means you've decided you'd like to stay."

"I think so." She looked at him for a moment before she approached his desk without being invited. "I have a question first, and I owe you a half apology at least. I wasn't in the best place to listen to your offer, but I won't apologize for standing up for myself. I'm terrible at it in the first place. But . . . I still don't know a lot about the Voice or the Mark. I can't tell you a lot about my past, there's a moment in time that I can go back to and that's it. About a year ago. I'm not trying to keep it a secret, it's literally not a part of my life. This life. Who I am now."

He stood and watched her as she spoke, taking in her tirade without commenting until she was finished. "That is . . . quite an extreme to have gone to in your dealings with it, especially for someone who claims not to know much about it. I can only assume that particular bargain did not . . . end as you imagined?"

"You could say that." She scoffed as she glanced down to her ribs where her Mark was. "I even took some desperate measures to try and get rid of it. Nothing that needed hospitalization, but . . . that Mark definitely doesn't disappear even when you hate it." She looked back at Darius again. "The man I loved gave it to me and I lost him trying to be more *for* him. I only know what I know from him and my own trial and error."

Understanding moved across Darius's features, and he gestured to the couches nearby where they'd had their first conversation, so that she could get more comfortable.

"There have been many traditions and rituals around the gift of the Mark recorded through history. Many of them, with good reason, involved long periods of contemplation and instruction, some of them even testing and rites of passage before it could be given, to avoid situations like what's happened to you."

As hard as the man's features were, and as merciless as she could see his soul was behind his eyes, there was still sympathy in his voice that seemed genuine. "I'm sorry for what you've lost. But you're right, it cannot be removed, or undone. Not in my experience, which has been extensive. I wish it were otherwise."

"Damn thing didn't even leave a scar. I wanted a scar at the time." She sat rigidly on the couch, since she was still extremely uncomfortable. "I've spent the last year being detached from everyone and everything. Inviting me into this . . ." Aimee still wasn't extremely sure what *this* was, but that was her life anymore. "Is exactly what I wanted to avoid. But I, um, well. Casey is a convincing person."

"He is that." Darius agreed readily. "So long as he stays in one place long enough to make an argument, it's typically a convincing one." He glanced up at Jacob, which the man seemed to understand somehow as an instruction to mix some drinks for the two of them.

The clink of glasses and ice made for a calmer backdrop to the rest of their discussion. "I've known many people who choose to go about their lives unattached in terms of having a covenant or a network to which they decide to belong. It can work, but I've never found it to be ideal. Bearing the Mark doesn't change the fact that we are still at least mostly human. I hope you'll find during your time with us that your life is a better place than it sounds like it has been."

"In the end, it was *my* mistake that cost me everything." Aimee gladly took the offered drink when Jacob brought them over. "I don't want to lose everything again." She stared down into the glass before she took a drink, hoping that she wasn't misplacing her trust by accepting a drink from a relative stranger. "My question . . . I don't . . . know the extent of my transformation. I was hoping you could help me find out." Eventually she looked at Darius again. "I don't think this body is immortal, but there are clearly magical boundaries that I can't pass in order to take it off course from perfection."

"Have you asked the Voice to clarify?" Darius was sipping his own actual beverage this time, some kind of dark amber liquid with a chilled stone in the glass instead of ice.

". . . No." She hadn't really considered having some kind of conversation with the asshole in her head. "To be honest, I avoid any interaction I can. I only have two active pacts."

"That's understandable, given your experience." He set down his drink and leaned with his elbows on his knees, sighing. "What may help you to understand . . . is that the Voice doesn't care. It has been loved and hated, even worshipped by some as some kind of god. It does not care either way. Just as it neither loves nor hates us. Any emotion you invest toward it, good or bad, is wasted."

"Easier said than done." She grumbled as she finished off her drink. "Sometimes I really wish I could get wasted. Might make for an easier conversation with the asshole in my brain. I begged and pleaded to get my life back. I self-harmed. I tried to negotiate other ways. It feels personal."

"So does the weather sometimes." He agreed. "The only difference is, the weather never listens in the first place, so it's easier to write off." He got up from his separate seat and moved to sit beside her on the couch with a hand out for hers. "I've been talking to it for a long time. I can speak to it along with you, so long as you give your consent for what I'm allowed to know and what I'm not. It'll mean you understanding the details of some of my own pacts in return, but that . . . particular wrinkle is always a part of acceptance procedures anyway."

Aimee looked down at his hand and hesitantly put hers into his. "You can know whatever you want or need to know. Anything that is a part of my life now doesn't have much depth and isn't a secret. And no one can know, per my pact, my life before. I only have one other pact, a luck pact."

It was strange to see another person besides herself floating in the void of gold and shadows that she had avoided for so long. The only other time she had seen anyone or anything else within it was the image of her perfected self, before she had been transformed. It was tempting to look around for her old self, but she already knew it had been destroyed, as utterly as anything could be.

Darius, for his part, appeared comfortable within the shifting tendrils of power, his hand holding hers loosely as the presence clarified all around them. "I've made many pacts over the years. There are two that you should be aware of, if we are going to serve in the same covenant together." She could feel an understanding of the pacts in question impressing itself on her mind, as the Voice facilitated the exchange of information between them.

For the first, he had altered his vision to make himself much more sensitive to light, with the benefit of being able to see much better in the dark, but with a much lower tolerance for bright days. That was the easy one for her to take in.

The second pact revealed to her by the Voice involved just how long Darius had been alive.

"Early on in our lives, my sister and I found ways of extending our lifespans, though we chose different methods." His voice was explaining, at the same time the Voice was laying out the balance by which he lived. "I was a soldier, when I was young. I was in a position to take a great many lives regardless of any pact I had made. So I made an arrangement that whatever life I took, I kept, and added it on to my own lifespan."

Aimee wasn't sure what to say to that, since it was many layers of fucked up that the man was a murderer to extend his own life. A soldier taking lives was understandable, especially in times of unrest and war, but it was a particular kind of ruthless to find a way to make death beneficial to one's own life. "I really hope you're a vigilante of some kind and not some sick, twisted . . ."

"Vigilante is a close enough word for what I am." He agreed. "Not everyone who takes the Mark does it for good or hopeful reasons. If I began reciting the list of people my sister and I have dealt with who decided to make magic into a weapon against others, we would be sitting here for weeks. I hope to have done more good than harm."

"I hope so too." She was even more nervous now than before. "After what Casey explained to me, I still think I would be safer here. As long as you're not going to suck my life next."

"I am not." He shook his head, smiling faintly at the vampire implication. "As for yours . . ." she could feel the knowledge of her own pacts moving through Darius in answer to what he had shared with her, and saw the curious look on his face. "You left it open-ended, not fully defined. It happens a lot, especially in early pacts, and leaves some things vague. You couldn't have made yourself immortal, since you didn't have that in your power to trade. But you specifically asked for perfect. In terms of the Voice's interpretations, that generally means it does what bodies can do, perfectly. You'll never get cancer, no heart or respiratory troubles later in life, you'll see as well when you're a hundred as you do now, but you will eventually grow old. Maybe a little later than most, all things considered, but you will get there eventually, barring any other troubles."

"Hopefully no one comes after me or anything. I don't really lead a risky life." She was relieved to have some answers, and he could feel her physically relax a little next to him. "So . . . what else do I need to know? What do I need to do to be a part of this . . . covenant?"

"We have a gathering once every month, here below in the ballroom." The eerie translucent world of the Voice faded slowly from their shared perceptions when they were no longer talking about it directly, and Darius got up to go back to his seat and give Aimee her space. "The next of which is this coming Saturday night. It's just a social gathering, food and drinks, nothing elaborate. But it is a chance for the entire covenant to recognize you. Once presented, you'll be a probationary member for a year, after which you're thought to be fully vested. The covenant is all of us, working together, so it requires the acknowledgement of a majority to induct someone new."

Aimee nodded slowly but there was no shaking the feeling that she was being inducted into a low-key cult. The Mark made all its bearers a part of a cult, she supposed. "Okay. Good to know. I guess I'll wear something low cut to try and swing some votes my way." She had to undercut some of her worry with humor. Another panic attack would not be fun.

Darius just smiled. Did the man ever actually laugh? "Dress as you like. It's a very casual event. Not everyone even comes, if they aren't in town at the time." He looked up at the windows nearby, nodding out at the lights of the other buildings in the complex at a distance. "In the meantime, I'll speak to Zeke and get a unit and a house set up for you. If you're looking to change jobs, you already know Casey. He handles most of that for the covenant, since he knows people all over the state."

"I'm determined to make him my best friend. Casey, I mean. I don't know Zeke." She got up from the couch slowly, though she felt a little lightheaded from whatever in-depth brain meld she'd just undergone with the mob boss and the Voice she still didn't like.

She grabbed onto the side of the couch for some added stability. "Oh. I have another question." She completely ignored the dizziness to try and appear less weak. "Is there some kind of gag-order on talking about the Mark with people? My prior . . . well, it seemed very hush-hush. So I've been very secretive. Also I don't want people to think I'm crazy."

"It's not an order, exactly, but it's usually . . . prudent. We don't tend to advocate for expanding with people who don't yet have the Mark. We've always been more about finding those who do and bringing them on board, if it suits them. But you've seen yourself how it's easy to . . . misunderstand what you're dealing with, from the outside. Teaching someone what it is, how it operates, trying to prepare them for it . . . that's never been something we devote ourselves to doing. Any time someone new takes it for the first time, there's always a chance of things going . . . spectacularly wrong."

"I would guess the odds are more in favor of going wrong than otherwise." She straightened her posture when the dizziness subsided and she gave him a small smile. "Good thing I wasn't wearing heels. Might have ended up on my ass." Aimee cleared her throat and glanced toward the door. "Good to know, anyway. If, um . . . is that it? I can go, a changed woman, yet again?"

"Not quite so much this time as the last one, I imagine." Darius stood up with her and saw her to the door. "We'll be seeing you around, Ms. Zimmerman. I'll let my sister know to look you up when she's back in town, likely the day after tomorrow."

"Sure. Sounds like a plan." Aimee looked at him for a moment longer and stepped out the door when he opened it for her. She figured that with a man like Darius, many people had reason to be scared, but for now . . . she had nothing to lose. Not really. Casey was chatting with one of the guards she saw before, and she smiled as soon as she saw them both. "Hey, I made it through round one."

"Oh good. That's when we start showing you the really weird stuff." The man grinned over at her past Casey, who just glared at him for his grin. "Chanting around bonfires, animal sacrifice, that kind of thing."

"Just because that's *your* usual Friday Night doesn't make it everybody's, William." Casey's tone was having none of it.

"Your loss." William was clearly making no apologies.

"Welcome to the weirdness."

Aimee held out her hand with a smile. It was only polite to introduce herself to the cute guy, right? "Aimee. Nice to see you again and make some kind of official acquaintance."

"Nice to see you too." The look on his face was a bit quizzical as she introduced herself. "That's . . . interesting. I don't know if I've ever met anybody who's both lying about their name and *not* lying at the same time. Huh. No judgment, just a curiosity. I look forward to seeing you around."

Her eyebrow raised but she actually smirked. "It's not an identity crisis. Just . . . used to be someone else and now I'm Aimee."

"Oh I wasn't trying to call you out on nothin', it's fine, it's just not every day I hear both at once. I figured it was either that or dissociated personalities. Seen that too." He nodded back over his shoulder. "You need a ride home, or you good?"

She looked at Casey and back at William. "Yeah, I could use a ride. I guess I'll be getting a place here, but right now I could use a ride home if Casey assures me you're trustworthy."

Casey looked a bit skeptical, but got a sarcastic look from William for the doubts on his face. "He's fine. Don't get crazy with the trustworthy bit. I mean, he's not a liar, I'll give him that."

"No, I am not." William nodded over his shoulder at a car parked nearby. "Come on, I'll give you a lift so bossman here can get back to whatever business he's running tonight."

Aimee quickly gave Casey a hug even if he didn't ask for it before she looped arms with William, even if he didn't ask for it either. "I'm really bad at being outgoing even though I'm a stripper. I figure I'll give it a try."

He gave her a second look over as she took his arm. "No shit? Man, apparently I get around to all the wrong clubs. You are fine as hell. I would not want to be the one to come up on stage after you."

"Thanks." She smiled as she held onto his arm. "Club G. I'm there all the time. Except tonight, obviously."

"Bet they're missing the revenue. Move over to this side of the city and you might bankrupt the place."

Aimee looked him up and down and shook her head. "You're dangerous for me. You're too good-looking. I don't know if I should flirt back."

"You can flirt all you like. The girl I usually hit it with these days is on security detail with me, but we're on-again off-again at best. But, fair disclosure, she's nuts. Not that I mind the crazy." Casey clearly hadn't been joking. The man had a level of honesty that bordered on the self-destructive.

"Maybe I don't want to cross a crazy sort-of girlfriend." She shook her head as they arrived at his car. "I have a feeling that if we flirt then you'll be honest with her and next thing I know, I'll have to watch my back all around the complex. You're on your own, hot stuff."

"Damn. Can't blame a guy for getting started." He slid into the car and got moving through the late-night Vegas streets.

SIX

Not quite a year later

Aimee ignored her alarm for the tenth time, but she heard Casey's voice getting closer to her room. He had a key to her apartment, one that she actually shared with Lydia, her other best friend. Lydia was away on covenant business, which meant that Casey was backup to harass Aimee prior to work.

She moved the covers just enough to yell, and not an inch farther. "Don't steal all our good coffee!"

"You don't have any good coffee! You drink shitty coffee! I'm doing you a favor!" She could hear telltale signs of Casey's presence downstairs, including footsteps that were too fast to be natural, slamming cupboards, and minor sonic booms as he raced around the room. Behind closed doors, the man never saw any reason to slow himself down.

"Goddamn it." She cursed as she got out of her bed in her skimpy pajamas, but Casey wouldn't care about that. She burst out of her room fully ready to wrangle him for some coffee. "You do this to get me out of bed, don't you? Lydia throws ice at me, and you steal my coffee."

"Well I'm certainly not doing it to get you *into* bed, am I? Come on, get your ass in gear, we're expecting the first of the spring break crazies to start trickling in today and it's gonna be all tits on deck. Also you're out of creamer." Rather than tossing the empty container across the room into the trash, it was faster for him to just run over to it and back again in a blink to resume stirring his coffee.

"All tits on deck." She rolled her eyes but approached him to steal a drink out of his cup first. "I'm extra grumpy without Lydia. I haven't had anyone to cuddle with for over a week." She also hadn't heard from Cody for close to a month. He was just . . . gone.

It had only taken her a few days after meeting him to get the guts to call him. They went on an adorable first date, held hands, he kissed her goodnight. But she was determined not to jump in head first.

So they went slow. Spaced out dates, tried not to be clingy. No attachments.

Right.

But in the last three months, she'd finally admitted to herself that she was head over heels. They had never defined their relationship, but maybe she should have asked. Hindsight made her wish she had asked to be official. Maybe she wouldn't have been ghosted by the first person she'd allowed herself to truly care about since Tony. "You and Issac will let me cuddle with you right?"

"He's in Vienna this week on a library dive, and I'm booked for the next five shifts straight at different hotels. Gonna be you and your stuffed animals for a while, sweetie." Casey glared at her for the theft of caffeine, but he got back into motion quickly once the cup had a lid on it. Necessary for both toddlers and managers who insisted on moving at supersonic speeds. "Come on, let's get moving, where is your uniform? You've showered relatively recently, yes? Let's go!"

"Alright, alright." She hustled to her room to change out of her pajamas and into her uniform. "I showered. You know I shower." She glared at him as she shoved her makeup bag into her bag as well as a change of clothes for after work. "If you're driving, I'll do my makeup at the casino."

"Where was that wisdom when you were deciding how many alarms to set?" He had the car already started up and ready for her by the time she got out to it, but the door didn't quite close all the way before they were roaring into motion along the Vegas streets.

As much as she didn't want to indulge in her misery, Aimee checked her phone as Casey drove. No missed calls. A text from Lydia that she answered with a smile. No social media posts that caught her eye.

It had been a month, why was she still torturing herself? She turned her phone on vibrate and shoved it into her bag before she grabbed her hairbrush. "Lydia looks like she's enjoying herself. I wish I could have gone with her." As a probationary covenant member Aimee was kept out of all official business, but three more months and she would finally fully belong.

"Keep talking about all the places you want to go and in a year you'll be making a bargain to take it all back when you're waist-deep in something unpleasant in a ditch somewhere. Not all the field trips Darius and Sophia send people out on are quite that pleasant."

"I know." Aimee countered defensively, as she turned to watch the blurry buildings. "It will just be nice to actually be a full part of the covenant. And maybe getting away from here even temporarily would . . . clear my mind."

"You need to clear your mind or your pants? Because you and I both know there's a wait-list for the latter." He spared a glance away from the rush of the road to give her a sarcastic glare, then looked back at the street just in time to take them around a curve hard enough to throw her across the car against his shoulder.

Despite being thrown around like a rag doll, she kissed his cheek given the opportunity. "My pants missed their chance unless some hot girl makes the right moves tonight. I think the ship for men has now sailed and is gone in the night."

"We are trash. No one knows this better than we do. But there's a line of women too. You want Rose up at the theatre desk? I swear that woman takes a bathroom break every time you come on shift and say hi."

"She does?" She smiled as she slid momentarily back into her seat, even though she was sure he would toss her around again. "That's hot."

"*How* are you still unaware of these things? Have I taught you nothing? I feel like a failure as an instructor. What have I been doing with my life?!?" He melted down in melodrama as they were forced to stop at a red light, but he recovered by the time it turned green.

"See, this is the problem. This is what I'm talking about. I need you *focused*, because I very much want the next few days *not* to suck. Can you do that for me? Can you please go work out whatever it is you and Rose need to get worked out in a stall or a courtesy room somewhere and get back on shift? You can do it on the clock for all I care, but I need you on *point*, if you please."

"I haven't had any action other than my vibrator since the last time I made out with he-who-ghosted me. But he and I never had sex. That's gotta be why he ghosted me. I was just waiting for a good time, I . . ." She shoved her brush back into her bag. "Yeah. Okay, I'll get focused."

"I'm telling you, the guy did more than ghost you, he's off the fucking reservation. I don't know what happened to him, short of alien abduction. And I feel like we would've gotten a memo if those were real along with . . ." he waved vaguely around them, "you know, everything else. I'll put in another call with Tracy and see if she's gotten any sign of him, but the guy seems like he skipped town. I've got half a mind to send the Porters after him, except somehow I doubt Darius would authorize a kill order just for being a shitty boyfriend."

"We never got there either. The boyfriend/girlfriend thing. If he wanted to be found, he would be. No use chasing after another man I've loved and lost. If you ghost me next, I will *definitely* take serious offense." Aimee heaved out a heavy breath. "I can really make out with Rose on the clock? Why have I been working so hard all this time?"

"First you need a ride to work, *then* on top of that you want me to dive into the twisted intricacies of your beautiful mind? *I do not know!* You're the one who called us the mob when you met me. Do you ever recall me saying explicitly that we were not? You think gangsters have a good work ethic while they're on the clock? No! They fuck the ticket clerk!" He was forced to slow down once they were inside the parking garage, and seemed to take the restriction as a personal insult, growling about it as he navigated the corridors to find them a spot.

Aimee put her hand over her mouth to hide her smirk at his outrage, but she started laughing anyway. "Okay, okay, mob boss. I'll fuck the ticket clerk to forget my broken heart and get my head back in the game." Her heart really was broken over Cody, but this time she wasn't going to let heartbreak turn her cold again. Not like before.

To both their dismay, Rose the ticket clerk was not yet on shift, and so they concocted a plan as they hiked the rest of the way through the casino corridors. Check on her schedule, take a strategic break in an hour or two, and then move along with business as usual once Aimee felt sufficiently readjusted. Casey had to get moving to check in on a few of the restaurants dotting the property, but she knew he would check in frequently. When he said he was all over the place when they met, he meant it. Even when he wasn't moving at supernatural speed, he still never stopped moving.

Once she was in the safety of the casino and not Casey's car, Aimee quickly freshened herself up, threw her bag into her locker, and hurried to get to the floor and start working. She left lots of her blouse buttons unbuttoned, her skirt was already short, and she grabbed a tray before she headed to the bar to get her floor assignment. Their job was to flirt, get drinks, food, whatever it took to keep people happy and gambling. She was good at her job and she enjoyed meeting new people, most of the time.

Casey hadn't been wrong about the spring break crowd, and the energy in the casino was starting to shift with every shuttle that delivered fresh guests from the airport. She was too busy on the move to do much more than keep drinks on the move, but she felt her phone go off several times before she had an opportunity to stop and check it. Had Rose come in after all? Had Casey just opted out of being the middleman and given Rose her number directly? It was the kind of thing he would have done.

When she finally got a breath behind a counter to check, though, there was no message from Rose or Casey. Instead, there were three missed calls, all of them from Cody.

Seeing the missed calls almost made her drop her phone. It had been nearly a month. Now he wanted to call her repeatedly? It wasn't like he didn't know where she was. Instead of calling, she sent him a text.

On the floor working. Sorry I missed your calls.

Aimee was fairly certain that even if she had caught his calls, she wouldn't have been able to coherently answer. She sent a text to Casey quickly after.

Cody called me. Three times. No message.

WHAT?!?!?

Casey was not known for restraint in his responses.

Are you going to call him back?

Aimee stared down at Casey's message but she knew she would need to get back to work. Eventually she typed out a reply back to Casey, but there wasn't an immediate reply from Cody.

I sent him a text. I'm working. I'm not going to call him. He ghosted me for almost a month. I need to get over him, right? I'm waiting for Rose, remember?

I know, she's still not in yet. What the fuck is he thinking, just calling out of nowhere? Alien abduction is just about the only valid excuse I can think of, and even then, I'd be pissed.

Aimee chewed on her bottom lip as she stared at her phone, willing Cody to answer back, but he didn't. She knew her break wasn't long, but now how was she supposed to work? How was she supposed to focus?

She took a deep breath and stepped further away from the noise and decided to return Cody's call, her pulse painfully fast as she pressed the phone to her ear. If he would even answer. He hadn't answered all her calls from weeks before, some of them drunk, some of them teary, some of them desperate.

His line rang through, but there was no answer. Unlike several of her past attempts, however, it did get through to voicemail, as opposed to just dying off as a disconnected number like it had the last few times she'd called. His voice sounded rough, and tired, almost like he had just woken up when he was recording it.

"Hey, it's Cody. If you're anyone but Aimee, leave a message and I'll call you back. Aimee, if it's you, I am . . . so, so sorry, and I promise I can explain. I won't blame you if the explanation isn't good enough, but I swear I . . ." *BEEP*.

Aimee's voice was caught with emotion but she left a message anyway. "It's me. I guess, um, I'll talk to you some other time." Aimee disconnected the call and roughly wiped at the tears on her face. It didn't make sense that he couldn't answer her call but he could change his outgoing to something so . . . heartbreaking. What could he possibly have to say, to explain, after all this time? She sent another message to Casey.

I called. No answer. Weird voicemail saying he was sorry. I don't know if I can handle this.

Well what the hell are you supposed to do with that? That's it, I'm calling the Porters. This guy needs a beating.

Do not. Wyatt is already too irritated about it on my behalf. I'm gonna get off the floor for a bit.

Aimee went to tell Tammy that she was going to need a longer break, but when she looked up, the floor was packed again with gamblers and her hope for privacy died in her throat. There were some people in suits, high rollers presumably, who were observing the area. Apparently spring breakers were a good reason for high rollers to lurk around.

Aimee grabbed a tray again and went to a table of suits with a fake smile. "Hello, I'm Aimee. Can I get you a drink or something to eat?"

It was easy to pick out who thought they were in charge of the overpriced formalwear in front of her, since he was the one who took it upon himself to speak for everyone. "Yeah, we need a bottle of champagne for the table, it's about to be somebody's birthday. And we're gonna be around a while, so here's for the tab." He handed her a card as a few others around the table rolled their eyes at the man's apparent sense of self-importance.

"Glad to do so. Is there anything else you need?" She looked around the group, a few who had eyes on her, but she was used to it. A couple of women hung around the suits like flies, but they didn't look thrilled to see Aimee. "This floor is lucky tonight, you know. I've seen some big winners already."

"Means there's been some big losers too, huh?" One of the others asked as he got up from his seat, apparently to stretch and have a long look at the blackjack tables nearby

Aimee shook her head and smiled at the big boss, but she reached out and ran a hand kindly over his arm after he handed off his card. "Well, good luck to you. Your friend seems grumpy, that's no way to win. Let me go get that champagne for you."

"Here's hoping you just got started. If the floor's as lucky as you say it is, maybe we'll end up sharing some of it around with you tonight." His hand casually rested at her waist by instinct after her own touch, but he clearly didn't mind the notion of picking up a cocktail waitress for the night.

She glanced down at his hand but her smile remained as she met his eyes again. "I'm often told I'm a good luck charm." Aimee gave his hand a gentle squeeze before she slid out of his touch and nodded toward the card tables. "Trust me."

Before a month ago, Aimee had the comfort of Cody watching her back when people like the high rollers came in, but since his disappearance, she'd been on her own with the risky flirting game. Tonight she hoped that the grumpy friend would bear the brunt of the bad luck, since she really didn't want to handle it herself.

Off to the side of the room, near a stand of slot machines that wasn't presently occupied, another pair of out-of-towners watched the exchange while expertly pretending to do no such thing. The man was maybe in his early fifties, maybe not so early, with a sour look permanently etched on his face and a growl to his voice that was the product of too much shouting as a matter of habit.

"Did you see it? When he lifted up her shirt like that?" He reached out to tug at his companion's shirt with a similar gesture, keeping her close to him as he watched where the redhead chose to go next.

"An old nasty fucker chasing tail? I saw that." The woman next to him was clearly younger than the sour-looking man, likely in her thirties, with dark hair pulled back and a give-no-shits expression among dark eyes and caramel skin.

The redhead went back to get drinks for the rich fools, and almost as soon as she returned to them with drinks, one struck big and his friend didn't. She could hear the jeers and curses simultaneously. "You think the girl is trouble? Not these rich fuckers we've been looking into?"

"Maybe one of them too, but she's the one I think I saw a tattoo on." He sipped at the bottle of water he carried around, watching their interactions. "Have to wait for another one to cop a feel to be sure, unless you feel like going and getting a hand on her yourself."

"You know she's not my type. Barrett." She gave him a look of annoyance as she tipped back her martini. They weren't supposed to drink on the job, but she wasn't much of a rule-follower. Especially out in the field, no one was going to uphold the rules anyway.

They were on a scouting trip, but backup was only just outside the strip, due to the incidence of activity in the area. Maggie, in her jeans and tank top, looked like an older version of the spring breakers around them . . . except she had a concealed weapon at her hip.

She sat down on her partner's lap, even though that was definitely against the rules. Hunters were not supposed to get flirty or romantic with their partners, much like police. "Are you sure you're not imagining it so you can stare at the redhead with her tits halfway hanging out?"

"I'm gonna be doing that anyway. Don't need excuses." He watched the group a while longer, one hand moving up and down her back idly, leaving a rough massage against her spine. "Let's watch the suit she's serving up. If his lucky streak holds, it's either him that's got it or her. I don't mind killing some cameras and mugging him in the ladies' room for starters."

"We have to be sure. Typical man. Rush, rush, rush. Don't you know by now that the fun is in the chase?" Maggie turned around on her partner's lap and looked him in the eyes before she distracted him by grinding against him. "The fun is also in breaking the rules."

"Hence the unnecessary roughness of the intended mugging. I thought you'd like that." He growled under the covert lapdance.

She leaned in and placed a kiss at the very corner of his mouth. If they got a surprise visit from backup or if they had to actually call people in, their time of being fuck-buddies would be over. She definitely didn't want it to be over, which meant not being entirely focused on the job. "Do you want me to flirt with her so you can watch and inspect?"

"She seems a lot more likely to let you get a hand on her than me. Go for it. And whatever you do, don't behave."

Maggie smirked but slid off his lap slowly and grazed her hand across his groin before she walked away. Her jeans hugged her curves as she strutted up to the waitress with a warm smile. "Hi."

Aimee was at the bar waiting for another round to deliver, but she turned around to see a slightly shorter, smiling woman. Aimee smiled politely but there was no mistaking the look in the woman's eyes. "Can I help you? Do you need a refill?"

Maggie shook her head and motioned back to her table. "I'm cut off for now. My friend back there told me I wouldn't be able to get your number, but a girl has to try."

Aimee laughed politely. "Forward, I see." She put a comforting hand on the woman's shoulder. "I'm seeing someone, actually, sorry to disappoint you. She works here. Very jealous type." She didn't know enough about Rose to actually know if she would be the jealous type or not, but oh well. "I'm flattered, though."

Maggie tsked and reached out to tug gently on the woman's shirt trying to hike it higher, with a sigh of disappointment. "I won't tell if you won't."

Aimee cleared her throat and stepped back just a little, but her back was against the bar. "So sorry. I'm not interested. But maybe you can get lucky out on the floor, it's hot out there tonight."

The dark haired woman looked back at Barrett and then out at the tables. "I'm not much of a gambler. Not with money, anyway. I was taking my chance on you, hot stuff."

Aimee's order was up and she hurried to grab her tray. "Gotta get these drinks out, let me know if you need anything!"

Just as she was stepping away with her drinks, she saw Rose coming toward her with a bag over one shoulder, clearly on her way to clock in for the night. She had clearly witnessed the exchange, and looked concerned. "Hey, Aimee, everything alright? You need me to go find Carlo? Looked like she was getting a little handsy."

Aimee was surprised to see Rose but she stepped closer and lowered her voice. "I told her that I already had a girlfriend. Who works here." She looked nervous as she chewed on her lip. "Mind making me an honest woman and helping me out?"

Rose's eyebrows shot high as her eyes widened, her cheeks immediately flushing as she looked around. Was she looking for hidden cameras? "I, I mean, um, I'm . . . yeah, I can do that. I just . . . I thought you had a, um, a boyfriend?"

She looked down at the drinks she needed to deliver. "Cody ghosted me a month ago. I don't know why, or what he will ever say about it. And we never . . . he never called me his girlfriend." She cleared her throat and felt her cheeks burning with embarrassment. "I'm sorry, I shouldn't have asked."

"Oh no, you should've asked as soon as he stopped returning your calls. Where are these going? I'm gonna pour one in that bitch's lap for putting her hands on you." Rose took the tray from Aimee and looked around for any sign of the woman who had gotten into Aimee's business, clearly motivated.

Aimee was surprised as soon as Rose took her tray, but she guided Rose to the high rollers and dropped off the drinks before anyone got angry. "I . . ." She still didn't know what to say to Rose, but it was actually hot to see Rose get all worked up on her behalf. Maybe it was because she had been psyching herself up to see Rose before Cody called her, left no messages, and then didn't answer her returning call. She wanted a distraction.

Aimee leaned into Rose after the drinks were dropped, and whispered into her ear. "I really was waiting for you to come in. Casey said you were interested in me. I had no idea."

She looked flustered at that comment, but leaned in closer, putting her lips against Aimee's neck. "Well I did my best to keep it to myself, since, you know, boyfriend and all. I'm sorry he was an asshole to you, but I'm not gonna lie, I'm not *that* sorry."

Aimee took a sharp breath when Rose kissed her neck, and her pulse kicked up. She desperately missed Cody, but she wanted to forget the pain of missing him. She also wanted to convince the handsy stranger that she had a serious girlfriend. Both could be accomplished by pursuing Rose. "I'm sorry I was oblivious." She gasped softly as she dropped a hand to Rose's waist. "Do you wanna disappear with me for a bit?"

"Right now?" Even though she sounded shocked, she was still grinning. "I mean, I'm half an hour late for my shift, but that's very much not a *no*. Where do you have in mind?"

"Casey will vouch for us." She assured Rose as she tried not to think and just act. Aimee noticed the strangers watching them again, but she just grabbed Rose by the hand and headed off the floor. Once they were out of the open, she pulled Rose into a hallway and kissed her against a wall.

"Mmmm, if you're gonna bring my fantasies to life, this uniform is gonna have to go." Rose moaned under the kiss, her hands reaching up to untuck Aimee's shirt and begin unbuttoning it as the kisses deepened. They could both hear footsteps coming along the employees-only hallway around a corner, but neither of them could bring themselves to care.

Aimee's shirt was halfway unbuttoned before Rose even

started, and it didn't take much for her shirt to open completely and expose her ample breasts and lacy black bra to the air. After too many months of stripping, she didn't care who saw her in her bra. Aimee's hands trembled slightly from both guilt and anticipation. She still felt guilty about Cody, even after being ghosted, but the attention from Rose was intoxicating.

She slid her hands up Rose's sides and unbuttoned Rose's shirt as well. "You're so beautiful. And soft." Girls were so much fun that Aimee wasn't sure why she cared so much about Cody.

"God, you're one to talk . . ." her moans escalated as her hands wandered down over Aimee's skirt, fingertips teasing at the hem without pulling it up in public. "You are fucking amazing. We need to get somewhere quick, otherwise Greg in security is gonna get a hell of a show that he didn't pay for."

Aimee nodded as she tried to breathe evenly, but her thoughts were frazzled. She looked down at Rose's breasts again and ran a hand along Rose's bra. "I'm . . . I can get us a room." Her phone was still shoved into her apron, even though it was askew, all it would take would be one text that she never had to utilize before but now was the time.

As she went to pull out her phone, the sound of footsteps down the hallway came closer, and then suddenly stopped. The abrupt halt drew Rose's eyes first, and as Aimee looked at her again, she saw her expression turning to a kind of guilty shock.

The source of the guilt was fairly clear. Cody was standing in the corridor in a casino-standard suit. He had cut his hair since the last time she'd seen him, and it was shorter than it ever had been, almost like it had been shaved completely after she'd seen him last. There was something off about the way his face looked, but she couldn't put her finger on exactly what.

"Right, that . . . right." Cody stopped and just nodded, looking at Aimee and coughing as he took a few steps closer.

"I'm . . . sorry, I got back over here as soon as I could but I'm . . . clearly interrupting . . . something."

Cody definitely didn't look good and her heart seized in her chest at the sight of him. Aimee's mouth seemed paralyzed for a moment but she eventually looked at Rose. "I'm so sorry. I . . ." There was no way that she could run off with Rose and lose her chance at some kind of explanation. "Cody, wait . . ."

"Cody wait?!?" Rose was immediately both flustered and appalled between Aimee and the wall. "What do you want him to wait around for, exactly?"

Aimee looked back at Rose with her own pained expression. "I can't. I need to talk to him. I need to know why . . ." She took a deep breath. "I'm sorry." Despite being asked to wait, Cody was walking away anyway, but she turned back to Rose. She kissed Rose once more, briefly. "I have to talk to him. I need an explanation. I'm so sorry."

Rose slipped away from Aimee with a glare, resetting her clothes in obvious insult. "You need to work out your fuckin' priorities. Whatever he says, he did it once, he's just gonna do it again. Don't find me next time, alright?"

At the sound of the fight happening behind him, Cody stopped and turned around to watch, clearly confused about what was happening. She had moved on to somebody else, why would she want to hear anything from him?

Aimee deserved the tongue-lashing that Rose gave her, and she didn't even have it in her to call out for anyone when Rose stormed off. She slowly buttoned her shirt and eventually spoke up. "I didn't know you even work here anymore, Cody." Her voice was soft but calm. Somehow. "I tried to text you and call you earlier after you called. You never responded. And now you're here?"

"I was on the phone with Hannah when you called, asking about my job. She said to come in and help cover for one of her new guys who's out and we'd talk about whether I've still got a job at the end of the night. I'm just here working on a chance." He was breathing heavily, but when she stopped him, he didn't rush away, whether his job was in jeopardy or not. "I had to try and find you first, I didn't know you were with . . . Pat said you were running drinks over here tonight, so I just . . . I'm sorry. For . . . a lot of things, but also that, on top of it. That sounded like it sucked."

"I'm not with Rose. Clearly." She held out her hand to the empty hallway and slowly made her way to him because she hated the sound of him struggling. "Are you sick?" Out of habit she apparently still had, she reached out to touch his arm, but she pulled away quickly. "Do you need to sit down?"

"I'm alright. I've . . . been better the last few days, they just didn't want to release me and the hospital gift shop doesn't sell cell phone plans." He stepped in closer to her, and she could see, now that she was closer, some bruising on one side of his head and neck, along with a few more healed-over scars than she could remember counting there before. "I think I woke up a few times and tried to tell people to get you a message, but I don't think I was very coherent for a long while."

"Coherent? Oh my god, Cody. What happened? Were you mugged? Attacked?" She gingerly touched his face and felt about two inches tall. He had been in the hospital and she didn't know? What kind of horrible person was she? "I tried to reach you so many times, oh my god, I didn't know . . ."

"I was up in Reno, you wouldn't have had any reason to look for me up there." He shook his head, then turned it so she could see. "I . . . they gave me all the medical mumbo bullshit paperwork, I've got it all back in the car, but it was a head injury. Some cocktail of concussion and bleeding and something about my spine . . . it put me in a coma for almost three weeks. Or, I mean, it put me in at first, and then they kept me in it until things got to where I wouldn't die from it. They didn't have my phone, I still don't know where that ended up. They had the car, at least, so I still have that. I left the hospital as soon as they would let me and grabbed the first phone I could find. Had to charge it in the car on the way straight here."

Aimee was crying as soon as he described his hospital stay further, and she felt sick with concern and guilt. "I should have been there for you." She didn't know how she could have, since she still didn't know what happened or why, but she felt consumed with guilt. "You were gone and I . . . I thought I did something to drive you away. We were going too slow, or I should have asked you to be official, or . . ."

"No. No! No." He stepped in closer to her with a hand on either side of her waist, holding onto her a little too tightly without meaning to. "Nothing you did. Nothing. It was my fault. You didn't know. You didn't . . . I hadn't even told you where I was going. You didn't know I would be out of town, let alone what I was doing. None of this was your fault. God, I didn't . . . I'm so sorry you've thought anything like that for a fucking month."

She looked up at him through her tears and stepped into him to wrap her arms around him gingerly. "I was . . . the Rose thing just happened today. Between trying to scare off some customers and trying to find solace in a pretty girl . . ." Aimee shook her head slowly. "You should be at home. Healing. Let me get a cab."

"No, I've sat on my ass for almost a month, I'm done sitting around." He stopped her from pulling away, hugging her tightly to let her know he wasn't fragile. "I've gotta work and make sure I can keep my job here. I just had to see you first."

Aimee definitely didn't try to pull away again, since she was so relieved and happy to be in his arms again that she sniffled in his embrace. "I missed you so much. God, I missed you." She clung to his shirt and squeezed her eyes shut. "I just kept thinking about all the things I should have done differently, and I'm . . ."

Her stomach twisted in knots as she thought over the

words she was still terrified to say. "After you were gone I wished that I had told you that I think I'm in love with you. And then it was too late." She felt like an idiot for not asking more questions of his situation, but she spent too many hours wishing she had said more about multiple things.

With her eyes shut, she reached out for the Voice.

What are the extent of his injuries? What would I have to pay to heal him?

She had gotten much better at speaking with the Voice over the course of her time in the Vegas covenant, due in part to some direct instruction from others around her who were more comfortable with it, including Casey and his husband Isaac. It no longer came to her with quite the degree of panic it carried early on, though some of the same fear was always present when it manifested itself.

The injuries can be transferred to you directly, though in order to satisfy the balance, you would endure them longer than he otherwise would, if allowed to heal in his own time. They could be removed entirely and suffered more acutely during a smaller window each day, by one or both of you.

Aimee opened her eyes to look up at Cody again, shaking off the conversation with the Voice momentarily, since she just confessed her feelings. She needed to know the extent, the cause . . .

The conversation had taken almost no time at all, instinctive as the Voice's requirements were sometimes. When her eyes focused on Cody's again, he was holding onto her in a clear kind of shock. "Did you . . . just say you're in love with me?"

She was trembling a little but Aimee nodded slowly. "I should have said it before, before you were gone, before when we spent every Friday night watching game show reruns. Before when we tried every conceivable pancake recipe on Sunday mornings, *before* when we would play 'would you rather' until late into the morning and fall asleep together on the couch."

She took a shaky breath. "I was scared to say the words

out loud because I was scared to lose you. Scared to get intimate because I was scared to lose you. I lost you anyway."

"You didn't lose anything." His large hand moved to the side of her face, resting against her cheek and neck to hold her so he could look her in the eye. "I love you too, Aimee. We've just got a lot to talk about and catch up on once we get out of this place tonight. Nobody's losing anybody." Cody had lost enough, in his opinion, to last a lifetime, and he knew she had too, though she had never come out and said explicitly what or how. "What time are you off?"

Fresh tears slid down her face and she leaned into his hand, and his embrace. "I want to just leave right now." She wrapped a hand around his neck and gently urged his face closer to hers. "Can I kiss you? Please?"

"Answer's always yes." He bent easily under her pull in spite of his bulk, melting against her as his free arm bent around her back to hold her close. If she'd had any trouble believing the pleading in his voice and the sincerity of the apology on his voicemail, there was no mistaking the desperation in his kiss.

She kissed him until she couldn't breathe, and she pulled away slowly, her breath uneven. "I guess we should go back out on the floor. I'm worried about you, though, I . . . want to take away your injuries."

He gave a weak chuckle at that comment, and shook his head. "I've always said you were magical, but I don't think you've got that kind of power, babe. I'll be alright. Doc said I need to stay hydrated and get as much sleep as possible and I'll be fine."

"You'd be surprised what I can do." She kissed his cheek gently and grabbed his hand. "Also, you're officially my boyfriend now. We're starting this off right." She slowly led him back to the floor and turned her attention to the Voice. *Can I take his pain for the day? The next twelve hours?*

Do you prefer to experience all of it in a single burst, or experience a heightened aspect of it for that duration?

A single burst. But I want to choose the time at which it occurs. Aimee had to make sure she was alone when it happened, and she would have to make sure Cody didn't know about it. *And I want you to tell me how long it will last.*

Both adjustments are acceptable, but will add to its duration.

After all this time, asshole. We will never be on good terms. But I agree to these terms. She felt the pact take hold and was waiting in the back of her mind for her say-so. Aimee squeezed Cody's hand as they made it out to the floor again. "I am going to go find Casey and talk to him real quick. Also I'm going to get us a room to stay here tonight, so we don't have to argue about where we're gonna stay after the shift is over. We both know the food here is better than both of our homes."

"Stay *here?* Did you get a hell of a raise while I was gone, or a big fat tip from a high-roller?" He had never asked too many questions about how she afforded a house out in the suburbs as a waitress, and his tone was still teasing. "I'm not gonna argue about not having to drive anywhere if you want to do that. I haven't even been back to my place yet, I've got no idea if my shit is even still there."

"I *do* get good tips." She gave him a reassuring smile. "Sometimes you just have to live a little and stay a night in the Bellagio." Aimee pulled him in for one more kiss. "Drink some tea. It will make you feel better." She let go of his hand and took a few steps. "Don't disappear on me again."

"It wasn't the plan the first time around, swear to god. I'll get some tea." He squeezed her hand as she let him go and started off, though as always, he lingered in place to watch her walk away. He'd made no secret in the past of how fond he was of doing exactly that.

Aimee was glad that she didn't spot Rose again on the way out, but she did see the extremely forward woman and the grumpy-looking man, both watching her closely. It made her nervous, so she picked up her pace and pulled out her phone to message Casey.

I'm headed to the front desk, can you get me set up with a nice room?

Oh thank god, you're still going through with Plan Rose. Yes, I've already got you booked for a room up on the 32nd. The key's waiting for you at the desk.

Well . . . I was making out with Rose, shirt open, in an employee hallway . . . and Cody showed up.

There was a pause before it showed that Casey was typing, something that almost never happened as far as she could recall.

Was he abducted by aliens?

He was in the hospital. Comatose. He looks it, too.

Aimee glanced backward once, even though Cody was long out of sight.

Rose told me to fuck off. Deservedly so. I can't lose him again.

This time, Casey's responses came faster.

Find out what hospital. I'm fact-checking this shit.
But also have fun in the room.
I may have sent rose petals.

I'll find out which hospital. Thank you. I love you, Case.

Apparently she was saying that a lot now, but she wasn't going to stop herself.

Barrett watched the redhead emerge from the employee corridor and head away past the slots, apparently in the process of putting both her wardrobe and her emotional state back together. He put down his drink and was about to stand and follow when he saw Maggie slip out of the same corridor looking smug. It was easily one of his favorite expressions to see on his partner's face.

With her looking that comfortable, Barrett leaned back again in his seat, resting an elbow over the back of his chair as he watched Maggie saunter toward him. "You look like you saw something you liked. Are we happy?"

Maggie resumed her place on Barrett's lap, and she mercilessly ground into him before she leaned in to whisper. "Red made out in the hallway with her 'girlfriend', and it was so damn sexy that the universe gave me a gift." She nipped at his neck, hard. "Red has a Mark. Right on her ribs. Didn't even try to cover it up or obscure it."

"I didn't know it was your birthday, getting presents dropped on you like that." There had been a time early on in their partnership when he had wondered how far PDA could go before the public intervened. Wonder had turned to mere curiosity over time. Different places had different thresholds. "No frame, no cover-ups, nothing? No one's that stupid and working in a place where you're bound to show off some skin once in a while."

"So stupid. What a stupid, hot, bitch." Maggie laughed against his skin before she moved her lips to his. "Time to stalk the redhead so we can see if she has friends. Can't just go for the kill right away."

"Of course not. What would be the fun in that?" He looked past the slots as if he could see through them to watch where the redhead had gone. He took a deep breath of the casino scent as if he could distinguish hers in the midst of it. "When she comes back on shift, you handle a badge swipe and I'll keep an eye on the suits. If she's favoring them, maybe she's some kind of 'in' they're using here. We'll see where it goes from there."

"Got it, boss." She smirked and kissed him again. "Tonight is going to be fun. You better be ready."

SEVEN

Aimee's shift ended before Cody's, mostly because she took two hours off early to scope out the room and take the cost of his pain. The half hour it took to take his pain was hell, and Aimee had to chase it with a few drinks and a shower after thrashing around on the fancy carpet in their ridiculously nice suite.

The shower and the stiff drink didn't remove the soreness, but Casey had been nice enough to send up three pieces of lingerie, so she picked a sheer black one and covered herself with a ridiculously fluffy robe to wait for Cody. After she sent him the room number, she sent Casey a text.

Thanks for the lingerie even though I know it was for Rose. Did you find out any information from the hospital in Reno?

Yes, but no. It's actually pretty frustrating. The physician's notes said he got into a car accident, but there was no police report filed for it. And I checked the news bulletins and the parking garage cameras, they show Cody's car as fine. So maybe it was the other guy's, but it all still smells sketchy to me.

That makes me . . . uncomfortable.

She looked around the room, and the smell of the rose petals permeated her thoughts as she gulped down more wine.

Why would he hide this from me? He didn't tell me what happened. Only that he was injured in Reno.

I don't know. And I'm not sure if it's better or worse that you're not the only one he's hiding it from, whatever it is. Just be careful about things for a bit, alright? Make sure his story checks out before you put, you know, all that, to good use.

How do I keep falling in love with secretive men? I took a temporary pact to take on his pain for a day. It was all compressed into 30 minutes. That was not fun.

Aimee walked over to the large window that overlooked the Vegas strip and allowed herself to be mesmerized by the view of the lights and the vibrant city. Leaving her old life behind was never easy, but she absolutely loved Las Vegas and never wanted to leave.

The lock of the door clicked with an accepted card before Casey could answer, and Cody came in, carrying a pair of bags in one hand. He got a look at her in the robe as soon as the door was closed, and he smiled brightly. It had been a long day, but strangely free from the pain he'd been enduring since he woke up from his coma a few days before. Maybe he was getting better quicker now that he was up on his feet and back to work.

"Good fucking god, a sight like that is worth any shift."

She gave him a small smile but was well encased in her robe as she walked over and greeted him with a kiss. "Casey helped me score this great room. You look like you're feeling better. Was it the tea?"

"I don't know. It was good tea. Also really good coffee.

There may have also been a really good energy drink in there somewhere, but I'll deny it in court." He put down the bags with a clink of some obvious bottles inside and a slight squeak of styrofoam carryout containers, so that he could wrap both arms around her. "D'you know I've never actually stayed over here before? Unless I was, you know, working dusk till dawn. That doesn't really count."

"That doesn't count. I've stayed a few times." Her whole body felt sore from taking on his pain, but she gladly melted into his embrace. "There's a few shops I stopped in before coming up. I got you some clothes, since you said you didn't have any. You don't need to worry about me. I saved up a lot of stripping money before I started working here. Not that we usually talk finances, but I didn't want you to worry."

"I . . . know I've done plenty of that before now. The whole worrying about money thing." He scratched at his neck as he stepped further into the room with her. "I'm . . . gonna be doing less of that for a while. That was part of what took me out of town in the first place a month ago."

"What happened, Cody?" She let him pull her over to the bed, and when he sat down, she sat on his lap. It gave him a peek of what was beneath, but she still wanted to talk. They hadn't ever slept together before, and they could wait longer. "I'm worried that you won't tell me the truth."

"It's just not the kind of thing I ever wanted to get you close to, so I never talked about it." He put both arms around the base of her spine to keep her close, his eyes raking over as much of her as the folds of the robe allowed.

"So I've . . . been in Vegas a while now. I think maybe . . . what was it, four years? Something like that? I wasn't lying about how I got here, drama back home, wanted to get away from it. But when I landed here, I started off bouncing, and . . . well, there was this one guy I worked with who said I could make some extra money on the side, if I was the type for it. So I checked it out, and I eventually got . . . involved. Nothing super-illegal, just . . . some underground fights."

He looked properly sheepish as he said it, clearly having worried for a long time what she would think of him for it. "Nothing that usually goes farther than tapping out, just some underground dirtier stuff so rich folks from out of town have someplace to go where they can feel like they're being dangerous and getting away with it. I do a fight maybe once every few months. Good money in it, and a hell of a kickback depending on how fat the people's wallets are who come to bet on things."

She didn't say anything right away, but she ran her fingers over his face, his brows, his nose, his lips. Aimee wrapped her arms around his neck and just hugged him silently for a moment. "I can't judge anyone for finding their way to survive here in Vegas. I did the same thing. The first time I saw you I was a stripper, why would you think I would judge you?"

"I didn't, I just . . . it wasn't that, I just didn't want you to worry. This is the first time it's ever landed me with anything worse than stitches." He reached up to rub at his scars, still a bit abashed about it. But as embarrassed as he was, he couldn't bring himself to regret it. "I also don't normally go out of town for them, but this fight in Reno was . . . I wasn't supposed to win. So the money was . . . is, insane."

"I would hope so, considering you almost paid with your life." She felt a wave of panic as she held onto him. "Are you . . . going to keep doing it?"

"I wasn't planning on doing any more for at least a year. Even after medical bills, I'm gonna clear plenty to see me through until next spring or so. Devina said she'd work out my paperwork to get me reinstated here, so with that, I should be set up for a while." He pulled her into a passionate kiss. "The plan was always to do this fight and then take a break. I just didn't realize how bad this one would end up."

"I keep spiraling and wondering what if you had died. It makes my chest ache." Aimee kissed him back just as fervently before she rested her forehead against Cody's. "If you fight again, will you tell me? I don't want to lose you. I . . . I've lost a lot in my life. I can't keep losing people who matter to me."

"I'll tell you. I should have told you before this one. Before any of them, honestly. I shouldn't have kept it back." His arms closed around her tightly as he rested her head against his shoulder. "I've gotten close to dying . . . I think that makes three times now in my life. I don't think it's something a person ever gets used to."

Aimee thought about the things she wanted to say, the things she wanted to tell him, but she didn't want to say anything without talking to Casey first. She was still trying to be a part of the Vegas covenant, and she didn't want to give them any reason to exclude her.

"If you had died, we would never get to sleep together. Naked. We've slept together all other ways . . ." Her nervous habit of talking too much always came back to haunt her, changed body did not change her entire personality. She loosened her grip around his neck slowly. "You worked too much to see me at Club G, and I quit right after we first met. I think I owe you a dance."

Cody's mind immediately froze up and locked on the feel of Aimee in his lap, all previous conversation forgotten at that prospect. "You, um, owe? Oh it's *that* kind of room!" He kissed her again once his brain was working just barely enough to move. "Have I mentioned I'm glad I'm not dead?"

"You have been the most patient man on the planet." She kissed him several more times. The fact that he had assumed they would just spend the night cuddling had her wanting him even more. "I've been with more women than men, since men make me nervous. But I . . . I was really nervous about losing you. I didn't want to rush things." She slid the rest of the way off of his lap and tugged gently at the tie in her robe. It opened slightly and he could see black lace underneath. "Please don't die."

Cody had spent hours just earlier that day on the mad

drive down from Reno thinking he had seen the last of Aimee for good, that his own stupidity had cost him the best thing that had ever happened in his convoluted life. He certainly had no intention of fucking up anything between them if she was giving him a chance. "I'd say I've got some fucking motivation not to. God damn, Aim, you are the most beautiful person I have ever seen. And that's just so far. My mind might not survive the rest."

There were a lot of women who would die for the compliments she got on her appearance, but it didn't really matter to her. She paid a high price to look perfect. What did matter was that Cody waited for her to be ready, he supported her, loved her, and he cherished her.

"I remember the first time I saw you, and I thought there was no way you were interested in me." She still felt like a fraud most of the time, but her appearance was no mask she had to worry about losing. Her personality, however, was another story.

"You're the kindest, sweetest, most patient . . ." she punctuated every compliment with a little less robe until she pushed it off completely, leaving her in just the lingerie. Her breasts strained against the lace, but they were perfectly perky and round. The sheer lace fell across unblemished, tanned skin, and when she gave him a twirl, he could see her equally perfect, pert ass, and the black thong begging for his attention. "You're the best man I know."

Cody quickly forgot he was in Vegas or even a hotel room as he watched her, unable to see anything but the amazing woman in front of him who decided somehow to forgive him for his mistakes and call him her boyfriend. As she turned and lowered her ass into his lap, his hand moved up her spine, caressing roughly over every muscle until he pulled her back against his chest by the neck. "I don't know about best, but I'm sure as fuck the luckiest."

She moaned softly at his initial touch, and when he pulled her back, she gasped gently in surprise, but she didn't stop. Aimee ground her ass into his lap, eager to see what else he would do. Her sexual experience with women was so different, softer, but her experience with men, well, she couldn't help but enjoy his large body taking her over. Cody was by far the strongest person she'd ever been with, and they'd never gotten to this point. She didn't know what he liked or wanted in bed. "Tell me what you want. I want to know."

"Right now? A photographic memory would be a start." He kissed the back of her shoulder as she ground on him, and his large hands slid over her waist. "All I want right now is you, Aimee. I want to make you shake until you forget I was ever gone and can't remember what day it is."

Aimee ran her fingers over the top of his hands before she twisted around and slid her hands up over her body and pulled at strings to loosen the top of the lingerie. "Photos. I could call someone and have photos taken for you." She turned around in his lap and the flutter of lace fell onto his arm as her top fell off. "I want you too, Cody. I want you so much."

"Mmmm . . ." he kissed her hard as soon as she was facing him, but his kisses quickly moved down to cover the perfect breasts now exposed. His face was rough from the growth of a day and a half, but his lips were warm. "Makes me wish I had your talent for taking pictures. I feel like you're the only photographer I've ever seen who could come close to doing you justice. You're an artist and a work of art all at once." The change in position meant she could feel how hard he was through the suit pants of his uniform, but he was too focused on exploring her breasts with his lips to even notice the fact that he was still dressed.

Aimee whimpered at the scratch of his facial hair, since it felt amazing against her sensitive breasts. She arched against him when he took one of her breasts into his mouth and explored with his tongue. She hadn't been this intimate with a man in almost two years, and the feeling of his cock straining beneath her had her aching. "I hope you don't break me."

He laughed against her chest, taking his time to taste and tease her as he listened to every little noise she made. "No, I'd say I've got a vested interest in keeping you in one piece. Only people I break are the ones I'm fighting." He leaned away from her long enough to undo the buttons of his shirt, pulling it back off his muscular torso until both arms were temporarily bound up in the sleeves behind his back.

They had joked, early on in their relationship, about having it in common that they each only had one tattoo, though Cody's was a great deal more extensive than Aimee's star. Covering the left side of his chest and down his arm to his elbow, his shoulder was covered in a tattoo of stylized medieval armor, with a pauldron and plate mail inked into his skin as if he was going to wear them into the colosseum in Rome to do battle for his life. The tattoo made a lot more sense given recent revelations, but had always served to make him look even more dangerous than he already was. For the time being, though, with his hands bound, it looked as though he was a gladiator surrendering to her instead of having any intention of breaking her.

"Now I'm the one who needs a camera." She whispered against his chest as she leaned in to take a few licks of her own. Her fingers explored every ripple of muscle, and she groaned in appreciation of his chiseled chest. "Let me know if I hurt you, I'm trying to be mindful of injuries." She squirmed against his lap before she *had* to slide off and tackle his belt. She was only in a thong as she went to her knees to remove his belt, pants, and boxers.

"I've felt great my whole shift, actually. It was mostly my head that got banged up. You're not gonna hurt me." He assured her as she tugged at his clothes. He tossed aside his shirt to free himself before he stood against her to facilitate the removal of his pants.

Seeing her down on her knees sparked other memories in him, of other times, and other women. The memories weren't Aimee's fault, but they made him nervous all the same. He knew she was nervous too, though, and he did his best to keep the other memories from interfering with the moment. All that mattered was Aimee. Everything else was in the past.

She stood up slowly as soon as she saw him looking nervous, and the only scrap of fabric that remained between them was her thong. "Did I do something wrong?" She reached out for his large hand and entwined her fingers. Being a stripper was an act, but she wasn't acting with Cody. She loved him. And deep inside, she was still the nervous, shy girl that just wanted to be liked. "I'm sorry if I did something wrong. I'm really nervous, I love you, and I just want to do this right."

"No! No. No you did not." He entwined his fingers with hers on both hands, leaning down to kiss her intensely with the heat of their bodies bare against each other. "It's just been a long time, that's all. You know what I came out of when I left Tennessee."

He had gotten himself tangled up with a couple of girls he'd gone to high school with, who had used him for whatever they wanted, played him between them both, and weaponized sex or the withholding of it for their own ends. He and Aimee had spent a long night talking about it early on in their relationship when Aimee said she wanted to wait on any kind of intimacy. Cody was happy to agree, wanting their relationship to be more than that before diving into something more physical. "I'm not nervous about you, I'm nervous about me. But I'm not gonna let being nervous get in the way of what we want."

She kissed him several more times before she said anything in response, though she did know his history and he knew as much about hers as she was able to tell. "I only want good memories." Aimee squeezed his hand and loosened one of her hands to tug down her thong and kick it away. "Also, to be upfront, I have an IUD. And I have been tested in the last six months, even though I haven't been with anyone since before I met you."

"Yeah, I got tested last year, and I'm the only one I've

been sleeping with for the last three. I've got condoms if you'd rather I did, though." He nodded down to his fallen pants, unwilling to take his hands away from exploring her body even to point.

Aimee shook her head as he backed into the bed again, and she climbed back into his lap. She kissed him roughly before she slid a hand down his side to reach between them and slide her hand along his hard cock. He was bigger than any man she'd been with, but she didn't want to think about anyone else. Just Cody. "I just want to feel you. No condoms."

"Ah, fuck . . ." he kissed her hard as she stroked him, his entire body arching and responding to her touch. His hands went down to her thighs and her ass to pick her up without even trying to readjust her against him. He was a big man, and her knees were spread open wide just to get her legs around him in the first place. The fingertips of one hand brushed down between her thighs to move against her in a slow and certain caress, one strong finger running along her folds to beckon her body into catching fire.

As soon as his fingers ran along her slick core, he could feel that their back and forth had already caused quite an effect. She was wet with need and her own body arched in response to his large fingers, followed with a gasp as she continued stroking him. "I've . . . literally dreamed . . . of your touch."

"Already lost some sleep about it?" He teased her both with his voice and with his fingers, long strokes growing more bold against her clit. He started to stroke inside her with each motion of his hand. "Plan on losing more tonight."

Aimee whimpered as he teased her, slowly, with measured circular movements that had her trembling. "I've dreamt of your tongue, your mouth, your cock . . ."

"If either of us need to be pinched right now, it's me. God damn, Aimee, you are fucking perfection." As he heard her gasps escalate, he put any plans of moving elsewhere on the bed on hold, focusing on her completely.

There was something to be said for having a history of being used for sex. He knew exactly what he was doing, and he loved learning exactly how Aimee wanted to be touched. "You're gonna get every single thing on that wish list and then some, baby."

"Will you . . ." She could tell he was watching her every move to see exactly what her moans and whimpers would betray, and she couldn't focus on touching him. Over the years of lovers that were mostly women, she had gotten well acquainted with excellent oral sex. "Lick me? Please?" His fingers were rough, and the idea of his tongue was something she *needed* in her life.

He grinned at the request, and kissed her one more time before he withdrew his hand with a last teasing brush along her clit. "Come here, I haven't had dinner yet." He laid back on the bed, bringing her down with him at first, but then pulled at her hips to move her up on the bed until he could hook his arms under her thighs, leaving her kneeling over his face.

Cody had never once considered himself a particularly shy person about anything he did in life. That included pleasing the woman he was with. Once he had her where she wanted to be, he went between her thighs eagerly with his lips and tongue, tasting every part ot her to deepen the torture his fingers started.

"Oh *god.*" Her eyes closed out of necessity as soon as his tongue explored her, and the warmth and slickness of his tongue had her curling her toes and white-knuckling the sheets. "Fuck . . . yes." Her moans sounded almost pornographic, but she couldn't stop the noises of pleasure, especially because he was so *eager.* "Yes, Cody . . ."

He couldn't have said anything even if he wanted to, but he didn't want to break from what he was doing long enough to speak anyway. His hands raked up over her sides to tease at her breasts as her back arched over him, rough fingertips reminding her skin of the scratch of his stubble moments before.

He had clearly not been exaggerating some of his previous experiences, even if those carried some baggage for him. Along with that baggage came a set of skills that, while not exactly on the level of some of the women she'd been with, was not to be underestimated.

Aimee could only take so much blissful torture before her body reached the peak of her orgasm, and she cried out loudly in pleasure as her knees buckled slightly. She was doing her best not to suffocate Cody as she tried to hold up her body, but the orgasm took over every thought with bliss. "*Fuck yes . . .*" she hissed several times as she reeled with endorphins.

She could feel him growl right up against her clit, which only made every sensation of her afterglow even more intense. His hands had a firm grip on her waist as she came, licking right through it as she shuddered over him, until she finally had to pull herself away to escape the blissful torture. Even then, he kept a hand on her to keep her from getting too far away.

Aimee collapsed into the bed and gasped as she tried to recover from the orgasm. She knew it was only the beginning, but she needed just half a minute before she rode him again in an entirely different way. Almost a year of no sex and he nearly killed her. No vibrator was good enough to replace the intense intimacy and a responsive lover. "We should . . . have done that . . . sooner."

"I'm mostly glad I haven't lost my touch." He moved himself farther up on the bed and grabbed a pillow to stuff it behind his head as she recovered, one hand lazily trailing over her chest and stomach, over her star tattoo. "You taste as good as you look."

"Thank god. It would be totally embarrassing if it was disgusting." She shivered at his gentle touch, but she eventually moved and crawled back over to him. Aimee curled her body into his as she ran her fingers over his muscled torso. "I'm going to ride you until you see stars."

"Don't be surprised if the stars pay a visit fairly quickly the first time around. It has been a long, long damn time." His fingers moved over her back as she writhed against him, relishing the warmth of her.

She kissed along his neck and down along his chest before she lifted her leg and straddled his body. She was slick and ready, definitely to please Cody. "I hope this will be worth the wait." Aimee slid herself closer and moved her heat up and down his cock, slick with want. "I can't wait to feel you inside of me."

"It's all yours, baby. Has been a long while now. Gimme everything you got." His rough hands massaged and claimed every part of her torso, every part of him as eager for her as he could be without exploding.

Aimee watched him as she lifted herself up and slowly lowered herself down on top of him. Almost as soon as the head of his cock was at her entrance she was moaning, since she had wanted him for so long. She was trembling, but her lithe dancer's body was more than capable of riding him as hard as she wanted. "Cody . . ."

"Oh *fuck* that's tight . . . holy shit, Aimee . . ." he was gasping, his eyes rolling back in his head even as she moved slowly to take all of him. Every bit more she took was a new moan from him, his hands trembling as he held her by the hips.

Somehow, even as large as he was, her body accommodated his entire length. Aimee was breathing heavily when she paused, only to look down at him with a lazy smile. It was the last thing he saw before she started to move, slowly, but she picked up the pace quickly.

"I love watching your face." She licked her lips as she watched every twitch of pleasure, wishing she could memorize the moment.

Cody had outed himself on more than one occasion as lacking any talent for deception or subtlety. The fact that he'd managed to keep his street fighting a secret for so long was an anomaly he couldn't imagine himself ever repeating, or wanting to try. He made no effort to hide any expression that came across his face, reveling in the heat of her and not ashamed to show it. "God, you're amazing. Go slow, go slow . . . *fuck* that's good, Aimee."

"Slow. Okay. I can . . . I can." She was gasping as well, her breasts bouncing with every movement. He was so deep inside her that the sensation had her squirming for an entirely different reason. "You're *so deep* . . ." Aimee was clawing at his skin as she tried to keep herself moving slow. "This is . . . so fucking hot . . ."

As she leaned down against him, he wrapped his arms around her back, pulling her in to take a small measure of control in rocking his hips beneath hers. His lips were hot against her neck, every gasp for breath caught up against her ear. "That right there . . . that right fucking there . . ."

It turned her on even more to hear him talking right back, and she moaned even louder as he rocked up into her. She didn't care where his mouth had been, she leaned in and kissed him, groaning against his lips. "I love you so much . . ."

He couldn't speak to answer her at first, but even as his moans began to pitch upward, he held her tight against him and sat up, carrying her with him in a single fluid motion. In just a moment, without any separation between their bodies, he had her flipped onto her back, pressed between his bulk and the too-soft comforter.

"I love you too, Aimee." He gasped the words against her ear as if he knew he wouldn't be able to speak afterward, then raked his hands up to the back of her shoulders and drove himself into her, with long, slow, steady strokes that were slowly increasing in speed.

Aimee wrapped a long leg around his waist as he drove into her, but again she white-knuckled the sheets as her red hair splayed out like fire on the bed. She was clearly falling into another orgasm as she arched against him, a string of curses falling out of her lips.

She could feel and hear it the moment he lost himself,

since he'd never been shy or quiet by disposition. His entire body shuddered against hers, gasping out half her name as his hips bucked by instinct over intention. His hands gripped her shoulders so hard it was possible she would have bruises afterward. A part of her would consider afterward that it felt like his body tensed for a great deal longer than her previous boyfriend ever had, but her mind wasn't processing that detail at the moment.

She wrapped her other leg around to keep him firmly in place while they both basked in the throes of pleasure. Aimee's heart felt like it was going to beat out of her chest, but as soon as she could, she let out a panting, breathy laugh as he finally pulled out and collapsed next to her. Instinctively she curled into him and rested her sweaty face on his chest.

His arm was heavy as it held her against him, his chest hard against her forehead as she cuddled close. She could feel his heart pounding against her face as they caught their breath, his hands running over her back in gentle caresses temporarily devoid of his usual strength.

"You . . . are . . ." he couldn't finish his statement as he held her, still groaning as he had to move his hips to adjust himself on the bed before he fell off it.

Aimee laughed softly as she traced the lines of his extensive tattoo, but really what flooded her thoughts was how much she cared for Cody, and that she would do anything to show it to him and be with him.

The Voice responded to her musings, clearly hoping that she would try to negotiate something, and oddly, she briefly thought of Tony. She wondered if he felt the same haunting things, the need, the desire to share and have the deepened bond between them, and the pain of loss that came by her complete ineptitude and vanity.

She held tighter to Cody's side and ignored the Voice, desperate not to lose Cody the way she had already lost one love of her life. "I love you." She repeated into Cody's skin, as if loving him would will the universe into allowing her to keep him, despite the feeling of unease that came with it.

"I love you too." His words slurred a bit in the contented sigh that partly deflated him, but he moved one large hand to brush back her hair out of her face. "You . . . are amazing. I've . . . you know my history. It's more extensive than I'd like. But none of it was like that. Like this."

"Your history doesn't matter to me. What is in the past stays there." She wiggled to move up his body to kiss along his neck and cheek before she rested her head on his shoulder instead. "We're going to do that again. Once we recover and eat the food you brought." She lifted up slightly and brushed his hair off his forehead to look into his eyes momentarily. "You're amazing too. I'm sorry I ever doubted you."

"I deserve the doubts." He leaned up enough to kiss her cheek, which was all he could reach at the moment, before he collapsed again. "Bold of you to think I'm ever gonna recover from that."

She laughed softly and wiggled her way to lay on top of him but it was all she could manage to do before she was relaxing against his body. His slow caress on her skin had her drifting off faster than she realized.

* * * * *

Maggie leaned against a brick wall in a dark alley not far from the Bellagio, looking down at her knife as she cleaned it slowly. She and Barrett split briefly at the sirens, but he knew where to meet her. She heard the crunch of footsteps and looked up to see her partner slinking into the alley like the criminal he was. "The cameras caught you. You had too much fun, it seems. I don't know if the cameras caught me too, but I don't think so. We'll have to get someone on it."

"If there'd been any kind of payoff, I wouldn't have minded the trouble." Barrett was more annoyed at the attention they'd been obliged to run from than anything else. He methodically took off the coat he was wearing, emptied the pockets and then tossed it behind an AC unit nearby to rot. Rolling up his sleeves and putting on a hat wouldn't confuse everyone looking for him forever, but it was a start. "Guy was clean, no Mark to be seen. So either he's an initiate waiting for it or he was as oblivious as he sounded when he was screaming. My money's on oblivious."

"Damn. I was hoping for more information." Maggie waited for the police lights and sirens to go some distance before she led the way through the alley to the sidewalks. She saw a bike parked nearby and motioned for him to wait while she quickly hotwired the thing and motioned for him to drive. "There's a motel nearby."

"I remember the prep." Barrett grumbled as he got onto the bike. He waited for her to get on the back and wiggle in close, but he gave her barely any time to get a good grip before they were in motion.

They hadn't been assigned to Vegas for very long. No assignment ever lasted more than a few months, just to keep people moving, keep a fresh set of eyes on any given situation, and keep their targets from being able to predict who was hunting them.

It had been years since Barrett had taken a shift in Vegas, but he had to admit, he liked the town. He appreciated how obvious most of the scams were, as if the place itself was admitting that it had a single strip of bright and shiny distractions to keep focus away from everything else that was terrible underneath.

The motel they found was no exception. No one pulling up to it would be under any misunderstandings about what it was for. It was no resort for a weekend getaway playing host to tourists. It was the kind of place that made Barrett feel an immense sense of gratitude that a blacklight was not a standard part of any given Hunter's travel kit. "What did you get on your end?" He asked once they ditched the bike a block away, beginning the quick hike through the backstreets to get to their room.

"The girl has been with the casino for almost a year now.

Used to be a stripper. The order has checked Club G before, though, nothing shady there." She pulled out her phone and put in a new chip as they walked, since she had long since ditched the old one.

"The strip, though . . . the Bellagio has been under investigation for a while. No leads yet, seems clean. I got a tracker on her phone, though, since the girl she ditched was angry enough to slip information when I asked. I sent her info back to HQ. They're going to watch her location, so as long as she doesn't ditch the phone, we're good. Right now they're still in the Bellagio, though."

"Could still be nothing more than a tattoo." Barrett admitted, since he had to remind himself to keep objectivity, at least until a target was identified. After that, all bets were off. "We need direct observation. Something HQ can't get their panties in a twist about later."

"Then we'll just have to wait until she moves. We can follow her and see what she does or who she associates with. Maybe the boy toy is in on it too." Once they made it to the motel, she unlocked the door and hustled in ahead of Barrett.

Their room wasn't messy, but it was clear who took up most of the space. Maggie fell back onto 'her' bed and stretched out. They typically shared a bed after wearing each other out, but they weren't supposed to do that. Even after being chased by the police, she looked calm. "Should we order a pizza?"

"Get two. If we're gonna be holed up on stakeout, we're gonna want leftovers." Barrett went through the methodical process of locking the door, both with the flimsy measures provided by the motel and the more secure means they brought with them. It was never about preventing access altogether; people who had magic would get in no matter what countermeasures were in place. It was about making sure their targets had to expend as much of themselves as possible in the effort.

Maggie made quick work of ordering the pizzas, his

favorite and hers, before she used the phone to log into their network and register her new chip. She scrolled through notifications as she lounged back on the bed. "They sure are keeping our numbers high and close to the strip. We haven't even reported anything. What aren't they telling us about this place?"

"Objectivity." Barrett laid back on the side of one of the beds with his fingers kneading his temples, thinking back through the altercation with the rich boys and considering how he would have to adjust because of it. "Means there's some kind of obscurement in place on the job at a high level, so they don't want us trying to coordinate yet. They want to coordinate remotely, so they need a few dozen eyes on the ground to triangulate. Only reason they ever pour this many of us into a city this small at once."

"I hate it when they do that. It makes me feel like cannon fodder." Maggie glanced over at Barrett and stared at him for a moment. "You've been in this longer than I have. Have you ever actually been in an area for a long time?"

She and Barrett had been partnered for about two years, but they always seemed to be on the move. They never stayed in one location for longer than six months and they were always the ones gathering intel that other people eventually capitalized on.

She was dying to make a big bust on her own. "I've seen some shit in my three years, but I will say that the moving around without any real accomplishment is annoying as fuck. You're a much better partner, though, than my last one. Once I cracked you with my sex appeal, anyway."

"Yeah, well, if you had managed to crack Warren with it, I'd have been amazed. For him to be any less interested in sex than he already is, he'd have to be some kind of inanimate object. Specifically the kind you can't fuck." He kicked off his boots as he relaxed on the bed, shaking his head at her question.

"Longest stretch I've been in one place in this job was three years, but that wasn't on assignment. The fucker cursed me to some kind of pocket space where they could do whatever they wanted with time. Left me there for three years while just a few days passed here in the real world." He grinned at her past his laces as he tossed them across the room. "The rest of that file's classified. That was a high Mark to bring in."

Maggie popped up from her bed and almost hopped all the way over to him as he took off his shoes. "Bullshit, classified. Are you really not going to tell me anything?"

"I hit up a Mark, got on his bad side, got fucked over into his own play-realm for three years, plotted my revenge, finally got out, strangled him with my bare hands, and wished I could've done it twenty more times just for fun." He shook his head as she came over, settling back on the bed with the shitty motel pillows piled behind him. "He was an old Algierian bastard. Not worth thinking twice about."

"Is that where some of these grey hairs came from?" She reached out to run her fingers through his peppered hair at his temple. Maggie smirked at him as he relaxed on the bed. "We really need to work on your torture tactics. But I'm glad you were able to give him his comeuppance."

"I'm not known for my patience. Your line of work takes a lot of that." He reached up and took her by the throat, not hard enough to stop her breathing, but enough to drag her up onto him.

Maggie smirked at him as he gripped her neck, but she squirmed on top of him as he dragged her. She couldn't talk with his grip, but she loved it when he got rough.

"But yes, that's where some of these grey hairs come from. Some of the others come from that fucking bottom-feeder that hit me in college and took half my twenties from me." He kissed her roughly with one hand behind his head to relax, before his grip loosened on her neck. "I'm a cranky old man. I've got my reasons."

She coughed a little and cleared her throat after he loosened his grip, and she fell onto his chest. "I can't eat my pizza if you choke me out." She tried to look indignant as she straddled his body. "Unless you want to fuck, cranky old man."

"Pizza would get here before I'm done with you." Still, he wasn't completely letting go. "Sight of you naked would be a hell of a tip for the delivery driver."

"He might call the police if he could see some of the fading bruises." She raised her eyebrows at him and his hovering hand. "You want me to beg, don't you, old man? You want the sexy partner to beg to be fucked?"

"You begged for the bruises the same as you did for everything else." He took a tight grip on her shirt, tightening it around her breasts to hold her close. "It's been a long fucking day standing around in a casino pretending like I'm just *pretending* to want you on my dick at all times, and I had to bail on beating that asshole in the suit who had it coming before I could finish what I started. Plus, we've got a hunt ahead of us as soon as that bitch leaves the hotel. So before we get busy chasing her ass all over town, I am gonna fuck you the way I've wanted to since I spent the afternoon thinking about throwing you over a blackjack table. Is that clear?"

Maggie grinned, since she knew the torture she put him through by grinding on his dick during recon. She licked her lips slowly as he held her close. "That sounds *so* much better than pizza."

"Oh I still want the pizza. I just want you first." He kissed her again, hard, and reached down with his other hand to take a firm grip between her legs even over the pants she wore, his strong fingers kneading through the fabric to beckon every part of her closer against him.

She groaned and growled as he teased her, but she struggled against him mostly because she wanted to kiss him again. She managed to get to his lips and press her own punishing kiss against them. "I want you to tie me to this bed. I bet the pizza delivery guy would love to see that too."

That got a full, growling laugh from him, and he let go of her enough to allow her to kiss him before he bodily threw her off so that he could stand up. When he got to his feet, he took hold of her pants, pulling them forcibly off her to peel them away onto the floor. "That'll be a story for him to tell back at the shop."

"Hell of a story." Once he peeled her pants off she pulled away from his grip, since she was fully aware that he liked a chase. She was half naked without her pants anyway, since she conveniently hadn't worn underwear. "Sexy old man and his kinky fucked up submissive."

"His brat, you mean." He took a handful of the bedsheets next, ripping them off to throw them on the floor, leaving the bed as bare as she was about to be, with only the fitted sheet straining to hold onto the mattress. A single step took him over to his own suitcase open on the low table next to the room's shitty television. The rope he used (which he packed for missions, certainly, there was always a professional need for rope) was ready at hand, and he quickly uncoiled it like a whip as he stalked her across the room.

Maggie was grinning like a cheshire cat as he stalked toward her, though she was still at the head of the bed, away from him. She pulled off her shirt and threw it at his face. He looked so serious and turned on that she was almost giddy. "Okay, brat. But I love being your brat."

He threw her shirt aside toward the door of the room where it hung on the hook of the pathetic door-bar without him noticing. Throwing her around the bed to tie her up involved him chasing her over the covers, throwing her down repeatedly until he could bind her arms behind her back with his knee pressed into her spine.

Her kicking and thrashing afterward was minimized once he had the rope from her bound arms looped under the mattress itself and tied back onto her wrists, pinning her face-down on the bed. Each ankle followed with its own expert knots as he blocked her from kicking at him, both left free to kick and squirm as she liked until he looped those ropes under the bed with the first, and began to spread them apart.

"That's what a brat gets." He growled once he had her restrained the way she wanted. "Put in her place, is what."

"Face down." She mumbled into the bed as she tugged against the ropes, but she knew from too much experience both in bed and in business, that rarely did anyone escape from Barrett's restraints. "Now I can't even see you."

"Don't need to see to come. Were that the case, you wouldn't like being blindfolded so much." She could hear clothes hitting the floor behind her, and his shirt actually landed on her back, long before the rest of him followed. He took one arm of it and wrapped it around her head to blind her as she felt the bulk of him move in close against her back. "How many times is it gonna take to mellow out your behavior for the night, do you think? Five? Six?"

"Mellow? Do you even know me, old man?" Maggie was bare except for her bra, which he snapped against her back, and she let out a needy whimper. She had fading bruises on her ass, but the way she presented her ass to him made it clear that she didn't care about the goddamn bruises. "I've been grinding on your cock all night."

"Seven, then. And sore enough you can't hardly sit down unless it's on my cock to get some more." He slapped the ass she presented, hard enough to set the windows and fixtures ringing with the sound, then took her roughly in hand again, his strong fingers brushing expertly against her clit and rubbing at her like a lamp that was about to grant every wish he asked for. The rough play already had her worked up, as he had known it would, but he slid his fingers into her anyway to take charge of her.

Maggie groaned loudly as his fingers sank inside of her, and she bucked against his hand, all of her limbs tugging on the rope. "Fuck." She hissed in pleasure, wondering how long he would tease before he sunk his cock into her. "I'm soaked for you already, big guy."

"You're soaked for yourself, don't give me that bullshit." Everything about Barrett relied on people thinking they knew what he was capable of at first glance. An older man with a sour disposition who walked with a vague limp and wore a suit like he knew how.

People expected him to be one kind of washed up or another, when in fact, he had never been sharper. He had never been more dangerous.

One hand pressed to the small of her back as the other tortured her soaking cunt, giving her nowhere to escape the building rush between her legs. Every twitch of her legs reminded her body that there was no avoiding what was coming. Because he said so. "You're out to take, and take, until you've got everything you want. But you're gonna give it to me first before you get to keep the rest."

Maggie writhed against the bed and felt so incredibly close when she heard knocking on the door, and she almost went feral with need. "Don't . . . you dare . . . answer . . ." Maggie wanted her orgasm and she didn't want him to stop when she was so fucking close.

"You'd better make sure he hears why, then." Barrett's pace didn't change in the slightest, keeping up exactly the kind of pressure on her that she couldn't escape, that her body craved after a day like they'd had. Some people made good Hunters because they could outsmart their quarry, or deceive them into a false sense of security. Barrett wasn't the strongest or the fastest or the smartest, but he would never, ever stop, until he got what he wanted. That included getting what he wanted from Maggie. Delivery guy be damned.

She pulled against his ties so hard that her wrists burned, but all of it was worth it when she finally cried out in pleasure and collapsed against his relentless touch. Maggie definitely wasn't silent about her pleasure, and it turned her on even more knowing that someone else was listening.

It seemed as though he had just stopped to let her orgasm run its course, leaving her twitching on the bed, but the sound of the chain on the door intruded on her afterglow as Barrett answered the door. "Twenty four, right?"

"I, uh . . . yeah, twenty four fifty . . . it's . . ." the college kid outside the door scrambled over his words and nearly dropped the pizza warmer.

"Whoa, hey, steady, man, you're gonna fuck up your tip. Here, keep the rest." Barrett exchanged food for money and leaned against the door. "You wanna finish her off, or you got more in the car?"

"I got . . . there's . . ." sneakers scraped on the shitty outdoor carpet outside the room as the man's voice cracked like a teenager's.

Maggie was still groaning a little on the bed as she laid on her face, but she turned her face toward the door. "Really? You want to watch instead of fuck? Pizza guy! Make a choice, here! I'm dripping down my legs!"

All she could hear afterward was the sound of receding footsteps and Barrett slamming the door. "Coward." He replaced the chain and set down the pizzas on the flimsy table by the window before coming back to the bed with her. "Finest piece of ass he's ever had half a chance to get into and he just walks away. Bet he leaves that part out of the story when he tells it later."

She smiled at his compliment, even though she didn't comment on it. Maggie took his compliments like candy whenever he actually gave them to her. "More for you, big guy. Come fuck me."

"Only order of yours you can ever expect me to take." He laid himself against her with a hand at the back of her neck, relishing her helplessness before he guided himself inside her with a satisfied groan. He dearly hoped the redhead took her time leaving the casino. He had better things to do than chase down a witch.

EIGHT

After a long day, Sophia's feet were killing her. All she wanted to do was walk into her apartment, kick off her heels, toss off her clothes and get into a hot bath. Instead, she unlocked the door to her apartment, kicked off her heels by the door with a moan, and then almost had a heart attack when she looked up.

Sophia and Darius were leaders of the Vegas covenant, and while Darius was the ultimate decider of Covenant matters, Sophia ran the business side and supported her brother in all the ways she could. Right now she wanted to curse him for ever hiring Zeke to run tech.

With a growl, she tossed a threatening look at her uninvited guest. She let down her long black hair from its tight bun and glared at him. "You're supposed to send me a warning when you set up shop in here. I know there are a lot of upgrades happening, but for fuck's sake, Zeke."

Sophia was a tall, beautiful woman with dusky skin, brown eyes that often were more dangerous than inviting. She had long, endless legs that went with her lean figure, but her attitude scared off most admirers and anyone who might be a friend.

"Sorry, it's protocol to start with your rooms and your

brother's when upgrading equipment. Also, in my defense, your schedule has you meeting with one of your warehouse managers on the east side in ten minutes, so unless you're getting piggyback rides from Casey these days, you're the one deviating from a schedule here." Zeke was already on the tall side, but being up on top of a fifteen foot ladder in the middle of her living room with vaulted ceilings only exaggerated that fact.

As usual, the man was in a simple, sleeveless gym shirt and a pair of basketball shorts, as casual as it was possible to be while remaining at least halfway decent. His spiked blond hair was hidden from her by way of his head being halfway inside her ceiling to work on her electronics. "A pair of Hunters got within spitting distance of a couple of our people at the Bellagio, which means it's time to change all the cameras and randomize all the locks again."

The defense of her change in plans died in her throat before she could start talking, since surprise won out at the notification of a new threat. "Darius didn't contact me. Is he not concerned or just slacking?" Sophia decided to detour into her kitchen and set down her bag on the table before she took out her devices so that Zeke could boost her security. She ran a hand through her hair as she headed for a bottle of wine next. News of Hunters meant her night was going to get even longer.

"Maybe your brother decided to take a vacation. For the first time in . . . how many thousand years? Don't answer that." He jumped down from the ladder, looking as though he hit a few invisible bounces on the way down to stall his momentum before he landed on his feet and went to her phone. Nimble fingers had the case apart in seconds, doing a standard sweep for any compromised components.

"Looks like an older guy and a younger woman this time. I'm not sure yet whether it's the older guy being punished by being put on a shit detail and the youngster is being dragged along, or if she's hot for a big score like us and dragging along the old man. I'll let you know if I get any data either way.”

“How did they find us? Who are they after?” She sipped her wine in her blouse and pencil skirt across from him, watching him disassemble with ease. “Also it irritates me that you knew before I did. I’m sure you take joy in that.”

“I know most things before most people. So the joy fades after a while.” He shrugged, then looked up and caught her death glare over the rim of her wine glass. “About current events, I mean. I’d never presume to know more in general. Actually, I would, just . . . present company excluded.”

Her glare turned into a smirk before she took another drink. “I do enjoy watching you squirm.” She motioned to her phone once he put it back together and he held it out for her. “So, smartass, who is our weak link? Did someone slip up?”

“I wouldn’t call it a slip up. They were caught on camera at the Bellagio, but they beat up some suits after hanging around most of the night just watching. We had twenty-six different members of the covenant inside the hotel at the time, but I haven’t finished running path analytics to see if they were trying to follow or watch someone. Having to backtrack and this took priority. You know Darius would shit a brick if he found out I did anything out of order. Ancient gods forbid.”

Zeke went to a tablet he’d brought and started in on some work remotely with the new camera he’d installed in her ceiling. “Casey and Aimee were closest at the time my software recognized them from known Hunter logs going back a couple years.”

“Hm. Well, we better tell Casey and Aimee they can’t come back here until we’re sure. I’ll contact Case and he can reach out to Aimee. They’re ‘besties’ anyway, and Aimee isn’t inducted yet, so protocol works differently for her.”

She finished off her glass of wine and looked for Casey’s number on her phone. She walked past Zeke and smacked his ass with a smirk. She doubted he would think it was funny. "Lemme know what else you find, Z."

The smack clearly got his attention, and he looked at her over the device in his hand for a few seconds to watch her smirk, before he leaned a little to get a look at her ass, well-defined in the pencil skirt she was wearing.

She stopped to look over her shoulder at him, not even turning around to impede his view. "Plotting revenge?"

"And enjoying the view. I'm multitasking." He finished up his work on the equipment in his hands and set it back in its case. "You know I have a weakness for skirts."

"Did I know that? I'm not sure I knew that." She was in the process of pouring herself a second glass of wine as she leaned against the countertop.

"July the tenth, four years ago, at the Mayburn club. We were talking about the waitresses and I mentioned I have a weakness for skirts. You were wearing that green one with the slit at the time." He put his equipment up on one shoulder for easy carrying and headed toward the door behind her.

"You were a little distracted at the time, but that's understandable, since we were there to kill somebody. I was mostly looking at your ass." He angled a solid smack to her own ass on the way by, but stopped against her shoulder as the echoes of the smack rang off the solid surfaces in the expansive room. "I'll let you know what I find, Boss."

Before she called Casey she watched Zeke disappear, her ass still tingling in a way that she minded not at all. Had he always been checking her out? They had known each other a long time, not to have shown interest.

There were probably several reasons why everyone kept their distance from her unless necessary, but one main reason kept Sophia from making friends. The cost of making friends was the risk of losing them, and while necessary, it meant she kept most people at arm's length.

Keeping them terrified to know her was the easiest way to keep herself functional in the Covenant. If the wrong person forgot who she was, well, it had caused some problems in the past.

Zeke had no interest in being her friend or knowing her beyond surface level, and it was best to keep it that way. She put Zeke out of her mind and tapped on Casey's contact to give him a call.

Casey answered the phone almost before the first ring was finished. The man had reflexes that would make cats jealous. "Okay, before you say anything, I know the carpet is hideous, I didn't pick it, it was a full staff meeting and they thought it would be funny. Don't worry, I plan on firing three of them."

Sophia looked down at the carpet in her apartment but it hadn't changed, so she had no idea what he was going on about. Half the time she didn't know what Casey was talking about. "Carpet is the least of my concerns at the moment. Has anyone been in contact with you about a sighting? Seems we have trouble in paradise."

"Sighting? What kind of sighting?" Casey sounded like a kid on Christmas with an oversized present by the tree. "Celebrity? Cryptid? Aliens? Please let it be aliens!"

"If only. Hunters." Sophia replied with a sigh of irritation. They dealt with Hunters every now and again, it just irritated her every time they had to turn their lives upside down to eradicate the infestation. "You and Aimee nearly brushed shoulders with them, and you know the protocol."

For once, there was a pause on the other end of the line, an uncommon occurrence from someone who talked as much as Casey. "Aw, shit, are you serious? Oh man, I *hate* lockdown! Fuck. Fine, fine, fine, protocol is protocol. I'll go round up Aimee, I don't think she's been through that brief yet."

"Zeke will be in touch with both of you. There'll be a team watching over you in lockdown, but since Aimee isn't inducted . . . we really, well . . . she's on her own. Obviously if trouble happens, she can reach out, but we can't afford to lead any trouble back to us." She shook her head even though Casey couldn't see her. "Make sure you have someone covering for you. Get to your house and lay low."

"Yes ma'am." He clicked off the call and took a moment to himself to sigh. Stupid Hunters. This was going to fuck up his whole week. Oh well, at least he'd get some sleep. He was starting to feel the need for a good long extended rest.

His first call was to Isaac, letting him know he'd be home soon for a week of lockdown, but he went to call Aimee next and got no response. After checking in with her very annoyed shift supervisor and finding out she had just disappeared, he made his way up to the room he'd reserved for her and checked at the door.

Alright, either she was in the process of being murdered by Hunters, in which situation, Casey would not be the most helpful person who could barge in, or she was currently having her mind rearranged by her boyfriend.

Casey's money was on the latter.

He sat down on a couch down the corridor from her room, putting his feet up to type a message while she finished with round . . . whatever it was for her that night.

So I don't really want to interrupt, since I'm in the hall outside and it sounds like you're having a great time, but I wanted to let you know, you and I need to leave the hotel and head home. I'll explain as soon as you get out of there, since I don't want to freak you out in the presence of a civilian, but whatever you need to do, you need to make some excuses, get some clothes on, and come out here to meet me. I'll explain on the way.

He waited until the sounds from inside the room had come to a crescendo and then to silence before he sent the message. Courtesy was important.

It was a solid fifteen minutes before Aimee checked her phone, and she only checked her phone because so few people had her contact information. She read the message from Casey with great confusion before she looked over at the sexy, naked man next to her. He wasn't quite asleep, but he pulled her into him after she scooted away to grab her phone. "Casey has some sort of crisis." She spoke softly as Cody held onto her. "I should go."

"Should? Really? I don't think *should* is the right word here. You should really stay. Casey can deal with his own crisis." He kissed her sleepily, but with a firm grip locked around her back to hold her close. "You might *have* to, but you're never gonna convince me you *should*."

Aimee whimpered as he kissed her, held her, and she couldn't help but kiss him back several times. The last thing she wanted to do was leave him after she just got him back. "You're not going to disappear again, right? I . . . I can't lose you again."

"Only place I'm disappearing to right now is la la land. Especially if this room is paid up through the night. If Casey's crisis ends up being temporary, you have my full endorsement to come back up here and get in the way of my beauty sleep. It's never gonna be as beautiful as you anyway."

Aimee blushed since his comments were so sincere. Aimee knew she was beautiful, she made herself that way. But it felt so different hearing it from Cody. She ran her hands over his defined chest and arms before kissing him again. "I love you, Cody."

"I love you too. Don't judge me if I'm snoring when you come back." He held onto her as much as he could in the process of getting up, but when she got out of his reach, his arm flopped to the bed and did not move again from where it fell, the man attached to it already out cold.

She smiled at him as he slept, though she wanted to kill Casey for pulling her away. She dressed quickly in the change of clothes she bought when she bought Cody's new clothes. Nearly a half hour after Casey's message, she stepped into the hallway in jeans, sneakers, and a tank top.

"I'm going to kill you." She growled at her friend quietly as the door clicked closed behind her. "I just got him back! I . . . what in the world could possibly . . ."

"We have Hunters." Casey front-loaded the

conversation, offering her his arm to walk her down the hallway in her fairly disheveled state. No way she was going to stand out in Vegas at that time of night. If a person walking around on the strip at three AM *wasn't* some kind of disheveled, they were the suspicious ones.

"I know you haven't been through those protocols yet, but whenever the covenant monitoring gets a blip on a set of Hunters in town, especially if they were close to anyone, protocol is to get back to your house away from the complex and lay low for seven days. Catch up on your streaming addiction, tip your delivery driver when he brings you wine and chinese, that sort of thing."

"Lay low?" She looked back at the door as Casey led her away, and more than ever she wished that Cody knew the truth. "Is Cody in danger? He doesn't know, I can't lose him again, Case."

"The fact that he doesn't know actually makes him safer than you or me. Hunters are a very *specific* breed of serial killers. They only kill the Marked. Or they're only supposed to, anyway." It had been a rare occasion when there was someone or a group of someones that Casey didn't like. For almost the first time in their friendship so far, she could hear in his tone just how much he hated Hunters, though his version of hate sounded a great deal lighter than most people's. "Just tell him you're sick or something and you'll see him in a week. It'll suck, but he'll buy it. Quarantine rules. Easy."

"Easy." She scoffed as they wandered through the casino to leave. "I told him I am in love with him. He said he loves me. We didn't even get to spend the night together and this shit happens. I should be with him and instead I'm being stalked by serial killers."

"Girl. Seriously. I let you out of my sight for five minutes and you start dropping four-letter words on a guy who just dropped off the face of the planet for a month. What am I gonna do with you?" Casey was back to needling her as they rode the elevator down.

Aimee sighed as she gripped tighter on Casey's arm and rested her head on his shoulder as they walked. "Can't I just stay with you and Isaac? Why do we have to separate? I hate staying in my house by myself, it was only fun when Cody would stay with me. I haven't been back there since he disappeared."

He shook his head. "It's protocol, I'm sorry. Everyone has to go to their own residence so we can keep an eye on who's following who. If the Hunters try and get a bead on my place, we'll know they were here for me and we can try and backtrack to find out where I fucked up. Also makes them work harder if they were after all of us, keep us all out of the same place until we know where we need to respond. It sucks, I know. But probably about a dozen more of us are likely to be going on lockdown too, since they spotted them here in the Bellagio tonight."

She couldn't help the whine that escaped her lips. "I barely even worked tonight, between making out with Rose and seducing my boyfriend. And yes, I know that makes me sound terrible." She gave him a weak smile but she still didn't want to go to her house by herself. "I guess if I have no choice, I better start a grocery delivery."

"You can phone it in to Zeke, he'll double up your pickup with somebody working security anyway so they can sweep your neighborhood." Casey heaved a disgruntled sigh of his own. "It's sad how many times I've had to do this. I heard the word Hunter out of Sophia's mouth and I was immediately picking out the pajamas I'm gonna wear to sleep for a week."

"Some rest will do you good." Aimee kissed her friend's cheek as they made their way out of the casino. "Should I be worried?"

"About me? Nah, I'm due for a long bit of shuteye, but not, like *over*due for it, just a part of the price, is all." Casey shrugged it off.

Aimee squeezed his arm again and remained silent all the rest of the way to Casey's bike, since he graciously offered to drop her off at her home away from home. Fortunately for him, he had Isaac waiting at home. "I don't have any weapons other than a handgun. What if they come after me? What am I supposed to do?"

"Well if you have one, do you really know how to use it?" Casey was doing his best not to look doubtful when it came to her proficiency with a gun or the lack thereof. He remembered when they first met that she mentioned taking self-defense, but he didn't know if she kept up with it.

"Not . . . with great efficiency. I know how to use it. I'm no sharpshooter." Aimee chewed on her bottom lip nervously. "Do you think this is a real threat? I uh. . . should I be scared? I'm scared."

He shook his head as he led her out to his motorcycle. "Do I look scared? No, these things are a problem for the security team, not for us. Just lay low in your house. The Hunters can't find it if they've never been there before. You know how Sophia's charm works on them. So long as you haven't been having Hunters over for brunch, and I think I'd have noticed if you had, then you're fine. Only reason we have to go on lockdown is to make sure they don't tie us to anybody else and they can't follow us anywhere. This is a problem for the security team to handle, not us."

"I didn't think Sophia's pacts would apply to me yet." Her voice was small as she got onto the back of Casey's bike after he got on. She was dying to call Cody, but she didn't know what she would even say. What would keep him away for a week or more? She didn't *want* him to stay away. "I guess I need to figure out how, if ever, I explain things like this to Cody. Just when I thought we were serious, he was gone. Now he's back and . . . what if things do get serious, I can't just keep lying to him about everything."

"We have people who do introductions like that for you, if you want, once you're fully inducted." He handed her an extra helmet and tapped on the radio for the two of them as he drove. "And no, the covenant doesn't apply to you yet, but Sophia's talent for hiding places is for your house, not for you."

"Right. The house. Not me." She clung tightly to Casey's back as he took off, since she definitely knew better by now. There was no sense in talking at his driving speeds, but she was still alive by the time they got to her house and that was all she could hope for with Casey.

When she got off the bike, she still looked nervous as she took off the helmet and handed it to him. "Expect lots of texts. Even if you are asleep and can't answer me, I hate being alone. Lydia is still too busy." She stepped in to hug him one more time. "Be safe, Case."

"You too, Aim. Don't worry, we'll be past this before you know it. And this won't be the last time we go under lockdown for Hunters. They're annoying as hell." He hugged her tightly and revved his bike before taking off again into the relatively quiet streets.

Aimee stared at her house before she begrudgingly went inside. Everything was untouched from the last time she had been there with Cody, and it made her ache for him even more. A pair of his shoes were at the door, a t-shirt of his slung over her couch. She went and picked up the shirt, and it still had a hint of his cologne.

When he disappeared, she didn't want to come back and face the fact that they had basically been living together and then he was gone. He stayed with her more nights than he ever went to his own place, and she stayed at her apartment in the complex when he went to his place.

She looked around before she stripped off her tank and put Cody's shirt on instead. It was going to be a long week, especially having to blow off her boyfriend.

* * * * *

"She moved." Barrett said from beside Maggie on the bed, where she was lying naked in an attempt to dry off and cool down from the shower she'd just exited. He had his phone over his face as he laid partly beneath her, checking in on their monitoring to follow their quarry. "She just left the hotel, heading north."

"Thank fuck I was genius enough to tag her phone." Maggie praised herself but didn't move from laying on top of her sexy bastard partner. "Should we go after her or give her a false sense of security before we go do some recon?"

"All sense of security is false. For anyone. It's redundant to say so. But yes, that." He nodded absently in her direction, looking at the movements of their prey's erratic progress through the late-night Vegas surface streets. "Little weird for her to shack up with somebody in one of the rooms of the hotel and then walk-of-shame it home at three in the morning, isn't it?"

"Maybe she was consumed with guilt." Maggie snorted a little at the idea since their redheaded prey had a stripper past, so she doubted it. "Or maybe the sex was that bad. That was probably it."

"Well, either way, if she's headed back to the burbs and staying there, it's as good a time as any to go do recon on the place, see what we're dealing with." Barrett looked across the room at his clothes with an annoyed growl, clearly not quick to get in motion with Maggie on top of him.

Maggie had his handprints all over her body and around her neck, but she looked as blissed-out as ever as she slowly rolled away from her partner in literal crime. "I hate it when playtime is over. But the chase is fun too." She ran her nails down his thigh as she sat up. "Time to catch a mouse."

"Dedication. And to think I used to like that about you." He watched her crawl off of him and get to her clothes before he reluctantly got up to do the same. "We'll take the car this time. If this turns into a stakeout, I'm going to have to sleep you off in the back seat."

"You make that sound like an invitation." Maggie smirked at him as she grabbed her clothes and dressed hastily, not caring about how she looked or if she smelled like sex. Who didn't smell like sex in Vegas?

She braided her hair quickly and grabbed a backpack,

one of several they had ready to go at a moment's notice. She grabbed her phone and checked their network. No movement from anyone else nearby. Maybe they would actually get to hold a victory flag for this one. "A girl like that isn't alone around here. She has to have a web or connections somehow. This could be big."

"We've gotta pluck this strand first before we can start thinking about a web." Barrett preferred to look at the immediate goal in front of them rather than getting too excited about leaps ahead, but she wasn't wrong. "We'll have to do some observation first and see what else she might be tied into."

"Let's go, old man." She made sure her gun was at her hip and she whipped open the door to their room so she could jog her way to the car. She was ready to kill a witch.

NINE

Two days without Cody and already Aimee was feeling it. Being alone in her house, Lydia out of contact, Casey unconscious, she was going nuts. She looked at her phone when it started ringing and she knew Cody wouldn't give up on calling her.

She had tried radio silence at first. That was horrible.

Then she tried to explain that she needed some space, that was horrible too.

After ignoring him all morning and afternoon, she flinched at seeing his face on her phone, even though she desperately wanted him there with her. Aimee answered tentatively, since she could only go on for so long. "Hey. I'm okay, but you gotta stop calling me. Please?"

"I'm sorry, I can't do that." His tone was still light, but she could hear the concern in his voice, just as there had been when she said she needed space. "If something had gone wrong, sure, I could understand the whole 'space' thing, and that's fine, but one night we're talking about needing to get groceries for the house so we don't have to leave and the next I have to stop calling? What happened? Is this because I disappeared for a month?"

"No, it's not you." Her voice sounded so small, even to

herself. "I miss you, actually. I just . . ." God, she didn't even know what to say? Where was Casey when she needed him? "Just need some time alone. That's all."

She could hear the wind blowing past his phone and the heavy fall of his boots on pavement. She could almost see him walking into (maybe out of?) the casino to talk to her under the sunlight. "Yeah, alright, that's . . . sure, I get that, I just . . . you can understand how a guy gets some mixed signals off that, right? If I fucked up some kind of way the other night, you can tell me, I promise, whatever it is, it's something I can work on."

Aimee's eyes were stinging with tears, since she did understand that she was giving off mixed signals, but she didn't know how to fix it or change it. He didn't know everything about her, but she wanted him to. If only so she could know if he would leave her in the dust after he knew the truth.

"I promise I'm not trying to send mixed signals." She sniffled and tried to keep it quiet. "Honestly, I . . ." She looked around her empty home and ached to have him with her, she knew she would feel a lot safer with him there. Even though she also knew that having him with her would just endanger him from things he didn't even know existed.

"I want to tell you some things, I just . . . now isn't the time. I know I'm being vague, and I'm not trying to be vague on purpose. You didn't fuck up anything. This is on me. I love you, I promise, my feelings haven't changed."

"Okay, you were being vague before, but now you've crossed over into either seance-medium, or politician. That's a whole new level." He walked a bit farther, and she heard a door open and close, quieting the world a bit. "Is it the mob? Because I can deal with mafia connections. I've dealt with a few of them before, they don't bother me."

"The . . . what? You've dealt with the mob?" She didn't know what to say immediately to a statement like that. "I don't know what the mob would want with a former stripper turned waitress." She ran her hand through her hair.

"You really wouldn't care if I was a part of the mob? That's unexpected."

"No? Why would I care about that?" He actually laughed, but she could hear how nervous he was beneath it. "The mob would be lucky to have you, if it did. I don't judge people for what they do for a living."

"I know. I don't either, I just . . . I'm not in the mob." Aimee hated hearing the nervousness in his voice, and all she wanted to do was cuddle with him. "There *is* something I need to tell you about me, but now isn't the time. I don't want to lose you. I love you." She wanted to emphasize how much she cared for him, just to make sure he knew she didn't drop off because of him. "I hate being apart. We live in Vegas. I have half a mind to have you meet me at a crappy Elvis chapel and make sure you're mine."

There was a brief but eloquent pause when she said so. "Alright, deal, but my terms are that we make up a different story to tell the kids one day. 'I panicked because I have a secret I haven't told your father yet' isn't the look we wanna go with. Needs to be some kind of full stripdown, roses-on-the-carpet, champagne-in-a-bucket down-on-both-knees shit. A man likes to be wooed."

Aimee looked at the phone just to make sure she was still connected before she put it back to her ear. "Are you serious? Would you really marry me?"

"You're . . . I'm sorry, are you surprised? You're really surprised right now? You're kidding me with the surprise, right?" She could hear the engine of his bike humming in the background. No wonder his voice sounded clearer, he was talking to her on his helmet.

"Yes, I'm surprised!" She wished she was with him on his bike, she wished she was with him anywhere. "I . . . I just never thought that anyone would want to marry me, or love me enough to ask. Except you didn't. I asked. Sort of. Oh my god. Are you really saying yes?"

"Shouldn't have joked about it if you weren't serious." He paused a moment, and she could almost see his brain short-circuiting at his own contradiction before he decided to just move on regardless. "Yes, I'm really saying yes. And I actually know a pretty awesome chapel if you were serious about that part too. A buddy of mine got married there a couple years ago."

"Oh my god, Cody." She was choked up, but she tried to clear her throat. "I . . . if what I have to tell you doesn't scare you off, then we can run off and get married. I don't have any family, and Casey . . ." she paused as she thought about her friends. "Well, Casey is still mad at you, I think. But I'll give you a proper proposal after all this crap that I'm dealing with is over."

"With all due respect to whatever you're hiding, baby, what the fuck could you possibly not be telling me that you think could get rid of me now? Are you in witness protection? Is that why the no-family thing?" Horns honked past him, but he didn't sound concerned.

"No. Not witness protection." She so badly wanted to tell him to come over to her house, but she knew better. "I'm not telling you for your sake too. You have to believe me. I want you here with me, but it's just not the right time, Cody."

"So the right time would be . . . when I'm there with you, right?"

"Well, yes, but next week. When it's . . . safer. Next week. Okay?" Aimee got up from her couch and decided she needed a glass of wine. "I need time to order you a ring, right? Next week. I'll make it up to you with so much sex."

"Next week." He knew he didn't sound very convincing, and he didn't really mean to try. "Uh huh. Next week. Or, *or* . . . hear me out . . ."

Now, which turn was it on this street? For some reason it was always confusing, even though he'd been through her neighborhood a hundred times. Was it . . . no, it was the second left. Down the row of houses that all looked mostly the same . . . yes, that was the one. Why was it always so hard to find? Just a trick of the neighborhood, maybe.

"Cody. Don't come to my house. Please. You can't come here, okay?" She put her wine down with the glass unfilled as she went to look out her window. She *did* want him to show up, but she knew she shouldn't want him to show up. Her tone wasn't very convincing. "It's not safe, okay? It's not safe for you."

This time, when he revved his bike to get up the last stretch of the street, she heard it at the same time outside her window. "You remember me telling you why I was in the hospital, right? It takes a lot to register on the scale of 'dangerous' for me."

* * * * *

"Two days." Barrett had just woken up from his turn to nap in the back seat of their car, which they had folded down to extend the space into the trunk, just to have somewhere to get some relief from the Vegas sunlight. "Two fucking days, and we can't narrow it down beyond what *neighborhood* we're watching." He shook his head, rubbing at his eyes. "She's onto us and put up some kind of protection bullshit. Her phone signal's here, which means she's still here."

"She has to be onto us. She hasn't moved. Not for anything." Maggie growled but it turned into a yawn, since she wanted to take another nap. It was boring as shit, watching and waiting for nothing. "Maybe we need to get someone here who can sniff it out. Or maybe we need to shake down an employer for exact information or something."

"Yeah, one of the other units tried shaking down a Bellagio manager yesterday going after one of their pit supervisors. They think he's a speedster." Barrett rolled his eyes. He hated dealing with speedsters. Fucking superhero wannabes, all of them. "Didn't go well. They got kicked out of their hotel and had their temp bank accounts emptied before they could even get back to their room. Somebody's tied in here and doesn't want to be sniffed out."

"Well shit. What about the guy? The one she was fucking before she split? Do you think he knows anything? The muscle?"

"He probably does, but if we're gonna use him, we'll have to have the office do it. Unless he happens to have been walking past here while I was sleeping and just holding his phone out to be bugged?" He rubbed at his eyes again as he lumbered himself into the front seat. "No? Didn't think so." He went rummaging through their supplies looking for a water bottle as he grumbled. "I fucking hate calling Saul. Smarmy asshole."

"All business, that guy. I'll call him." Maggie stole a gulp of Barrett's water with a smirk before she made the call. "Hello, sunshine." Maggie said when the phone finally connected.

"You only call me that when you're in a good mood or you want something. Which is it?" Saul didn't sound like he was awake yet. The man kept strange hours, like all Hunters.

"The second one. I'm actually pretty cranky after a two-day stakeout. We need a bug or a tracker. We've got a girl dodging us by hiding her place. Her muscle boyfriend is a bartender at the Bellagio, Cody something. We need your help."

"You've already got a bug on the girl's phone itself, what's the problem with that? Just follow the GPS." Saul was still clearly in the process of getting himself conscious.

"Yeah, thanks, we didn't think of that, boss." Barrett grumbled without the phone even being on speakerphone.

"I heard that. You're saying she's got some kind of masking on it, then." He sighed. "Have you got any basis for thinking the boyfriend is Marked?"

"Only by association. We've seen the Mark on *her* and if she's strutting around with that, he's gotta know, right? Or he's in on it. We're not after him until we get confirmation. We're after her. And we need something. We keep trying to follow GPS and end up going in circles."

"So you think she's got something to keep herself from

being found, but if you can track the beefcake, you might be able to actually do your jobs." Saul's sleepy brain finally caught up to where they were going. "Cody, works at the Bellagio, muscular. That should be enough for the office to go on. Give me some time, I'll get the information connected to you when it comes through."

"Thanks, Sunshine." She really wanted to say asshole, but he agreed to help, and she didn't want to rock the boat. Maggie sighed once the call disconnected. "Hopefully he works quickly."

"He's been out of field work too long to remember what 'working' means, let alone quickly." Barrett laid himself back in the seat as if to go back to sleep in annoyance, though he started sitting up again when she repeated her yawn. "This kind of shit is almost enough for me to stop one of these assholes and have them give me the Mark for myself. At least then I'd be able to find them easier and kill them at their own game."

Maggie looked over at Barrett at that kind of statement, but she'd never met a Hunter like he was describing. Although she knew they existed. "If you go getting Marked, that's a suicide mission. I didn't know you were that dedicated to the cause. I heard those fuckers are something else entirely."

"I've heard the same, but if I turned into one, it wouldn't be because I'm dedicated. Don't give me that look." He physically shoved her face away from looking at him, but not rough enough to actually hurt. "These people have whatever they feel like wishing for, whatever they feel like finding a way to take from everybody else. They didn't earn shit."

"Well. If you are feeling that insane, please warn me if you're going to get one of those Marks before you do it. I'll give you a head start, old man, but you better run fast." She smirked even after being shoved, since there wasn't much that got her down. Especially not for long. "Think you can outsmart me?"

The look he gave her could only have been more sarcastic if he'd been more awake. "If you gave me a head start, the only thing I would do with it is go get coffee while I wait for you to shoot your shot. There's nothing about you that scares me."

Maggie glared at him as they waited in the car for anything from Saul. "Cocky bastard. I am capable of killing people, you know. I have killed several people."

"Oh, you can kill with the best of them, there's no question about that. You just never killed *me*." He only grinned more at the sight of her glare.

"I would rather fuck you. So be grateful to your cock." She continued glaring at him and stole his water to guzzle some down until her phone pinged with a location and a short message.

You're welcome.

Maggie showed her phone to Barrett and her scowl was gone. "Let's stalk the muscle. Looks like he's on the move."

"Finally, some good fucking news." Barrett reached down into the bag beneath the seat to check their guns while Maggie started the car.

* * * * *

When Aimee opened the door and Cody was there, she dragged him inside immediately. Once her door was locked, she jumped up onto him and wrapped her arms around his neck as she kissed the breath out of his lungs. "You're not . . . supposed to . . . be here." She scolded between kisses.

"Says who?" He leaned back against her door as she attacked him, dropping his keys on the tile before he even had a chance to kick off his boots. "Says you? Because that's not the takeaway message I'm getting from this."

"It's not safe." She whispered against his lips before she kissed him several more times. It felt like an endless two days without him after she had him back, and she didn't want to be without him again. "There . . . there's some things

I should tell you. Especially now that you're here."

"Like about your mob connections?" He kissed her into silence as he walked them farther into her living room, his hands under her ass holding her tight against him in a grip that was in no way interested in letting her go. "Tell me later. Whatever it is, I'm not going anywhere."

Aimee groaned against his lips as he carried her into her living room, and she felt comforted as he held her tight and simultaneously soothed her worries without even knowing the truth.

She kissed him several more times as her legs wrapped tighter around his waist. "It's not the mob." She countered breathily but she leaned back slightly in his embrace, his strength always astounding to her. Aimee wasn't petite by any means, but she felt light as a feather as he held her. "It's . . . magic. Witchcraft. Whatever anyone wants to call it. Otherworldly."

His head snapped up a little, having clearly not expected anything like that to come out of her, but she could already see the rationalization on his face as he thought about it. "So . . . yeah, okay. I didn't know you were into all that, but that's not a deal-breaker. I knew a Wiccan girl in high school, I've got no problem with that. It's not like I'm religious on my own. She always made it pretty clear everybody's practice is gonna be their own, so I don't know what that means for yours, exactly . . ."

"God, if only it were like that." She sighed and buried her face into his shoulder. "It's not a religion, at least not for me. It's . . . a curse, most of the time. But especially right now, there are people who might be out there after me. I haven't heard anything from security in days, but . . ." She knew all of that didn't make sense, but she lifted up her shirt just enough to show him the tattoo that she knew he was already familiar with.

"It's called a Mark. It's not ink, it's magic. I know I sound insane, I . . ." she looked around and chewed on her lip. "I don't really have any way of showing you. I actually don't have a lot of magic. On purpose. Maybe Casey can show you sometime. Oh! Remember the night we . . . well, you were in pain and I . . . I took some of it. I still have a bruise from accidentally flailing a little too much."

"You did what?" He had moved to her couch, and sat in the middle of it with her still straddled on top of him to show him her tattoo. "I mean, I remember feeling better, but how would you do that? And why? I thought you said you got that tattoo on a dare before you dropped out of college?"

"It wasn't really a dare." She looked appropriately ashamed for lying. "You winced when you moved, and I wanted to help you. Turns out you were a lot more injured than you let on too." Aimee looked all across his features and ran her fingers across his jaw before she forced herself to meet his eyes again. She knew as he looked into her eyes, he wasn't looking into the brown ones she was born with.

"My last boyfriend . . . gave me the Mark. This tattoo. Because I asked him to. I . . . was so insecure, I changed my body through magic to look like this. And I know it sounds *insane*, like truly insane. I would show you if I could." She was trembling out of fear for a lot of reasons but mostly she was afraid of losing him.

"He could . . . move things with his mind. Much easier to show." She cleared her throat as her eyes burned with fearful tears. "I don't want to lose you too. Please don't leave me because I sound crazy."

"I'm . . . I don't . . . I admit, I'm not following, at all. You're not making a lot of sense yet. But I'm not going anywhere." His arms remained locked around her back as she stumbled over her explanation. "You're talking a little like you're somebody out of a comic book right now."

"Yeah. I get that." She sighed but she kissed him gently afterward as tears slid down her face anyway. She was grateful for his reassurance, even if she wasn't convinced. When she buried her face into his neck, he could see the current state of her life. Aimee wasn't that messy of a person, but there were still some errant snack wrappers laying around. Most notably, though, there were a pair of handguns on her coffee table. One of them was pink. Whatever threat she was worried about, it was real to her.

He looked at the guns and she could feel his grip at first stiffen a bit, then tighten around her. "Alright, alright, it's . . . yeah, okay." He was doing his best to sound reassuring, but he was sputtering and repeating himself. "So if . . . right, so if you're magic, or you have magic, or do magic . . . what kind of trouble are we talking about? And are, um, are the guns really going to help?"

"Better than nothing." She lifted her head to look back at the guns and realized quickly why he had gone tense. "The people that might be after me are called Hunters. I've learned a lot about them in the last couple days. They look for people like me, who have the Mark, and . . . eradicate us. It's some kind of religion . . . cult . . . I don't know. But I was near a couple of identified Hunters at the Bellagio the night that you came back. So they think the Hunters might be after me. I don't know how they spotted me or if they even did, it's not like I was stripping while delivering drinks."

"Wait, they who? You keep saying 'they' think they're coming after you, who are you talking about?" Cody was still clearly having trouble keeping up, but the notion of someone coming after her was enough to have him looking past her shoulders at her door and windows.

"There was an older man and a younger woman." She slid off of his lap to grab her phone and she pulled up a picture to show him, though it was grainy from the security footage. "These two."

He looked at them for a while, but shook his head, not recognizing them. "There's thousands of people in there every day, I don't remember them, but I'll take your word for it. Dude is strapped, though, it's impressive he got that onto the floor." He pointed under the man's arm to where the barest hint of a holster could be seen poking out of his shirt.

"Who knows how they did." She thought she heard something outside, but she was flinching at all kinds of noises in the last couple days. "I almost never use my magic. I'm no threat to anyone." Her voice shook a little bit as she shoved her phone into her pocket. "This house is supposed to be impossible to find if you've never been here before, so hopefully . . ."

Her words died in her throat as the whole house shook on its foundations, and the front door was smashed in off its hinges.

TEN

Two gunshots rang out in quick succession afterward, as Cody plunged to the floor behind the coffee table with Aimee under him. Two more shots quickly followed, making the couch and the coffee table shudder with the impact. A moment later, Cody rolled under the coffee table and threw it in the vague direction of the door, letting it spin wildly as it impacted the intruder.

"Run!" Cody had no idea what was happening, but he'd be damned if he was going to let anybody just break in and do anything to Aimee, magic or otherwise.

Thankfully the guns slid to the floor next to them after he picked up the coffee table, and Aimee grabbed both before she gave one to Cody and they got up and ran. His keys were still by the front door, but she had a packed bag by her back door in her escape plan.

As soon as she grabbed the bag, someone shot at them through the back door. Aimee screamed and ran toward her stairs to go upstairs, though there was nowhere to escape from there except up to the roof. She shot clumsily at the back door.

"Cody!" She saw the older Hunter take aim at Cody and she used her luck to deflect the bullet, and the Hunter tripped. Thank god some things went her way.

Cody shot back at the older man once on his way up to the stairs with her, and once through the shattered glass of her back window before he rushed up out of easy targeting range. "Shit, they must've followed me!" Cody caught on a little too late as he rushed up with her and ducked around a corner, looking for a good vantage point for a standoff down the stairs against the intruders.

She grabbed her phone out of her pocket and texted SOS in a group text before she threw the phone to the ground and shot it twice. She couldn't take the chance of being tracked, and she had an unused burner phone in her bag. "We have to go to the roof, it's the only way out. Or the bathroom window." She didn't know how many people were around her house, if they were utterly surrounded or not. Aimee panicked as she dragged him up to her bedroom and toward the attic door in the ceiling.

"Window would be closer to the ground, but the roof means more options." He fired twice down her stairs, discouraging the man in the living room from coming any closer. After the second shot, he ran to follow her, putting down his hands to vault her up into the attic rather than waiting for the ladder.

Aimee squeaked as she made it up into the attic, but she knew the house well enough to know all the places to get out. She didn't know how long it would take for help to come, but she made it to the tiny window on the outside of the attic and pushed it out. When it went crashing to the ground, she looked out to see if anyone was waiting to shoot her. No one was waiting.

She pushed herself out the window, swiveled up to the roof and then pulled her bag after her. Cody would barely fit through the window, but she used her luck pact to help him through, even though he said he wouldn't make it. She lost her balance on the roof after he made it through and nearly fell off, but she caught the chimney before careening to the ground.

Cody was there throwing himself against her chimney, which thankfully was made of solid enough stuff to hold them both as he pulled her back up to safety. A gunshot came from the far side of the house, setting them both running up the slope of it to the apex. "It's the other one from the picture you showed me, she's got two pieces, I think." He was looking around frantically. "Your front entry is gonna be the easiest way down unless you want to break something on the way."

"You go, I'll use my luck on you. If anyone breaks anything hopefully it's them and not me. If you catch me maybe it'll be okay?"

"Yeah, that's a plan. Use luck?" Another gunshot went off and he turned away, forgetting about the question in favor of heading down away from the sound. He tumbled the last few feet and rolled off the roof head over teakettle.

Aimee gasped and rushed after him, holding herself over the edge only to watch him somehow land perfectly and roll without breaking anything. He looked shocked when he looked up at her, but she didn't have time to respond as a bullet nailed her in the shoulder.

She gasped in pain but turned around to see the woman on the roof, though she wasn't sure how. She fired back at the woman and her shots went wild before she yelled out to Cody and jumped, hoping he would catch her.

He grabbed her out of the air and immediately started running as he got her readjusted and onto her feet. "Are they magic too? What'd she do, teleport on top of the house?!" He quickly vaulted the low fence between her house and her neighbor's, running to get behind a shed.

"If I use my luck, then the bad luck lands randomly on someone else. It must have benefited her somehow so that I would have bad luck." Her shoulder was on fire but she couldn't think about it in her panic. "We have to break in, call the cops. Something!"

"You're the one talking about magic! Are cops really gonna help against people who are out to fight magic?" He paused long enough to shoot back at the pair following them, and he thought he clipped the woman in the leg, but he wasn't sure. She might have been starting to tumble off the roof even before he fired.

She didn't have a lot of neighbors on purpose, since the covenant chose quiet neighborhoods, but they were starting to draw attention. Aimee shot again and aimed with her luck, hitting the man in the shoulder. One of her neighbors followed up with a scream as a shot went wild and shattered a window, but sirens could be heard in the distance. "We just have to run!"

"I can do that, can you? You're bleeding." He kept pace with her, darting around corners and over fences to get as much distance from the gunshots as possible. He wanted to stop and look at Aimee's shoulder, but the shouting behind them was still coming closer.

They made it out to a main street outside her subdivision, her lungs on fire along with her throbbing shoulder. A sleek black car cut them off and Aimee nearly ran into it as it stopped.

She wanted to scream, worried that more Hunters had cut them off, but a familiar face was inside, yelling at them to get in. Aimee darted in and Cody followed her lead, slamming the door behind them as the car peeled away.

"Get down, both of you." A gruff voice barked from the driver's seat, while the man himself did not look away from the road. "Two rules. Number one, put that blanket on the seat down at your first convenience, I will be mad as hell if you get blood on my seats. Number two, if this car gets shot up with bullets while I am rescuing yo' ass, you will agree to testify in court that I was elsewhere all day when I'm brought up on charges of killing these motherfuckers." Wyatt Porter was not usually the more animated of the Porter brothers, but apparently the man had strong feelings about the state of his vehicle.

"I agree, Wyatt." Aimee said with a groan as she reached out for the blanket but Cody put it down for her. "You're saving our lives, why wouldn't we agree? Oh my god, how are we still alive?!"

"Because I have immaculate fucking timing and a bad habit of listening to police scanners for fun. Fucking hell in a haversack, how did they get to your house?" Wyatt was focused on driving, while Cody tried to comply with laying out the blanket as instructed and helping Aimee get comfortable.

Aimee looked up at Cody but she shook her head. "I don't know, to be honest." She looked down at her blood-splattered backpack and was grateful that she had prepared herself enough to have an escape plan. "I got rid of my phone. Put some bullets through it. Cody? Did you get rid of yours?"

"No. Shit." He reached into the pocket of the motorcycle jacket he wore, and pulled his phone out of one of the front pockets. As he did, he had to yank on it to get it out of the pocket. He stared briefly before he moved it so she could see the shattered phone screen and the bullet embedded in one corner of it.

"Holy . . ." He stared at the insanely unlikely bullet stop and then rolled down one window to toss his phone into some landscaping that was overdue for a trim.

"Guess you had some good luck." She laughed weakly, but she was still in a lot of pain. "Wyatt, what . . . what does this mean now? For us? For me?"

"Well, it means they weren't after Casey, that's for damn sure." Wyatt finally glanced up from the road long enough to look at her in the mirror. "Also means you need a different place to lay up for a while until they can be dealt with. Can't really do that with the whole damn neighborhood watching a firefight."

Aimee nodded but she wasn't sure what she and Cody could do on their own. "So are you taking us to some motel somewhere? Is there another place the Covenant can send me?"

"The what?" Cody was in the process of trying to look

at her shoulder, but the title made him look up.

Wyatt glared at her by way of the rearview, then heaved a sigh. "Yes, I'm taking you to a motel. What are you doing with this guy? Are you bringing him on? What's the plan?"

Aimee looked at Cody with a warm smile, even though she was sweating, bloody, and in pain. "I'm marrying this man. He also just risked his life for me. He's going to know the truth."

"You're what?" For the briefest moment, even Wyatt was distracted from the fact that they were speeding away from a gunfight. "When did that happen?"

"When I asked if I could marry him at a cheap Elvis chapel and he said yes." She laughed but it hurt to laugh. "Not sure how he feels about it now that I'm being hunted, though."

"I mean, I'm . . . I didn't wake up this morning expecting to get shot at, but I'd be lying if I said this was a first for me." He held his hand to her gunshot wound to stop the bleeding, but she had an exit wound on the back of her shoulder, so he was having trouble keeping both from bleeding at once.

Aimee should have expected that Cody would rethink his options, but it silenced her at first. "I have a first aid kit." She motioned to her bag on the floor. "Sorry, I didn't think about it."

"I didn't say I had changed my mind. I haven't." He went through her bag quickly to find her first aid kit, though he kept looking back and forth between her shoulder and the bag, concerned about the blood.

Aimee popped some painkillers and chugged some water but it wasn't long before Wyatt pulled up at a motel. Apparently arrangements had been made, since Wyatt ran in and got a key for them with no issues. Covered in blood, Aimee and Cody couldn't do much.

Cody patched up her shoulder temporarily but she knew she would need stitches. After Wyatt handed her the key, she looked up at him, her injured shoulder slumped. "No one else is coming to help us, are they?"

He didn't meet her eyes as he answered, watching the entrance to the motel and listening to the traffic on the street beyond for any signs of pursuit. "I was in the neighborhood. And the room is on the covenant's dime.

"We're still gonna track the Hunters, especially now that we've got confirmation that they were targeting you, but you're still probationary. If we can find a good way to throw them off completely, get them to leave town, or get them caught by police for disturbing the peace, we own some of the local PD, and we can get them put away long enough for their order to know to keep away. Having Hunters in town is good for nobody."

Aimee felt like crying for an entirely different reason, and now she felt like there was no way she would be allowed into the Covenant. They had rules. They had expectations. All she had to do was make it a year, and now she felt like she was losing her whole family. When Wyatt showed up, she thought it was a response to her SOS, and now she wondered if they would have just let her die.

"Sure. I guess, um, tell your brother I'll miss him." She didn't know if they could even stay in Vegas at this point. They were on their own.

He walked them to their room and gave her as much cover as he could along the way, tall and broad as he was. When they were inside with the bag she grabbed during her hasty exit, he mostly closed the door to talk to her through it.

"Look, none of this kicks you off probation. Any of us could've been picked up by Hunters. I've had them after me half a dozen times. Normally because I picked a fight, and mostly before I joined up here, but still. It's just . . ." he shook his head, heavy with the weight of the situation as he looked her over. "Covenant's got a lot of its own reasons for doing things the way it does. We'll handle the Hunters. You two just lay low and order delivery."

"I can't imagine getting busted on probation exactly

looks promising. Especially for someone who doesn't bring much to the table." Aimee looked weary when she looked at him through the slit of the open door. "My phone is gone anyway, so I don't have contact with anyone. Be careful, Wyatt."

"Zeke already knows what room you're in, don't worry about the phone. You'll be alright. I'll see you in a few days." He closed the door, and they could hear his heavy footsteps down the walkway back to his car before he drove off.

In the room, Cody was getting out the small suture kit in her first aid kit, looking it over with trepidation at the thought of having to do stitches on her. "I'm not gonna pretend I understood any of that. Come here, I'll get that closed up as well as I can."

Aimee took off her shirt and sat down in front of him, since the shirt was ruined anyway. She looked back at him and she felt bad for putting him in the position of fixing her up, so she stilled his hand. "I'll make a pact for it. I mean . . . I'll fix it with magic."

"Wait, what? You can do that? I thought you said you didn't have much magic?" His head was still spinning around every aspect of what had happened.

"I don't have much magic because I don't want to. All of it comes with a price that you have to pay. In my case, changing my appearance to this . . . . my price was my entire life. Everything and anyone I ever knew. I didn't understand it completely at the time, and it was a huge mistake." Her shoulder throbbed as she turned around completely to face Cody. "There's a voice in my head. It negotiates magical terms with me. And yes, it sounds utterly insane, but at least I can prove it."

I'd like to negotiate a pact to heal my wound.

That is possible. The Voice was present immediately upon her summons, without hesitation or apparent annoyance at having been ignored for so long. The constancy of it, the overwhelming sameness of its presence was like reliving a bad dream.

In order to heal the wound, I propose milder shoulder aches for a week longer than it would have healed otherwise.

The balance is not met. If the wound is to be healed, the mild shoulder ache will persist for a year under your own faculties.

That's not balanced. A year? This wound would take a month to heal of natural causes at most. A year is unjust. She opened her eyes once she realized that she had closed them and saw Cody staring at her but she gave him a nervous smile. "The Voice and I have issues. Just gimme a sec."

Moderate aches for two months. She countered again.

Moderate aches for two months, in addition to undergoing the majority of the bodily stress of healing in an accelerated format immediately. She could feel the threads of the recent pact she made on Cody's behalf to condense the pain of his own injuries into an excruciating and almost timeless void that had thankfully passed.

Again? Goddamn it. She opened her eyes for just a moment and she closed them again. *I get to choose the moment the pain starts. Within the hour.*

That is acceptable.

"So it's . . . talking to you right now?" Cody was watching her as if he was looking for any sign of the supernatural shenanigans she was undergoing.

Aimee nodded simply at first to respond to him while she finished her negotiations.

I agree to the terms.

She opened her eyes and looked into his eyes again. Aimee sighed and frowned a little. "I made a deal to heal it, but I have to go through an accelerated healing process, which includes intensified pain. I just wanted to let you know, so you don't freak out."

The pact is made. The Voice's presence in the back of her mind seemed content to be dismissed.

"Accelerated . . . what? How is that a deal?" He looked back and forth between her eyes and her shoulder, where she had still clearly been recently shot.

"Well, I don't want to keep bleeding out, and I don't

want to end up in the hospital." Aimee leaned in to give Cody a gentle kiss. "I'm gonna get a towel and lay on the bed. It'll be easier."

"Towel, right." He put a hand on her good shoulder to keep her still and headed to the bathroom to grab some towels for her, seeming to forget the part where she said she would get it herself.

Aimee went to the bed and laid down once he laid out the towels, since she didn't want to get blood on the bed. She stripped down to her underwear and laid down in the bed. "I promise I'll be okay. Please don't call anyone. Or if you think it will be easier, you can go take a walk or something."

"Now I know you've lost too much blood, you're talking crazy. I'm not going anywhere." He settled next to her on the bed and held onto her hand, still not really sure what to expect from whatever she had . . . done? What was she about to do?

"I'm going to think about our getaway wedding. Cuz you're the best thing to happen to me in this new life that I've regretted for so long." She smiled at him and closed her eyes again. *Okay. Now.*

The pain that shot through her shoulder felt as though someone was taking a hot poker and was attempting to cauterize her flesh in a singular moment. Getting shot had hurt, but almost too much for her mind to take in at a single impact. The pain of healing was more precise, blisteringly conscious, making her feel like that whole side of her body was on fire.

When she opened her eyes, Cody was there with a swab from her kit, cleaning off the last residue of the wound with wide open eyes, staring down at where the blood had been just a few minutes before.

"It's . . . it's gone." His face was frozen, and he kept swabbing the same area over and over again even after it was clean. The cool of the swab felt good on what had felt like searing heat just before. There wasn't even a scar. One more side effect of her perfect body.

"Yeah . . ." She replied through gritted teeth, since there was a lingering pain that remained, and she knew it would for two months. "It's gone. Still throbs like a motherfucker. I'm wondering where childbirth falls on the pain scale after these healing pacts. Maybe it'll be no big deal after all of this."

Cody continued staring for a while before his mind caught up to what she'd said. "Chi . . . ch-childbirth? Oh, we're moving on to that, now? Magic, Marriage, and kids all in the space of about an hour and a half? Sure, yeah, we can go there." He was still staring at her shoulder as she watched his entire conception of reality falling apart behind his eyes.

Aimee sat up and reached out to put her hands on his cheeks and kiss Cody soundly. "I'm sorry." She apologized after the kiss, clearly concerned about her boyfriend (fiancé?) having a mental breakdown. "This wasn't exactly how I envisioned having these conversations."

"You mean you didn't plan on getting shot today? Weird." He gave her a playful look, but his face was still a mess of uncomprehending attempts to catch up with the world in front of him. "That . . . you . . . that . . . was the most bat-shit crazy thing I have ever seen in my life. That was . . . I mean, it's like it never happened!" He had one hand absently on the side of her neck to keep her close, but he was still staring at her shoulder. "Are you okay? I mean, did it just . . . cover it up? Does it still hurt?"

"I'm okay. It's healed, it's not covered up. But yes, it still hurts a bit. That was part of the deal. Less pain, instant heal, longer time of dealing with the pain. Sorry it took me a minute to negotiate, I hate messing with it."

She looked around their motel room and looked Cody up and down now that she wasn't actively bleeding. He was definitely covered in her blood. "Let's get cleaned up. Then you can ask me whatever questions you want. I'm going to have to negotiate how to keep us safe . . . I don't know what my . . . friends are going to do, *if anything,* to watch out for us."

He took off the shirt he had on, briefly considering whether it could be saved or just needed to be thrown away. Washed and then thrown in a dumpster somewhere would draw the least attention, he imagined. "Your friends . . . you said coven? So are they other . . . witches? Is that a thing?"

"Covenant. Yeah, everyone, well mostly everyone involved has access to magic. Witches, Wiccans, Wizards, Sorcerer . . . whatever you want to call it. Mostly we go by the Marked, because we all have the Mark. My tattoo." She got off the bed and led him into the bathroom, but she turned on the shower and stripped as soon as it was nice and hot. "You can literally ask for whatever you want from the Voice, but you have to be willing to pay the price to have it. It's less thrilling than you would think."

"If it all ends up with a person screaming on a bed for the wrong reasons? Yeah, no, thrilling isn't what I would call that." He stripped along with her (a bit awkwardly, since the room was clearly set up to be a one-person bathroom at max), his mind still reeling. "Still, 'whatever you want' is a seriously broad field of what magic could do. Anything? Actually anything?"

"As far as I know, there isn't a limit as long as you can find a way to pay the price of balance." The shower was small, but they fit inside snugly, and she pressed herself into his chest with a low moan as the water hit them both at once. "I'm glad you're here with me. Even if you may be regretting it."

"The only thing I'm regretting is that you got shot." He turned them so the hot water would mostly come down on her, reaching behind her to smooth her hair away from her face and gather it down her back. "I'm sorry I was hard-headed. If I hadn't gone to your place when you told me not to, this wouldn't have happened."

"We don't know what would have happened. They could have found me alone and killed me and no one would have known what happened to me." Aimee pulled his face into another gentle kiss. "I'm sorry I didn't tell you sooner. I'm sorry I kept you in the dark, or that I gave you mixed signals. I didn't mean to. Or want to."

"No, you've . . . I mean . . . it's magic. That's a damn good reason." He shook his head as he stroked her hair, his mind still racing even as he felt his heart rate finally start to go down.

"It's a lot to take in, but I'm sure it's also a lot to live with. You said something about giving away your whole life. That can't have been great. I get why you don't talk about what came before much. I used to think it was the stripping, like something had gone sideways there and you didn't want to talk about it anymore. Which I can understand too. This is . . . a lot. And now with people coming after you just because you have it . . . that's bullshit I can't even wrap my head around."

Aimee hugged herself to Cody and enjoyed the intimacy of the moment. Prior to a few days ago, she and Cody had never slept together and never showered together. Today they were alive, together, and he was holding her close. "It is a lot." She pressed her cheek to his chest and closed her eyes. "I love you."

"I love you too, Aimee." He initially hesitated about putting his arms too tightly around her shoulders, but he seemed to remember a moment later that she wasn't injured anymore, and squeezed her tighter against his chest. "If I see those assholes again, you're gonna see me get a lot more violent than just flipping a coffee table. I hope you're alright with that."

"I have a sinking feeling we will probably see them again. I hope I'm wrong."

"I hope you are too. Just this once." He ran his fingers through her hair again as if he could wash away the stress of the day with just a gesture, taking deep breaths of the scent of her as the steam rose around them.

* * * * *

"Sit still and stop being a fucking bitch." Maggie growled as she reached out for the bottle of whiskey with bloody fingers and held out the liquor to her partner. "Drink this and let me fix this gaping hole." Maggie sewed up her own wound, but it was a graze, whereas Barrett's injury was worse. After picking the bullet out of muscle, she was trying to sew him up.

"Just work fucking faster, we're wasting time." He winced again and got another glare from her, but grabbed the bottle anyway, gritting his teeth at the burn as it went down. At least it was a distraction from his shoulder.

"Those motherfucking . . ." he hadn't stopped swearing and growling about the way the fight had gone for half an hour, even though the back seat of their vehicle had long since soaked through with his blood from all his restlessness.

"I didn't think the bitch would be smart enough to be prepared. Also I didn't think they'd get on the motherfucking roof." Maggie stitched his skin as fast as she could, which wasn't very fast, but it was a clean and neat stitch that would hold. When she tied it off she cleaned the wound so he wouldn't end up with an infection. The last thing they would need would be a hospital visit.

"We need to recoup and call Saul again." They managed to disappear before the police showed up to the scene, but they couldn't go back to their motel just yet. They were going to have to ditch the car and hot-wire a new one. "You've lost a lot of blood."

"He's seen the police reports by now. I'm surprised he's not calling us incessantly as it is." He let her finish what she was doing with his shoulder and sat up, groaning at the fire raging in his shoulder. "We need to figure out where those two assholes ran to hide and cut them off."

"I told you she has to have connections. If I can get to her, I bet I can make her sing. She seems like a weak little bitch." She wiped off her hands and cleaned up a little before she grabbed his keys. "I'm sure we can find the boyfriend's apartment somehow and they'll pop up there."

"You think they're that stupid?" He moved to the passenger seat, since he would let her drive with two good arms for the time being.

"I do, actually." Maggie quipped as she started the car and made sure that the coast was still clear before she started driving. She was still concerned about her partner, but he had suffered worse. Maggie picked up an obliterated phone from the floor and held it up. The screen was shot to hell, but the body of the phone was intact. "There's a chip in here. I wanna know what information she left behind. Only an idiot would leave it behind."

"Is it hers or his?" He looked over the phone and then dismissed it, putting it into the bag at his feet for processing later. "Only an idiot leaves it where we can find it, but still means we're gonna have a harder time tracking them."

He rubbed at his face, his other hand squeezing into a fist against the pain in his shoulder. "Did you see any full confirmation? You know Saul's gonna be a pain in the ass about it. Only evidence I need is that those fuckers actually got away from us. No way they did that on their own."

"No, but she told him to jump off the roof and the fucker didn't get hurt. That's something too. The whole thing reeks of Marked bullshit." Maggie looked in the backseat briefly. "Do you need some more whiskey to take the edge off?"

"Any more of that along with the blood I've already lost, and I'm not gonna be in any shape to beat the magic out of those fuckers. I've had worse." He stretched his shoulder to test the wound, gritting his teeth the whole time.

"We can't go after them today, old man. Whoever scooped them out of danger is gonna be looking for us too." Maggie shook her head at her partner. "And I'm not dragging your blood-deficient ass around until you get some sleep. That's asking to lose my partner and I'm not about getting reassigned."

He didn't have the energy at the moment to fight with her, and so instead he pulled out his device and started looking for a motel close to the boyfriend's apartment. "Fine, you deal with Saul, then. I'll find us a place. Turn east here."

Maggie let him lead her to a new motel, she paid by cash with no questions asked, and got Barrett comfortable in the room, even though he resisted all of her help. With a final glare at the grumpy, ungrateful asshole, she called Saul.

There was an audible sigh before the phone even reached Saul's ear. "Am I sending one hearse or two?"

"If Barrett keeps up his bitching, just one, but we may end up killing each other. I assume you know already about the shit that went down. Or do I have to confess our sins?"

"No, the police report confessed plenty already. Fuck almighty, Margaret, an open shootout in a suburb based on what amounts to a hunch? Tell me you at least got observable proof of an active Mark." Saul's voice was both strained and exhausted, even though he'd just woken up when they spoke to him before.

"Of course I've seen it. And the shit she pulled in order to get away, no one is that lucky, Saul." She usually gave people all kinds of shit for calling her Margaret, but she wasn't going to get into that right now. "Her boyfriend is a fucking hulk. We had to make a bold entrance. He threw a fucking table at Barrett."

"Who hasn't, given the proper motivation? I've got a poker table in my back room with Barrett's name on it the next time he mouths off." Saul's sigh deepened into a growl. "It's fucking thin, Margaret. You might as well be hunting civilians and having a bad day, and that shit doesn't fly. Not with me, and definitely not with Jade. You'll be lucky if she only kills you for it if it's found that's what you're doing. You two need to back out. I'll tag in another team."

"Back out? What the fuck?!? This is our discovery, Saul!" She hissed and growled into the phone, since she couldn't imagine losing another case when they were so close. "You have got to be fucking kidding me!"

"What you've 'discovered' might as well be a tattooed civilian and a bodybuilder boyfriend. Do I sound like I'm fucking kidding? Cool off, Margaret." Saul didn't even sound surprised with her outburst.

"This is the entire problem with you two. I thought you had something solid to go on, but even you admit you don't have anything tangible. We'll find you two something confirmed that you can sink your teeth into. Until then, you know the protocols. Two states away in whatever direction you please, and for fuck's sake, get Barrett to a decent hospital. I'll at least keep you posted if anything comes of this case, then you can feel free to you-told-me-so to your heart's content."

"Fucking asshole." Maggie growled into the phone before she hung up, even though she knew better than to hang up on a superior. She tossed her phone aside and looked over at Barrett. "They're sending us away, but I'm supposed to take you for some medical care first, old man."

He heard most of her outburst and was sitting up on the edge of the bed. He was changing the bandage over his bullet wound, since the last one had soaked through with blood. "Saul can say whatever the fuck he wants, we're still not leaving. Not till the job's done."

"I agree with you on that. But I agree with him about getting you some help. At least some stitches. I can't be dragging your ass if we're going to get these motherfuckers." Maggie went to help with his bandage, her touch surprisingly gentle. As much as they abused each other, she had a fondness for her partner and fuck-buddy. "We can hit up a small clinic, then you get some rest, I'll see what I can track."

He was clearly in no mood to fight her on any point in particular, staring straight through the opposite bed as he finished changing his own bandages.

"This is the part of the job that Saul and every other fucker in the office forgets." He forced himself to take a deep breath to try and maintain any sense of calm. "They like to tell themselves it's numbers and protocols and probabilities from their desks, but that's not how it is out here. He knew that once."

"Thank fuck people doing the actual work know how to get shit done even without the office." Maggie grabbed some painkillers and a glass of water before she dared to try to convince him to move. "We make a helluva team. And we're going to show them why."

ELEVEN

"I recognize I'm riding a line here, boss. Other boss." Wyatt looked between Darius and Sophia without looking the slightest bit repentant for what he'd done. "But I wasn't on shift, I didn't expose us unduly, and if I hadn't been around, we'd be making funeral arrangements right now instead of paying a hotel bill."

"Our main concern is exposure." Sophia responded patiently, but she didn't look angry. Honestly, Sophia didn't know what to think or feel, since she liked Aimee but the situation was precarious. It also didn't bode well for them that the Hunters found Aimee easily. "You did the right thing at the time, no one wants harm to befall Aimee. We also want to make sure you weren't followed or tracked."

"I stayed down the block from the place I dropped 'em, had a good meal, went out the back, had William come pick me up. I'll have somebody else pick up the car and run the usuals on it. Not much I can do about traffic cameras, if anybody was watching everything happen in real time, but I assume Zeke's been all over those." Wyatt looked between them at that assumption, and got a nod from Darius.

"He didn't brag about scrambling anything in real time, so that tells me he didn't do it, but he went back and poked holes everywhere he thought necessary to keep your trail from being easy."

Sophia paced a little as she considered their situation, though she clearly didn't know what to do. She glanced over at her brother and back at Wyatt. "Thank you for stepping in, Wyatt. We'll still need to discuss what to do from here, if anything. If I could figure out why Hunters keep sniffing around, I would be less uncertain. It would be grand to be rid of the infestation."

"Just to leave my own two cents, ma'am, I don't know if that's possible." Wyatt got up to leave after that dismissal, lingering by the door. "If there's ever a case that just won't crack, then most people forget about it, but it's always somebody who never will. They know something's going on here, and I expect they'll keep coming until they find out what."

She gave Wyatt a nod of agreement as he stepped out, but as soon as he opened the door, a different imposing presence stood there in Wyatt's way. Sophia raised an eyebrow and stood still in her heels as she glanced at her brother. "I didn't know we were expecting company."

"We weren't?" Darius turned to look at Jacob, their ever-present shadow and servant on the far side of the room. He shook his head, and checked the gun hidden under his arm just to make sure it was still in place.

Sophia went up to the door and opened it wider, but she didn't reach for a weapon as she smirked at the person standing there. Sophia didn't have much use for weapons anyway. "Look what the cat dragged in."

The man at the door was one of the few creatures Sophia or her brother knew who could easily dwarf them in height. He stood just over seven feet tall, but that was only where the strangeness of his features began. He had long, straight hair that fell back from his face over his shoulders. It appeared black at first, but the color shifted slightly as he moved, making it hard to be certain. At one moment it looked like a very dark blue, at another some kind of deep gold. He had sharp, powerful features that commanded attention and a bearing that looked like it would have been perfectly at ease even on a firing squad.

He was wearing stone-washed grey jeans over biker boots, with a plain, unadorned black t-shirt hugging his lean torso. At first glance, his eyes were a bright gold, more appropriate to cats and other predators than humans. They seemed to move even when his eyes were focused, black lines and shadows in the irises swirling along with the gold.

Sin was not a presence easily forgotten.

"Hope this is a good time, though the look on your face suggests otherwise." His voice was a rich baritone that rarely had to rise to be heard.

Sophia closed the door behind Sin and shook her head slowly as she glanced over at her brother. "We have Hunters knocking. It's true what they say, one roach gets in, you'll always be fighting them."

"Two, in this instance. They are rarely assigned on their own." He nodded to Darius and then to Jacob, his unsettling eyes lingering on the man briefly before he went to have a seat in a chair at Darius's gesture.

"Are you here to warn us about the Hunters?" Darius went to retrieve the drink Jacob was already pouring for their guest, so as to deliver it himself. "We're very glad to see you, you just don't make social calls much of a habit these days."

"No, I haven't recently, you're right. I should really make more of an effort in that respect." He took the offered drink, but didn't sip from it yet. "You were in the middle of a difficult decision when I came in, please don't let me distract you."

Sophia finally stepped out of her heels and grabbed a drink of her own before she sat down across the coffee table corner from Sin. "You can't help but be distracting." She smirked at their friend before she looked back at her brother.

"I'm not sure I'm ready to make the decision that needs

to be made. We're not actually interested in being exclusive to those who fit in here, but we also can't invite in a threat. We don't actually know Aimee, other than what she has shown in the last year. She has an extreme aversion to the Voice, which is concerning but not unheard of. However . . . we don't know if she's a plant and how would we?"

"No matter how long she's here with us, she's going to carry that kind of risk." Darius took his own usual seat across the coffee table from Sin, clearly feeling weighed down by the subject himself. "Her pact is genuine, she erased all ties to her former life. Which means even if she did have ties to the Hunters before, those would have been severed."

He took a sip of his drink, sighing as it burned its way down. "Of course, that doesn't mean they didn't exist, or that she couldn't have the same interests now, in helping lead them to us. Her old life being cut away could be the deepest of deep cover possible, even if that's not the most likely explanation for what's happening here."

"Casey trusts her and I trust him, but this is . . . the Bellagio hasn't been breached in some time. We have extra protections there, how did we not flag them as soon as they came through the door? Did they have help?"

"Zeke claims they weren't on any of our lists. Guy was supposed to be dead, and the girl is new to his records. If we had known they were Hunters, they'd have been flagged as soon as they drove up, and our people would've been alerted. The fact that they were far enough off our radar to get that close is just . . . one more piece of all this that doesn't sit well." Darius wasn't easily unsettled, but they had spent years cementing their position in Vegas and making sure all possible avenues of approach were covered. To have missed something and created a vulnerability was concerning.

Sophia rubbed at her temples and groaned a little, but she ignored the troubles to look back at Sin. "No comments from the peanut gallery? I know you always know something."

Sin shook his head, the look in his strange eyes unreadable, even after lifetimes of knowing the man. "I always know quite a lot of things. But no, I'm here this time because it seemed like a good time to be around friends."

Darius' attention moved over to him immediately, his head turning slowly. "The last time you said something like that was the day before we heard about the beginning of the first World War."

Sin's drink touched his lips before his answer did. "Was it?"

"Fuck." Darius rubbed at his eyes, standing up to pace near the couch.

"Asshole." Sophia muttered as she finished off her drink quickly and leaned her head back. "Well. Right now we don't have enough evidence to damn anyone, including ourselves. The Hunters are a credible threat, there's a new pair moving in from Reno. So for now, we can't know if Aimee is with us or against us, but we can't risk the compound. So . . . the choice is to let her be, and focus on the Hunters to see what they do. We can't afford a rat."

Darius agreed, which she knew he would, given the situation. "Agreed. But we also need to be thinking about what kind of placement we're going to set aside for her if this whole thing blows over and it turns out she still seems to be what and who she says she is. If she even decides to stay."

He was already thinking through the implications of the choice, but it was the right one to make. Covenant security had to take precedence over someone who hadn't yet been fully accepted and therefore didn't share in their risks. "She's got her boyfriend with her, after all, and he should be all she needs against a couple of Hunters."

Sin gave an appreciative nod. "Cody is an exceptional fighter. But so is Aimee, oddly enough. You would not think it to look at her."

Sophia didn't look convinced by Sin's approval of Aimee's fighting skills, but she did look surprised that he knew about the two of them already. Sin knew a lot of things. Too much, really, but she still hadn't figured out how he had the time. "If she's true to us and we have to apologize, then we'll worry about that later. She and her boyfriend can join up or not, once we're sure one way or another."

"I'll contact her." Darius didn't sound happy about the duty, but handling the personal side of covenant business was more his job than Sophia's, for a multitude of reasons. He looked over at Sin once the discussion was clearly closed. "I don't suppose you could tell us when, or if, the Hunters will ever *not* make themselves into everyone's problem?"

Sin gave half a shrug. "It's not generally a good idea to ask too hard about what I could or couldn't do. It's not a question I even ask myself, if I can avoid it." He took in the two of them with a subdued smile. "It's good to see you again. It's been too long, and the last few years have been . . . unpleasant."

"Iz will always give you hell. I'm sorry." Sophia consoled their friend and arguably their leader, before she got up and moved closer to give him a hug. He didn't invite affection, but neither did she, except from people she knew were safe to her. "You should come visit when we're not mid-crisis. We could go out. Get drinks."

"You're right, I should've called ahead to check on whether there would be a crisis or not." Sin stood up for the hug, glad for it even though he didn't tend to initiate such things. "We'll have a reason to see each other more often in the next few years. And the Summit is coming up fairly soon, so there is that."

"I'd rather deal with an army of Hunters knocking at my door." Darius's face turned even more sour. "Anything we can do to help with your unpleasantness?" There was never any point in asking Sin to be less vague on any given point. If he wanted to be precise, he would have been.

"Not this moment, no." Sin's eyes weren't quite focused on the room around them, seeing through his drink into places and events far removed from Vegas and its covenant. "There are a number of dominos you'll see falling soon, and picking up speed. When that happens, I'll need your help to make certain at least a few of them remain standing at the end."

Sophia fought down the instinct to ask more questions for the thousandth time in the span of her acquaintance with their walking enigma of a friend. "Always causing trouble." She gave him another gentle hug. "You always have our help. You know that."

"It is still good to hear." He looked between them with a sigh that seemed to take an hour leaving his chest. "For today, the only help I need is a place to stay, if you have an empty unit I could make use of for a few nights?"

"Of course." Sophia looked toward her brother before she headed toward the door. "Darius is going to make the uncomfortable phone call to Aimee, but Zeke should know what's available and I'll be glad to escort you. We always make sure to have spare units. Let's go, almighty Sin."

"Almighty." He shook his head as he followed after her. "I admit, it's never been my favorite word, in any language."

Back in his living room, Darius got the number for Aimee's burner phone from Zeke, and proceeded to dial. With the decision made, he wouldn't allow himself the luxury of delay. Whether Aimee was an honest applicant to the covenant or she was an elaborate plant, clarity was in everyone's best interests.

* * * * *

Aimee looked at her phone from across the room they were holed up in, since she honestly hadn't expected a phone call but anything was better than nothing. "Hello?"

"It's Darius. How are you two holding up?" He paced to the windows of his apartment that faced out over the city, one of the few units in the complex with a view over the high privacy fence surrounding their property.

"How are we holding up?" Aimee's voice was full of incredulity as she parroted back the question. "At least two people are actively trying to kill us, I would say I've been better. Wyatt told us to stay put."

"Good advice. And yes, having someone trying to kill you is . . . not the easiest thing to deal with the first few times it happens. I assume you've at least had no further sight of the Hunters since you were dropped off?"

"No. Maybe they were tracking us before somehow, I don't know. But they shouldn't be able to track us now, I don't think. They don't use magic, right?" Aimee didn't know a ton about Hunters, but she did know that they were not good for the Marked.

"Almost none of them. Their leaders keep a special pack of Marked to do certain jobs the rest of them can't." Darius kept his details thin, listening closely to her tone for any sign of her knowing more than she was letting on. "So the odds are very low that either of these after you right now is Marked. We're working our way through the hotels and hiding places of the city to narrow down where they might have gone to ground after the shootout."

Aimee took a deep breath and let it out slowly as she looked across the room at Cody. He was listening as intently to her as she was to Darius. "If you're calling me, then either things are worse than you're letting on, or you are cutting me off. You're not exactly known for check-up phone calls. No offense."

"I'm not, it's true." She could hear him sigh on the other end of the phone. "There've been no further developments in terms of the Hunters. When there are, we'll be sure to let you know. For the time being, though, you are outside of direct covenant protection. It's my hope that this status won't last very long, and once the Hunters are dealt with, things can return to the way they were a few days ago."

The chill of knowing she and Cody were definitely cut out was ice in her veins, and she bit on her bottom lip to distract herself from crying. "Go back to the way things were? Now? When I'm expendable?" She scoffed and her eyes burned with the tears she didn't want to shed.

"I was living my life here on my own before you forced me into this, and now that I have a family here in the Covenant, it's all business." Her tone was acid, and the hurt of betrayal emboldened her even though she knew so many feared Darius and Sophia. "We're not going to wait around. Don't bother."

"Any movement right now makes you a more visible target." Darius warned, but his tone wasn't urgent. "But that's only my advice."

"As opposed to sitting ducks with no backup?" She scoffed as she glanced at Cody again. "I guess we're not your problem anymore." Aimee snipped before she could even think about it. "Goodbye, Darius." Aimee hung up the call and made it to Cody before she collapsed into his embrace. "We're on our own."

The force of her collapse drove him back into the headboard, but he latched his arms around her regardless, sighing into her hair. "Even if it felt that way in the first place, it sucks to have something like that confirmed." He ran his fingers through the stray hairs that had escaped her ponytail at the nape of her neck. "Time to decide which way we're heading out of town, then?"

Aimee moved in his arms so she could curl into him but eventually she sat up in his lap so she could look into his eyes. "This is insane, and I can't believe you're still here with me. That you're . . . willing to just . . . drop everything. For me. They're not after you. I'm the witch."

"You're not *the* witch. You're *my* witch." He was very slowly coming around to understand that he was dealing with something outside the reality he had known that morning, but he still had a long way to go. "I came out here with nothing in the first place, and I've had almost nothing ever since. But even if I did have something to my name out here, it's you. I wouldn't hesitate. If we've gotta skip town, then we go get my bike out of your driveway and we get lost.

Head for the west coast or something, get lost in the sprawl out there. I've got friends in Tijuana who would love to have us come down and hang out a while."

She wrapped her arms around him and kissed him with everything she had, since he *was* everything she had. Cody was her world now. "I'm sorry I ever doubted you. And that I didn't tell you sooner how much I love you."

"You had good reasons. Magic would mess up my ideas about people too." He looked at their door out of rapidly-developing paranoid habit as soon as he crushed her against his chest, shaking his head. "You got nothing to apologize for. Though I'm not gonna stop you if you feel like making it up to me later. Right now, we need to decide on our plan from here."

Aimee looked at the door after he did and sat quiet for a moment, tired already of the paranoia. They needed help, except the Covenant had abandoned her. What she still had, though, was magic. "I'm going to try and negotiate our own protection, without the Covenant. I have as much access to magic as they do. Maybe if I do it out loud, you can kind of watch? You won't be able to hear inside my head, obviously."

"More's the pity. I'd love to get a look at some of what's in there." He leaned his forehead against hers and rubbed her arms. "Don't . . . push too much. Or do too much. I like all the pieces of you, don't go giving any of them away just to make a deal."

"I learned that lesson the hard way." She laughed softly before she kissed him again. "I'm not going to sacrifice myself only to lose you. Nothing is worth that." Aimee ran her hand along his cheek before she pulled away just enough to give herself a little bit of space in his arms.

As much as she hated working with the Voice, they needed protection. She closed her bright eyes and took a deep breath before she willed herself to engage with the Voice. "I need to negotiate a pact of protection."

That can be arranged. What is the nature of the protection you require?

Many possibilities swirled through the power around her, physical immunity to gunshot wounds, visions of people walking through flames without being burned, or breathing at the bottom of the ocean without a suit. One image of a man drifting weightless in a blank void but looking ahead made her wonder if there was someone moving through space itself without harm, all under the Voice's auspices.

Aimee already didn't like all the noise in her mind, and she waved off the suggestions the Voice made, although immunity to gunshots probably would have come in handy. "We, both of us, require protection from being found."

All previous scenarios disappeared from her mind, replaced by just as many possibilities with regard to them being hunted and found. *Permanently being erased from the perceptions of every other creature would require the loss of much of your own sensory capacity.*

"Okay, that's a little much." She grumbled as she thought about the options she was looking for. "Okay, so we don't want to be found by people who are looking for us. How about . . . for a day? We don't want to be found by anyone looking for us for a day."

The Voice immediately readjusted itself based on her parameters. *For such a protection and such a duration, you will experience a period of time in which you are more susceptible to be found by such actors as were blocked from doing so for the day of your protection. In this, there is balance.*

"Twenty-four hour protection for twenty-four hour susceptibility." Aimee opened her eyes and looked at Cody before she nodded. "Sounds fair, what do you think?"

"Sounds like we'd have an eventful day after tomorrow, if it's going to stop them from finding us for one day only to help them the next." Cody thought about it for a while. "But we can do a lot in just a day to make it a lot harder for anybody to find us later, even with some help. Maybe make sure they find evidence that we skipped town so as to draw some heat off your friends and make them expand where they're looking for us."

Aimee nodded as she looked at Cody. She searched his eyes for a moment before she kissed him again. "Twenty-four hours is a lot of time to be free, to do what we want before we have to run for our life. Twenty-four hours to be . . . just us."

"I'd take it. It's a hell of a head start. We'll make the most of it." He kissed her forehead and looked her over as if he would be able to see some physical manifestation of the magic she was working with.

"I agree to the terms of the pact." She said out loud, just to seal the deal, even though she always felt like she was making a deal with the devil.

The pact is made. The twenty-four hour term of protection begins now.

Aimee breathed a sigh of relief, even though she knew it was temporary. "It starts now. They won't be able to find us now." She peppered him with kisses as she let the temporary relief crash over her. "Where should we start?"

"Well, they're definitely gonna be still watching your place, so while we can do the impossible, we should get my bike. Unless you've got a car we can use to get out of town?"

"I don't have a car. Never needed one, really." She nodded and looked around their hideout room. "Yeah, let's go get your bike. I'm going to miss Vegas, you know? So much for our Vegas wedding." She laughed softly despite the situation as she slowly slid off of his lap.

He was a little slow in following her, getting up with a pensive look on his face. "Then let's do it." He picked up his shirt, bloodied as it was, and pulled it over his head, stretching it across the bulk of his torso. "Vegas wedding. Before we leave Vegas. Do things right for the night before we hit the road."

Aimee's eyes widened as she looked at him, partially because she could never get over the look of him shirtless, but partially out of surprise. "Really? Get married right now?

You want to do that?"

"Yeah, I do." They didn't have much of anything with them to even carry out of the room, but he went to get his boots back on to get ready to go. "We'll get a cab over to your place, or maybe a block away from your place, grab my bike, maybe grab some clean clothes from what's left at your house, then go find a chapel and get you a new last name."

He grinned until recognition seemed to hit him and his face fell again. "I mean, if you want to do that. I don't know if that's something you wanted to do or not, we didn't really talk about it. You know, in the last . . . four hours since we got engaged."

"Yes." She breathed the word as her eyes stung with tears of happiness. "Yes. I want to do that." She stared into his eyes for a moment before she grabbed his hand and laced her fingers with his. "Let's get married and run away. Ride off into the night. Just like a fairytale."

"Alright then. Hope Elvis is good and warmed up for us by the time we get there." He kissed her hard against the door before he resigned himself to opening it and facing the world. Aimee seemed to have trust in her magic, even if she disliked it, and that was enough for Cody.

Getting a rideshare over to her house was easy enough, and they got out a block over, so as to sneak the rest of the way between patches of garden and stone that passed for yards in Vegas. It didn't seem as though anyone had done much to her house, though there was still a police cruiser down the street watching the area. It made sense, since even the police wouldn't have been able to find Aimee's home to respond to the reports if they hadn't been there before themselves.

Cody's bike was still in the driveway tucked up against her garage, and the front door was still an open doorway from where the Hunters had broken it down. They had to go a little out of their way behind a few other houses to get to hers without being seen by the police, but soon enough they were inside, surveying the wreckage of what the

Hunters had done to her home.

It was difficult for Aimee to look around and realize that someone wanted her dead. Her walls were riddled with gunshots. They still had the guns they had managed to snag during their escape, but she felt the need to rush as soon as she saw blood. Probably her own, maybe that of her attackers.

"I have more weapons in my room. We'll probably need those too. And if I'm gonna get married, I probably need my legal documents." She cleared her throat as she tried to center her thoughts. They were protected, even from the Covenant, momentarily. "Some of your clothes are still in my closet. From before."

"Oh good, you didn't throw those out when I disappeared for a month. I'm grateful." He went with her, putting himself between her and the rest of the shattered room as if to help her get a little more distance from the attack. "I don't think I ever left a tux here, so I'm sorry in advance for just how casual these wedding pictures are about to be."

"I don't care about that." Aimee plucked out a white sundress and held it up. "I'm not wearing a gown. But thanks to Casey trying to get me to get over you, I have lots of lingerie." She laughed softly as she shoved said lingerie into a duffel, along with some other clothes.

She rushed around her room, mostly untouched as it was, to get toiletries and whatever she would need for a trip, and she did it quickly. "I do want to stop at a jewelry shop, though. I'm putting a ring on it. You are taken and every woman, man, and non-binary person needs to know it."

"Good idea. I hope you've got expensive taste." He grabbed a dress shirt that had been a part of one of his uniforms at the Bellagio and changed into a better pair of jeans that didn't have any blood on them. He just hoped they would stay that way. "I haven't been back long enough to do anything with the prize money I got from the fight except get it deposited."

"Don't waste it on me. I don't need that. I just need you." Aimee smiled at Cody as she rushed into the bathroom to freshen up. She changed into all clean clothes, including the white dress. Aimee put her dark red hair into a braid that hung over her shoulder and came back out to give him a twirl.

"Marriage material?" He could see her lacy underwear underneath her skirt when she twirled and she smiled at him with fresh gloss on her lips. Her shoulder, which had been shot through with a bullet only hours before, looked perfectly fine.

"Always, and in every outfit and state of crazy makeup." In the time that she had been freshening herself up, he had gone over the weapons stored in her room and finished packing for them. He had also gotten back into his jacket to get ready to drive, and had found a pair of sunglasses he'd left at her house before with some of his clothes. "You look amazing."

Aimee went to pick up her duffel, but he had it before she could grab it. She grabbed onto his hand again and let him lead her out, even though it wasn't easy to leave her house behind. She didn't really have a lot of emotional attachment to the house, but she did to the Covenant she was leaving. "Let's go get married."

It took some shuffling to get their bag settled on the back of the bike along with Aimee, but eventually they were on their way, watching the Vegas suburbs flow past them like raised dunes of the desert landscape with red stone roofs. It wasn't the side of Vegas in which either of them had spent the majority of their time in the city, but for some reason, thinking about leaving it behind, it was harder to imagine leaving the quiet life of it than the side that glittered.

The wedding chapel on the strip wasn't hard to find, and as both of them presented their identification, there was more crazed laughter than questions asked. The officiator made so many jokes about Cody having clearly kidnapped Aimee and carried her off to be his trophy wife that it was clear he mostly believed it, or at least thought it was more likely than her actually wanting to marry him.

"I mean, if anything, she's the one who put a spell on me, Reverend Presley." Cody just squeezed Aimee's hand, grinning like a fool at his own joke. "You wouldn't believe some of the shit she can do even if I told you."

Aimee laughed but she squeezed his hand just as tightly. Anyone could take one look at Cody and know why she would fall head over heels, but it was much more than that. She wasn't the prize. He was. "I assure you, I'm the winner in all of this. Cody is my everything."

"Well alright alright, that's what I like to hear." The impersonator officiator was back and forth between concern and keeping up appearances, but he led them inside to one of several chapels in the building, decked out with flowers and painted backdrops that would look good in pictures.

For Cody's part, he was glad to vaguely remember that the officiator had said something about a video recording of the ceremony being a part of the wedding package, since he couldn't focus on anything but Aimee. They faced each other beneath a trellis arch of flowers, and he couldn't stop smiling.

Aimee obviously hadn't had any time to plan anything for vows, but everything she had to say was from her heart. "I'm glad I'm going first, since I know I'm going to cry." She laughed softly as she stared up into Cody's eyes.

"The first time I saw you, I thought I had no chance with someone like you. Every time we would go on a date and you would kiss me like I was something precious and special, I fell harder for you. All of my insecurities, you find a way to build me up. My parents never did that. Most people never did. You do." Aimee squeezed both of Cody's hands as she held them. "We have been together almost a year, and I want so many more. I love you, Cody. With my whole heart."

A distant part of Aimee's mind picked up on the

officiator giving her an incredulous look when she mentioned insecurities, but he quickly got himself back on track and shifted over to Cody.

"Aimee, you are . . . my favorite person in this world. Before I came to Vegas, I came out of a situation where everybody I knew, all they seemed to know how to do was play games. You see the world so differently from all that. You look at the world and you see beauty in it, you see good in people. That's not easy to do, but you make it look easy. The more I've learned about you, the more I've wanted to be close to you. Whatever we do, we're gonna do together, and wherever we go, it'll be a better place because you're there making it one for everybody."

He squeezed her hands, unable to look away from her beautiful eyes. He knew what she had said about them not being her own, but the soul behind them was hers, and that was all that mattered. "I love you. Everything I am is yours."

Aimee cried even harder and was thankful for waterproof makeup as the officiant looked between them with part confusion and amazement, but pronounced them man and wife. She let out a happy squeak before Cody full-body hauled her to him. She kissed him with every ounce of passion she had in her. She wrapped herself around him like a cat and let him hold her in the air until the kiss broke.

There was a world beyond the chapel they were in, and Aimee didn't know what their life would look like beyond it. She didn't know if the Hunters would find them or continue pursuing them. She didn't know how long they would have to hide. What she did know was that moment was the most special of her life, and she would do anything to protect Cody and what they had. Even if she had to tangle with the Voice, or share it with Cody if he wanted. He was everything to her.

He held her with no effort at all, swinging her against him as they settled together in the aftermath of the pronouncement. He spoke to the officiant even with Aimee still clinging to him. "You understand if we're in kind of a hurry to get our paperwork and get going, right? We didn't exactly bring a wedding party to wait on or a reception to go to. This is very much just a party of two."

"Uh huh. We can get everything worked up and tied off in just a few minutes, absolutely. I'll go and take care of that for you, you two go ahead and take a few minutes with our photographer, she'll get some shots of you to treasure forever."

Aimee knew that they didn't have an endless amount of time, but she also knew some pictures wouldn't hurt. She kissed him several more times as he carried her to the photographer as if he was carrying her over a threshold. Her smile in front of the camera was wide, genuine, and filled with overwhelming happiness. "I can't believe we're really married."

"It's gonna take me a while to catch up too, not gonna lie." The photographer had clearly spent her fair share of time around rushed wedding couples, giving them dozens of joking poses and a quick succession of mostly-serious ones. There were several in front of a replica of the Welcome to Vegas sign, and a whole bevvy of different scenic shots taken from all the major hotels of the Strip.

"No, we don't have rings yet." Cody laughed back at the photographer when she asked about doing close-up hand shots. "That's the next stop. Unless you all have one of those on-site too?"

"No, but there's a nice shop not far from here. Tell 'em I sent you." The photographer snapped a few more pictures. "I can print these for you here, it won't take long. How about you go get some rings and swing back by for the prints?"

"That sounds good, actually. We'll do that." Cody looked through some of the digital pictures all the while holding Aimee back against him with his hands around her waist. His thumb moved over her ribs where her Mark was hidden by the dress she'd chosen, as if it was a physical manifestation of just how strange the moment was.

Something that couldn't have possibly been more normal against a backdrop of being hunted for Aimee's magic.

She shivered from his gentle touch, and she leaned back into him easily before she tipped her head back slightly. "Come on, let's go get some rings. And then we should splurge on a hotel room again because . . . well, my husband is sexy and I want to see him naked."

"Naked husband, coming up." Cody promised with a light, teasing kiss. "After rings. We've got what, twenty-two hours left in the day?" The photographer was looking deeply confused at the notion that the two of them only had a single day, but Cody didn't seem to notice.

She nodded. "Twenty-two hours left." Aimee gave the photographer a warm smile as she pulled out of his embrace to grab his hand. "We'll be back for the photos! Don't lose them!"

Bewildered photographer in their wake, they made their way quickly out of the chapel and down the street to the jewelry store they'd been recommended. They clearly weren't the first spur-of-the-moment wedding shoppers the staff had dealt with, though there were plenty of comments about not usually getting sudden shoppers either during the day or sober, let alone both.

Cody had to take a step back as he watched Aimee browse the racks in her white sundress, letting his thoughts wander over the insanity of the day. It felt like a dream he was about to wake up from at any moment, but he knew better. His dreams weren't this good. Every playful swing of his wife's hips as she looked over the rings was further proof that reality was better than his imagination.

She looked back at him once as he watched her, blushing as his eyes devoured her. She never would get used to the way Cody looked at her, not with only lust, but actual admiration. "I'm picking out your ring only. And you're making me blush."

"If you feel like getting any redder, I can get more detailed about what I'm thinking over here." He moved from the case to join her, though, and started looking over more feminine engagement and wedding bands, all the while stealing glances at her off to one side. "I think that one looks like her. With sort of the matching spiral to it . . . yeah, that one."

Aimee was still flushed when she tapped on the glass above a ring and nodded. "This one. Can we pay extra to have it sized now?" She smiled when the salesman nodded and she looked over at Cody again. "I did wonder once. If mind-reading was something to consider."

"You think you're blushing *now*, you start reading my mind, you're gonna have bigger problems." He was leaning on his own display case and grinned a promise of impure thoughts across the bright lights at her. "I think that finger's a size twelve, if this sizer thing is right." He handed off a selection of sizing rings to her while the attendants procured their abrupt choices. "And yes, definitely that one." He carefully kept the ring box facing away from Aimee so that there could be the slightest surprise still left to the day.

"Seven." She declared after she tried out the ring sizer for herself, but she didn't try to peek at his selection even though she wanted to. "Now you're making me want to read your mind even more."

"Alright, fine, take a look if you want to be so nosy about it. I won't answer for the consequences." He looked her up and down and then started talking to the clerk about price, never looking away from her for more than a few seconds at a time.

Aimee chewed on her bottom lip as she watched him as well, his ring already in the process of being resized, since she hadn't even tried to haggle over price. Men's rings were always much less to worry about. *If I let him hear my thoughts and he has given me permission to hear his, is that a fair pact? The ability to hear each other's thoughts when we want to, and to stop when we don't want to?*

He does not carry the Mark. The Voice answered succinctly, as if that explained everything she would need answered. *If you desire to perceive the thoughts of others when you choose, others will become aware of your thoughts concerning them at a time not of your choosing.*

That doesn't make sense. Random people aren't who I'm negotiating with. She shook her head at what seemed like nothing to anyone else, but she sighed. *I said he would give me permission to hear his thoughts and in exchange, he could hear mine. The exchange would all be through me. You make no sense.*

It didn't seem to feel the need to respond to her insult directly, and spoke as if she hadn't included it at all. *You will be able to choose the times in which your thoughts will be open to each other, specific to him. That is balance.*

Aimee was lost in thought as Cody approached, and she startled a little when he reached out and touched her arm. She smiled up at him afterward. *Good. So long as we both agree, then it works. I agree to the terms.*

The pact is made. She could feel a kind of window open in the back of her mind, waiting for her to look through it in the very specific direction of Cody's own thoughts. But more pressing at the moment was the sensation of a ring box being placed in her palm.

"These seemed like you." He was smiling as he closed her hand around it, leaning on the counter to watch her open it for the first time.

Before she opened the box she looked into his eyes briefly, and she leaned in to kiss him gently first. No better time for her to test out opening her thoughts to her new husband . . .

Hearing the full and present thoughts of another person all at once slammed into both of them like a set of bricks, with nothing gentle or easy about it. The intensity running through them both was had been sky-high for most of the day, and Cody's thoughts were jumbled accordingly.

There's no way all this is really happening. Her shoulder looks perfect, just like usual. This is the most time I've spent staring specifically at her shoulder since the other night when she was riding my dick at that one weird angle on the bed. Fuck, that was good. Nope, try not to get hard in the jewelry store, still gotta get to the hotel room. These cases wouldn't support both of us, don't want glass shards anywhere near what I'm about to do to her. God, that dress hits her tits just right, those pictures are gonna be amazing but I'm just gonna stare a little longer. What the fuck is happening, why does my head hurt so much right now? Am I hearing her thoughts? Holy shit, you actually did it? You absolutely gorgeous insane person, I love you for actually doing this. But spend five seconds in here and I'm gonna make sure you soak through that lingerie with every plan for how I plan on edging you into oblivion until you're sweating and begging on the edge of the hotel bed . . .

Aimee gasped loudly after the kiss broke. Just as he guaranteed, her face and all the way through her neck was flushed with heat after hearing his unfiltered thoughts. She couldn't even focus on the ring he was trying to present to her at first.

I can't believe this is real. He loves me enough to marry me. He really loves me. I can feel all the muscles through his shirt. God that's hot. I want to lick them. He's my husband. How did I get a husband this hot? I don't want to lose him. I hope he never leaves me. I don't deserve him.

She let out a shuddering breath as she tried to focus on the ring. When she actually looked down at it, she gasped again. *Oh my god. This is beautiful. It's too much. I don't deserve this. Oh my god.* Aimee trembled as she stared. "Cody, this is beautiful. Are . . . you sure? This is . . ."

Instead of answering her out loud, he just took the pair of rings out of the box and slid them onto her hand, massaging her palm with his thumb as she examined them actually on her finger.

Not half as beautiful as you are. I'm sure about this. I've been sure about you for months, I'm just nothing but a fighter and an idiot and nothing I'm ever going to do is going to give you the kind of life you deserve to be living. I couldn't even protect you against those two assholes who broke into your house, but I can go with you and get out of town and I really hope Carl is still in Tijuana, he kind of moves around a lot but he said the last time I talked to him that if I ever needed a place to crash, he would put me up and you'd like him, he's funny, he's gonna flip his shit when he finds out you're my wife and . . . his thoughts went on in constant ecstatic disbelief at the entirety of the situation.

Aimee started crying again but she kissed him frantically as his thoughts tangled with hers, both of them in disbelief that they had the other to call their own. When she managed to look at her ring again, at the beautiful twisting, braided design in white gold and glittering diamonds, she still couldn't believe that all the pain of the last couple years of her life had led to someone as incredible as Cody. He trusted her and was willing to jump in completely, even when he didn't know everything that was going on. She couldn't ask for someone better.

When the salesman slid another box her way, she smiled and reached out for Cody's ring. "This made me think of you, how you brighten my world, the whole world, and I love that about you."

He worked the ring onto his finger immediately, smiling at the bright metal that he never would have chosen for himself. It wasn't how he thought of himself, but it was what he wanted to be for Aimee. For his wife. "We need to pay this bill and get out of here." *Otherwise the security footage of this place is gonna go for a small fortune on some porn sites I can think of.*

Aimee smirked but her cheeks flushed again. *God I love your dirty thoughts.* She held out her debit card as she insisted on paying for Cody's ring, and she had plenty to cover for it. Covenant life had been good for her, even though stripping had amassed her a good savings prior. *I want to lick the muscles I can see through your shirt.*

They're all yours. He similarly paid for hers, waving off any talk of financing, though that clearly shocked the salesmen working the counter. *Yeah, I know I don't look like the kind of guy who's got money, fellas. You try kicking the shit out of people for money. Pays better than you might think.*

She snorted at his thoughts and beamed at him afterward, both their rings glittering on their fingers as they exited the shop. They made short work of getting their photos and then ran together to get back to his bike. "Which hotel should we stay at? I want to enjoy a ridiculously frivolous honeymoon suite."

"I would say the Bellagio, since I liked that suite, but maybe we go and hit up the Sahara or something. Unless your people had a piece of that one too?"

"We can go back to the Bellagio. They can't stop me from going in now, after they disowned me. I'm a paying customer." She got onto the back of his bike and the skirt of her dress hiked up dangerously high on her thighs. *Unless you want to fuck me on your bike.*

I absolutely want to fuck you on my bike, just not for the world to see. Stripping is one thing, and I've got no problem with it, but I'm not giving anybody a free show of you. He paused with the bike already purring beneath them to lean back into her and run a hand up her thigh, looking back over his shoulder at her.

Aimee smiled at him and wrapped herself around him so that all of her front was pressed against his back. Every corner of her thoughts focused on all the time they'd been together without having sex, and how ruthlessly she planned on making up for lost time. Especially because time wasn't on their side. *Get moving, you sexy husband.* She pressed her ample breasts into his back in encouragement.

The bike growled loudly as he raced off, with more than enough encouragement to get back to the Bellagio. It felt strange to park in the usual place and walk in as if they still worked there. Maybe they did, but it didn't feel like they did after the events of the afternoon.

Another casual extravagance the likes of which Cody never would have indulged in under normal circumstances got them a suite near the top floor overlooking the fountains. A little quick talking got them a bottle of champagne to be delivered to the room later, and within just a few minutes, the two of them and their duffel full of possessions were in an elevator taking its sweet time climbing the height of the hotel.

Aimee was restless as they stood in the elevator, but she kept tugging on the hem of Cody's shirt as if she was just waiting to rip it off of him. She hooked her finger through a belt loop in his pants and kept chewing on her lip. "So long to the top."

"Too long, but if we stayed too close to the ground, they'd hear you over the slot machine jackpots." He pressed her into a wall of the elevator until the car shook a little around them, sending a quick thrill of danger through their already racing hearts.

"Ambiance." Her voice was breathy as he pressed her into the wall, but she could play fire with fire. Her fingers slipped from his belt loop and brushed across his groin. She glanced up at the security camera in the corner before she looked up into Cody's eyes again. *I really want to get on my knees and taste you right now.*

Elevator ride's taking too long, but not near long enough for that. He pulled up the hem of her dress as he pressed himself into her, tucking one of her long legs up against his hip as if to have her right there in the elevator. *Elevator's taking too . . . damn . . . long.*

Her chest heaved with measured breaths as she felt him through the fabric of his pants and her thin lace underwear. She was about to say the hell with waiting when the elevator jolted to a stop. She didn't even want to move, but when he released her leg slowly, his hand glided across her skin, and she felt like she could combust. *You're trying to kill me.* She felt like she was already soaking wet from all his touches and promises.

I haven't even gotten started with you yet. I want both of us to live a long, horny life together. That starts here. He pulled away enough to pull her by the hand and run down the hall toward their room, just because it meant they would get there faster by running.

All their belongings in tow, they rushed to the room and Aimee was quick to scan the card and open the door. They flung everything inside and the door had barely closed before she was clawing at Cody's clothes like a feral cat. Too much teasing had her needy.

He didn't bother to look into the room to see any of what was waiting, let alone the view that came with it. The only view he was interested in was Aimee. The bag was dropped, his boots were shoved off his feet, and she had his shirt off within a matter of breaths.

With his hands finally freed, he grabbed at her dress and lifted it off over her head in a single motion, throwing it to the floor behind him as if it had offended him. *I might've ripped the dress, I'm not sure, and I'm damn sure not gonna stop and check.*

I don't care. She whimpered as soon as his hands were on her skin, and once his pants were down and kicked away, she jumped up onto him. He caught her easily, and even though she was curvy, he always held her like she was nothing. Aimee wrapped her legs around him and kissed him until she was panting for breath. *Rip it all off.*

Instead of even taking her anywhere, he let her back hit the textured wall of the entryway as his kisses moved down to her neck. His hands moved up to the sides of the lacy underwear that still clung to her and effortlessly destroyed them where they rode at her waist. A quick tug removed the scrap of fabric entirely, brushing the soaked lace against her clit in the process.

His thoughts no longer bore any resemblance to words, as all he could feel or think about was the touch of her against every part of him, the softness of her, the heat of her as she was finally bare against his cock, the taste of her skin as he felt her heart pounding against his own chest.

Aimee wrapped her arms tightly around his neck as he buried his face against hers, and she was lost to the feeling of the hard planes of his body and muscle. She squirmed against him as his cock teased her, desperate for him in every way. He was her husband, and her feelings for him made her chest feel like it was going to explode.

I love you. I love you. He could hear her desperation for his affection and his cock, her core slick with need as he teased her.

The teasing didn't last long. She could feel in his thoughts just how much he wanted to be inside her, to hear her crying out in relief that he was the cause of. Hearing the feedback loop of her thoughts against his only made him more impatient, reaching between them only long enough to guide himself into her before his arms took her legs again to slam her into the wall. *God, you feel like fucking paradise.*

She groaned in pleasure as he filled her, and her head fell back against the wall in pleasure as he filled her completely. *Fucking biggest cock . . . I've ever had.* Again and again she wondered why she was so nervous to have sex and why she waited so long, because he was right, it was paradise. *Feels so good . . . so full . . .*

Hearing her thoughts changed the way he moved against her, the way he held her, touched her. He sought in her frenzied thoughts for every yes that his touch provoked, every caress that he had never realized she enjoyed so much. When she wanted it a bit rougher than she was already getting, she could hear the surprise echoed back to her, but only for a heartbeat before the rest of him obliged.

God, this is . . . fuck . . . do that, please, all of that . . . keep it like that . . . don't stop . . . the best sex I've ever had. Aimee was sure everyone who couldn't read their spouse's mind was missing out, since anything she might not have communicated effectively, Cody knew instantly. When she finally hit the precipice and orgasmed, she thought she might black out from how intense and incredible it was. Her toes curled and her fingers dug into Cody's shoulders. "Oh god . . . Cody . . ."

Holy shit, so that's what that's like for you . . . Cody was both fascinated and intrigued by it as he followed her mind's instructions on how she wanted him to move or not move in the aftermath. Her legs were shaking against his sides as her orgasm tore through her, and he stopped moving as she cried out. He stepped away from the wall to carry her across the room to the bed as she caught her breath, and sat on the edge, still holding her in the light of the cracks in the curtains nearby.

Aimee felt boneless and content when her orgasm started to fade, and she opened her eyes to look up at him dreamily. She looked so content. "So good. Oh my god."

"Certainly helps to know what it is you want the second you want it." He laid her out on her back on the bed and kissed her hungrily, savoring the languid way she moved under him and every gasp his movements elicited.

"Mhm." She agreed with a smile before she returned his kisses just as hungrily. Aimee ran her hands along his muscles as she wiggled her hips. *Now I want to hear you moaning my name.*

Mmmm . . . even his thoughts somehow moaned against hers, his scattered brain noticing every aspect of her, the way her hair clung to her neck and forehead with sweat they worked up between them, the way it felt to have her thighs clutching his hips to welcome him, the feel of every heated breath against his cheek as he drove himself into her.

His arms latched around her back, hot and hard, but comforting after the scrape of the wall from moments before, clutching her against him as his breathing turned ragged. *Oh fuck I'm gonna come so hard, Aimee. I can't believe you're my wife. I am the luckiest son of a bitch ever born, god this is amazing. All I want to do is be with you until I die of a heart attack, it would be a great fucking life with no regrets.*

His voice itself was much less articulate, his moans only rising against her shoulder and her ear as his body's movements turned more to instinct than to purpose. "Oh fuck I love you, Aimee . . . I love you so fucking much . . ."

As if she couldn't love him enough before, Aimee was sure that she loved him with more passion than she thought possible as his thoughts crowded hers. His chants of love on the precipice of orgasm drew a sharp gasp from her as he finally let out a groan and came inside of her. Aimee moaned as her body gripped his body with a surprise orgasm, all worked up from his body and his thoughts. *This is perfect. He is perfect.*

Cody had the kind of voice even under normal circumstances that tended to fill a room, and he was not shy about being loud when Aimee's body demanded it from him. His growling moans filled the room and rang in some of the light fixtures as every one of his considerable muscles locked up tightly and then slowly began to melt into a deeply satisfied puddle.

His thoughts were incapable of any form of language, racing through the absolute relaxation and satisfaction of their lovemaking. His mind was as fully blank as it was possible to be while still mostly conscious.

When he collapsed to the bed, Aimee immediately curled into him, both of them gasping and sweaty, but sated. His arm draped around her as she slid into him, and she felt protected as his large body encased hers. The world outside that room was a viper in wait, but the world inside that room was perfect. Aimee was grateful for the calm before the storm, and she would do whatever it took to keep it.

TWELVE

Cody had never felt as drunk in his life as he did that night, and the only alcohol he had to drink was part of a bottle of casino champagne. Aimee was intoxicating. Hearing everything she thought about him, watching her hear everything he thought about her, was the sexiest thing Cody had ever experienced. Even when she chose to end the connection between them so that they could get some sleep at last, he couldn't stop running his hands over her, first to lull her to sleep and then just to savor every perfect part of her.

When he did eventually wake up, it was to a knock at the door, and a voice that had clearly been repeating itself for some time. "Housekeeping!" The knock repeated itself over and over again, increasing in volume with each iteration.

Housekeeping didn't start their rounds on previously occupied rooms until after noon, what the fuck?

A glance at the bedside table explained the circumstance.

"Oh shit. Babe, babe, we gotta go." Cody slapped Aimee's ass beside him to wake her up, looking at the perfectly-drawn curtains on the far side of the room as if in accusation. They had kept the entire morning's light from waking them.

Aimee groaned in her sleep but she turned toward Cody with a sleepy smile, though her eyes were still closed. "Again already? I feel like I just fell asleep." She giggled softly as she reached out for him. "How many times is that?"

"Eight, but that's not why we need to get up. It's almost one o'clock. We slept *way* the fuck in. We need to get moving." He kissed her hard, taking time for that no matter what other threat they were under, but after that he was up and out of the bed and racing for his clothes, then for the bathroom, thinking better of his priorities.

Aimee shot up as soon as she heard the time, and cold panic ran through her as she got out of the bed as well. How had they slept away so many hours? It was the sex. Amazing, incredible, *exhausting* sex that had apparently made her oblivious of the world and the hours they had spent having a honeymoon not on purpose.

Aimee rushed around after her new husband, getting dressed and putting up her hair as quickly as she could. "We still need to go to your place. We don't have much time. Oh god."

"I don't have much to get. We'll still be out of town before time's up. What've we got, two hours? Three?"

94 minutes. The Voice immediately chimed in Aimee's mind in answer to the question, supplying the information coldly and clinically.

"94 minutes, says the demon in my brain." She supplied as she hurried to get her shoes on. At least she had packed jeans and sneakers. Her white summer dress was shoved into a bag. Her glittering ring made her smile in spite of the urgency, and the vow of it made her think back to some of their conversations the night before.

"We were going to discuss the Mark again this morning." It seemed like the safer, smarter option for Cody to be Marked too, but she didn't want to pressure him into it, and she knew he would need time to make his first pact. Now they didn't have that time.

"You bring this up after calling it the 'demon in your

brain'? Nice timing." He jabbed at her as they grabbed their things and ran for the door, brushing past the housekeeping cart on their way without excuse or apology for their tardiness. Cody would call the hotel later and settle up. Or maybe he would forget. He had bigger things to worry about. "We might have to talk more about that on the road when I can just drive and we've got time to think things through together."

"Think together. I kind of forgot we can do that." She laughed as they ran together through the hotel, familiar to her as always. There were recognizable faces as she ran through, but she didn't stop. She didn't have the time, and the Covenant had abandoned her, whether most of them knew it or not.

It should have been a short drive over to Cody's apartment, but he had to wonder if the traffic was the Voice's method of making sure they got there too late. She had been to his apartment a few times, but there was a reason why they had spent most of their relationship at Aimee's house. Cody's apartment was tantamount to a slum, but he rarely spent any time there himself, so he had never seen a reason to move.

He parked up on the sidewalk instead of even looking for a parking space, looking around the entire time for any sign of anyone who resembled the pair who attacked them the day before.

"We still might be okay." She assured him as they rushed toward his apartment to get anything he might need. "If they're still looking for us, we'll be easier to find. Who knows if they are still looking for us."

"It's only been a day. And if your former people had knocked them off, they'd have let you know about it, wouldn't they?" From the way the door flexed after Cody unlocked it and shoved it open, it was clear he probably could have just pushed it open and it would have obeyed just as well, but the key made things less violent by a small margin.

"I honestly don't know anymore." Aimee said sadly as she followed after him. "Divide and conquer. What do you need me to get?"

"I've got a tablet I left on a charger somewhere in the living room, there it is." He pointed over at a corner where the tablet was sitting on the floor with a frayed cord attached to it. "I need that and there's a couple extra pairs of boots and jeans in the closet. I'll get my paperwork and my savings." He went into the bedroom and got to work on one of the floorboards near the window.

Aimee rushed to grab the tablet and shoved it into his backpack before she left the bag and jogged to his closet to get the boots.

When she opened the closet, though, someone reached out and dragged her inside and instantly covered her mouth, trapping her in the darkness as the door closed them in.

Maggie's voice was a hiss at Aimee's ear, and Aimee could feel the chill of metal against her throat. "Scream or struggle and I'll cut through this pretty neck right now."

A wrenching sound came from the floorboard as Cody pried it up and tossed aside the hammer he had grabbed to do so to leave it on the bed. When he saw the hammer move a moment later, he turned, wondering if Aimee had come into the room for some reason to get it, and immediately saw the same hammer coming at his face.

He managed to duck before it connected, but he wasn't prepared for the followup knee to his jaw, knocking him on his ass on the floorboards. Right beside his head, there was a single enormous dresser that had clearly been in the apartment since the complex was built. Barrett took the opportunity of the fall to wrench the dresser away from the wall, toppling the heavy piece down on top of the much larger man to give him something else to deal with.

Cody screamed out from under the dresser as something audibly broke on impact. Part of his arm was hanging out from under one heavy corner of the dresser, fingers still twitching as the man they were attached to howled in pain.

"Not a hulk then, huh?" Barrett growled down at the struggling man, harrumphing at the attempt to move the dresser with no clear hope of success. "Just picked the wrong witch to fuck, looks like. Poor bastard." He picked up the bed and levered it on top of the dresser, just to make sure the man stayed down, but then crouched near the mostly-shattered arm. "Hey, were they wearing wedding rings when we first saw them? We'd have seen a marriage license in Basics, right?"

Maggie marched the redhead in from the closet after she heard the crashes and screams, but she was grateful that they were in a part of the city where it was unlikely anyone would call the police. Or that the police would be unlikely to show up in a timely manner.

A trickle of blood edged down Aimee's neck as Maggie kept the knife pressed firm, but she looked down to see a ring on the redhead's finger too.

"Huh. I thought for sure we would have seen a marriage license." Maggie made Aimee look down at her struggling husband. "Well, short-lived marriage indeed." Maggie pressed the knife into Aimee's skin until Aimee gasped. "Do you want to help me get her tied up? We have some questions for you, Red."

Barrett watched the dresser and the bed for another moment to make sure Cody wasn't just faking being pinned, but he was soon satisfied the man was stuck. He retrieved a few extended zip-ties from one pocket, and bound Aimee's wrists and then her elbows, binding her arms behind her awkwardly and painfully.

A whimper escaped Aimee's lips but she didn't dare say anything or fight, since she didn't even have a weapon, let alone the mental capacity to try and negotiate with the Voice. She looked over at Cody as tears burned in her eyes. This was entirely her fault.

Maggie released the knife from the redhead's neck while Barrett tied her up, and she stepped back to survey the husband. "Huh. I really thought we had a two for one deal, here. Guess he hitched himself to the wrong woman."

She took the knife and moved so Cody could see her. "Red bleeds red too. Lookie here." She smirked as she saw the man struggle before she turned around to face the witch again and pointed the tip of her knife toward the woman. "Want to give your man a final kiss goodbye? Once I'm done with you, he won't want you anymore."

Aimee bit her bottom lip as she let out a shuddering breath. "If you think this is goodbye . . ."

"I'm being charitable, Red. Barrett and I can hobble you over and let you kiss his thigh. His legs are sticking out. Your knees aren't tied up. Might be kinda hot for a final kiss."

For his part, Cody just kicked violently at the underside of the dresser where he was pinned, unable to get the leverage he needed to shove it off him with only one good arm. "Aimee, just get out! I'm not . . . I can't . . ." He could barely even breathe under the weight of the hardwood over him.

"I want the kiss." Aimee finally said with a voice so small that she didn't recognize herself. *Cody. I'm going to Mark you. Save your strength so you don't pass out. The only way you can get out is if you can negotiate something.* Barrett hastily shoved her to her knees, and she hit the floor hard. She looked back as both the captors stared at her, Maggie smirking as she had to struggle her way to Cody's legs. *I love you. I won't give up if you won't.*

Never. I love you. Do it. He had hesitated before, but there was no part of his thoughts that didn't want a way out, a way to save his wife. She could hear his thoughts already churning through the pain of his shattered arm, trying to come up with things he would be willing to give up for sheer strength, for his arm to be healed. But the pain was blinding.

Aimee was in pain from the way she was bound, and she nearly face-planted into his thigh, but she kissed it soundly through his jeans. She had never given anyone the Mark before, and she was panicking with her arms bound, thinking back on what Tony had done to give it to her. He had just touched her, traced the lines, but her arms were bound. Could she even share it, under the circumstances? Did it take too long and the Hunters would notice?

Even as her thoughts flailed in the kiss to his jeans, she felt the presence of the Voice flare in her mind, more eager and insistent than she had ever felt it. Was it . . . excited? No, the Voice didn't experience emotion. But the rush of its presence through her was unmistakable, tingling under the kiss as if she had scalded Cody's leg in the frantic touch.

The Voice supplied the means of its own sharing, in a formula that leapt through her thoughts into Cody's. *I share with you the Mark of those empowered to hear. May the Voice bring you balance.*

She heard him hiss at the heat that came with the Mark but she slowly managed to sit up, thanks to yoga and stripping, making her more flexible than she would have been otherwise. "I love you, Cody." She cried the words as Barrett brought her to her feet in the most painful way he could have, wrenching her upward by her bound arms.

"Alright, Red. Time for business." Maggie taunted as she readied her knife. "You're gonna tell me who helped you get away, and who helped you hide from us. Or I'll carve it out of you."

Cody's head swam in pain and light and shadows, and there was nothing feigned about the howl of pain that escaped from him.

What do you desire?

I desire this fucking arm to be fucking healed, I'll deal with the pain of it later, the same as you did for Aimee's gunshot yesterday. Just spread it out to a dull ache for however long is fair.

The pain of such a healing at such a low threshold will last for not less than three years. Do you accept the terms?

Cody could hear the Hunters threatening Aimee somewhere he couldn't see, could hear her crying out at something he couldn't stop. *Yes, I accept, I fucking accept, heal it already!*

Unseen by the Hunters or Aimee, the dresser rose a few

inches as Cody's arm knit itself back together with an agonizing squelch that drew a fresh howl of pain from Cody in spite of the improvement.

Alright, Voice. Now, for my next trick . . .

* * * * *

Maggie had been serious when she decided to carve the truth out of Aimee. She was pressed down over a shitty trunk in Cody's bedroom, the sharp knife lingering and digging deeper at the most painful points where her screams were loudest.

It *felt* like hours passed for Aimee as Maggie carved her own name in Aimee's arm, completing a new letter every time Aimee declined to give any answers for the questions asked.

Who are you with?

Who helped you?

Are there more of you around here?

Who Marked you?

Is anyone watching you?

Where is the hideout?

Aimee's arm was dripping with blood and flayed open behind her, still tied behind her back. She didn't answer a single question asked of her, but as she started to pass out from the pain, Maggie's knife was at her neck again.

"No, no, no, Red. You don't get to pass out on me. Wakey, wakey. I need some answers or next I'm taking off your fingers. Maybe I should start with the one that has this pretty new ring." Maggie glanced over at Barrett but he just looked bored with the redhead. "Do we keep trying? Haul her off somewhere?"

"We should haul her off, I'm thinking. There's a chance, though not much of one, that someone in this shithole thinks the cops are worth calling. They'll have done it by now with all the screaming, if they're going to. Better to get her gagged and hauled off somewhere else for the rest."

"I guess so." Maggie wiped off her blade before she shredded one of the blankets in the room to create a gag. She tied it around the redhead's mouth tight and looked over at Barrett again. "Is the husband unconscious now?"

"He must be, he's not moving or howling anymore." Barrett considered kicking the man just for the fun of it, but with only his legs visible, there wasn't even a clear shot at the man's crotch for a dick-stomp, otherwise he was sure the redhead would've taken the open window while she had it.

"Let him bleed out here, testament to Vegas police response time. Come on, girl, don't act like this is your first time about to be face-down in a trunk." He took another strip that Maggie had carved out and blindfolded her.

Aimee couldn't even whimper or struggle as they blindfolded her and pulled her off the chair. She felt her body hauled over someone's shoulder, but she was so close to passing out that she couldn't try to decipher what was happening by sound. *Cody, I'm so scared . . .*

Just waiting for you to be clear of the room, baby. I'm honestly not sure what this is going to be like, but I'm definitely not getting back my security deposit.

As soon as Maggie manhandled her out into Cody's living room, it sounded like the bedroom behind them exploded.

The dresser was thrown from the floor across the room to impact the shoddy drywall around the space formerly known as his bedroom closet, sending the bed flying with it and crashing through the timbers with a crash that shook the entire slum. Cody leapt up from the floor and stumbled, both arms clearly and suddenly unbroken. Another leap sent him rocketing like a meteor at Barrett and Maggie, colliding with them both like a freight train and bearing them to the floor with a punch each. He spared a moment to turn around and rip Aimee's restraints off with both bare hands, though the plastic cut into his palms a bit as he tore at it.

"Get the gu . . ." was all he got out before a gunshot rang

out and hit him in the leg, at which he turned around and returned to the fight, momentarily prioritizing Barrett, who had been the one to fire the shot.

Aimee's arms were shaky and the one bleeding profusely was barely able to move without blinding pain. She pulled off the blindfold with her usable arm, but both her arms had been restrained so harshly that it was painful.

Aimee pulled the gag down off her mouth, but Maggie was barreling after her with a knife, all intention of taking her alive forgotten. Aimee threw herself out of the way of Maggie's deadly attack, but she didn't have a weapon or the strength to do anything except try to run.

The fight between Cody and Barrett was as brief as it was brutal. Barrett did his best to back away and try to keep out of Cody's reach, having clearly had a problem with strength in the Marked before, but he had been caught too far off his guard.

Cody managed to grab his hand and divert the next gunshot he fired off, but instead of throwing it aside, Cody just squeezed down on the man's hand, crushing the bones and part of the metal structure of the gun itself as Barrett's firing hand turned to agonizing jelly.

Barrett rolled away as he cradled his hand, but Cody was too fast, already leaping the distance to the door to pick Barrett up by the back of his shirt. The fabric ripped as Cody spun him bodily through the air, hurling him face-first through the living room window. Glass and dry-rotted wood exploded outward from it, and Barrett's writing form sailed a dozen feet past the sill into thin air before his fall to the ground below began.

Maggie managed to get to the redhead and hold a knife to her throat before the hulk husband could get to her. She had Aimee by the throat, and fresh blood was dripping down Aimee's chest. "I'll kill her, you fucked up piece of shit. Both of you are demons and the world is a better place without you. I'd rather keep her alive for information, but I don't mind cutting her open right now and watching her bleed out."

Cody was breathing heavily as he stared the woman down, but he didn't look away as he leaned down to one side, picking up a splintered piece of wood from the wreckage that had spilled in from the other room. "The way I see it, we're not the ones out here hunting other people for sport, bitch. I think your definition of demons needs some work."

"You just shattered your apartment and tossed my partner to his death. Try harder to convince me you're not a demon." Maggie taunted as she pressed hard enough into Aimee's throat that Aimee whimpered. "Seems like you're into making deals now. I won't kill her right away if you leave now."

"I'm fond of gambling. Sort of the reason I ended up in Vegas, if we're being honest." He looked at her sideways, moving a few steps to the side. "Only reason you're still standing is because luck's never been particularly on my side when it comes to darts." His eyes moved from Maggie's to Aimee's as his newly-strengthened fingers twitched at the splintered closet fragment in his hand.

Aimee, through the haze of pain, met Cody's eyes momentarily and she took a small breath as she used her luck pact, hoping that Cody's good luck wouldn't mean bad luck for herself and the knife at her throat. She didn't bob her head or give him any other indication other than the silent movement of her lips mouthing the word "now".

As soon as he saw her mouth the word, Cody kicked one foot to send part of the coffee table flying toward the wall just to make Maggie flinch, then threw the dart in his hand as hard as his considerable strength permitted, aiming for Maggie's exposed side beneath the arm holding the knife.

The knife at Aimee's throat fell away and clattered to the floor when the dart embedded itself into her captor's arm, and as Maggie screamed, Aimee collapsed to the floor. Aimee sent the knife away and toward Cody, but now both her neck and her arm were bleeding and she didn't know how much more she could take. She heard Maggie swearing and screaming as she tried to crawl away from the fight.

Maggie had to use considerable strength to pull out the dart, and blood gushed as she reached for her gun. Fuck the knife. "You motherfucking piece of shit!" She opened fire haphazardly, not caring at the moment who would fall victim to her gunshots as long as someone suffered for it.

Speed carried Cody across the room quickly as Aimee fell and more shots rang out. He didn't stop to notice whether the pain in his side and in his shoulder were from gunshots. The strength surging through him was distracting.

He slapped aside the gun so hard he could feel Maggie's fingers crack under the force between his hand and the gun metal, then followed with a single punch through the woman's face. It hurt his hand to crunch through so much solid bone at once, but he watched her fall as he shook it out, her body beginning to twitch from the brain damage she clearly suffered from a dozen shattered fragments all embedded backward into what remained of her skull.

He didn't waste much time watching to make sure she was dead, hurrying over to check on Aimee after her fall.

Aimee looked up at Cody from where she collapsed on the floor, but she was afraid to try and talk, since she didn't know how deeply the knife had cut into her throat. Everything hurt. *You saved me. It's so hard to keep my eyes open, though.* He could tell, acutely, how much pain she was in and she was fading fast. *You should call the Covenant . . . let them know . . .*

They've got no reason to listen to me, I wouldn't know how to even get in contact with them. I can take this. You contact them. She could already hear him negotiating with the Voice in his own mind, though the specifics of the communication weren't open to her. The Voice kept its deals private unless explicitly told to do otherwise, it seemed.

Cody, you have to be careful, it will take too much away from you. Aimee closed her eyes since it felt good to close them. *I can't lose you. Please.*

You're not losing me. All I'm taking from you is some injuries and some blood loss. I'll tell the Voice to put it on the tab I started with fixing the arm. He leaned down and kissed her gently, either holding himself back considerably or suddenly very weak.

Cody nearly collapsed next to her as she felt her wounds closing and consciousness returning, as her injuries transferred to Cody's significantly-larger body.

"Cody." She wheezed out of fear as he nearly collapsed next to her, and while she felt immediately better, she rolled over to inspect him. He didn't look great either, and there was definitely a bullet wound in his side. "Oh god. Oh god." She whimpered as she looked around, spotting either his burner phone or hers on the floor, but it looked intact. She scrambled to it and dialed, not knowing who or if anyone would answer, especially after how she had spoken to Darius.

The line rang only once before it stalled and beeped a few times, before it was finally answered. She had spoken to Zeke only a few times during her residence with the Covenant, but she recognized his voice. The man was deeply unpleasant and frankly insulting most of the time, so there wasn't much reason to talk with him any more than absolutely necessary. "I thought Darius was going to talk to you? You're still calling me from inside the city, so what is it you want?"

"They came after us. They're dead." She croaked as though she had been screaming for hours. Maybe she had. Maybe her voice would never return. "We're at Cody's apartment if someone wants the bodies . . . I'm calling 911. He might be dying." She looked over at Cody. He was breathing, but he was still bleeding from his side.

"Do not call 911. Casey is faster. He's my next phone call, then Lydia and the Porters. Stay there and keep him alive, they'll be there shortly." He hung up the phone without waiting for her to respond, and the line went dead in the too-quiet apartment.

Cody just squeezed her hand, much weaker than he

typically was, his fingers barely able to squeeze hers. "So this . . . is what it feels like . . . not to fight, for a while." His breathing was deep, at least, as his heart rate slowed down, eyes closed against the hissing pain in his side and leg.

Aimee leaned into him, her forehead pressed into his temple. She was crying as she draped herself over him, especially since she had never seen him so weak, not even when he first returned to her only days ago. It felt like a lifetime ago. "I love you so much. Someone is coming." She ran her fingers across his forehead and his face as she cried.

* * * * *

Outside the apartment, in a nondescript four-door at the back of the parking lot, the passenger's head moved slightly while talking on the phone held up to his ear.

"I counted thirteen total. One initial volley of two, then a whole lot more in a secondary flash. But that was after somebody put what looks like a bedpost or a dresser corner right out through the wall and siding of the place." He didn't sound either happy or impressed about the outcome, his tone short and sharp and businesslike. "Something went wrong in there, and I rather doubt it went wrong in our favor."

The female voice that responded to him was smooth and unperturbed, but eager for more information. "I knew Barrett and Maggie were impulsive and eager but I really thought they had learned some patience."

The sigh that followed was as if she was speaking about petulant children. "Well, they did accomplish something, even if they did pay with their lives. Now you have visual proof of a Covenant. Any sign of anyone recognizable?" Jade, their boss, had a vested interest in a particular party. A mysterious man who was almost impossible to pinpoint, but she was convinced that most large covenants that aimed for peace instead of chaos belonged to Sin in some way. "Or a large and imposing presence?"

"Nothing so far, but I do my best to keep an eye out for large and imposing presences, as a rule. I'm going to check out of here back to Barrett and Maggie's last checkpoint in the unlikely event that they had something there they were working from. I'll let you know if I'm followed."

"Good. Anything else you find, I want to know it all. We need to proceed carefully in this city." Jade looked at a map above her desk and drew a big star on Las Vegas. They would be back, and next time they would be ready.

THIRTEEN

Lydia got the panicked phone call from Casey with wind blasting past the speaker of his phone. The fact that he maintained a grip on it at all meant he had slowed down significantly just to talk to her. It was a short conversation, a panicked burst that Aimee and Cody needed medical assistance at an address on the south side of town and nothing more.

Rushing out the door of her apartment, Lydia found an inhumanly tall presence sitting on the steps leading down to the lot where her car was parked. Sin turned his head slightly as she came down the steps, not quite looking at her because he knew how his eyes unsettled her. "Do you mind if I tag along?"

Lydia put a hand to her chest at her surprise, but she should have known that Sin's appearance never came with a warning. "You really shouldn't give me a heart attack when I'm responsible for healing. It doesn't bode well for those who need it." She chastised lightly as she nodded toward her car. "Tag along if you want. I'm in no position to say no."

She smiled gently as they jogged toward her car, but her smile faded quickly. "I just got back and she's gone. Darius and Sophia wouldn't tell me much of anything except she wasn't going to be inducted. She's one of my closest friends. My roommate."

"I'll catch you up on the ride. You know where you're going?" Sin somehow fit into her passenger seat, which in itself had to be some act of magic.

"Yeah, I've picked her up from Cody's place a few times. He lives in a, um, difficult part of the city." Lydia didn't have Casey's speed or his accuracy, but once the car was going, somehow along the way her path was always open and no one got in her way as she hurried.

"I didn't even know she was back with Cody. Darius sent me on assignment and I didn't have any personal effects with me. Last I knew I was still hating the dude for disappearing on her when she was clearly in love with him. Now he helped her kill some Hunters? I feel like I'm missing an important part of a movie plot."

"He fights in the kind of underground boxing matches that don't get advertised on television. He had a rather serious accident in such a match and was out of contact for some time, so she very reasonably thought that he had . . . what is the word the kids are using these days, 'ghosted' her?" Sin smiled, without looking quite at either Lydia or the road. "They were about to leave the city and run away together when the Hunters found them. They may change their mind about that now, they may not."

"I want to ask how you know that, but I think I know better. If you knew, though . . . you must have some reason for your silence?" She glanced at him momentarily before she sighed. "The psychic who enjoys keeping his secrets, you are. Sometimes I wish I could get some answers out of you."

"I spent a very long time thinking that things functioned more smoothly when people had answers." He smiled, not quite directly at her, but at least mostly in her direction. "That perspective didn't last. I could go into the ifs and conditionals, but those things didn't happen. Knowing about them after the fact doesn't help."

"I could use a nudge in my dating life, if you're feeling generous." She teased as they got closer to Cody's apartment. She could only go so fast, but they were close.

Sin's chuckle was both sympathetic and unhelpful. "That, interestingly, will require absolutely no assistance from me, for once. I will have business elsewhere when all that ends up happening, so please accept my congratulations in advance and my apologies for missing any events you may or may not choose to have."

Lydia shook her head and focused on the road leading up to Cody's complex. "Well, I guess that rules you out as my love interest, then. That's one step closer to the truth. And Darius, well." She had a lot of feelings she kept deep down about Darius and their precarious friendship. Or what could possibly be called a friendship. "He pulled himself out of the running. So two down."

"Only three billion, three hundred seventy-seven million, four hundred eighty-two thousand, six hundred and thirteen to go. Nineteen. Thirty-four. Thirty-three. Forty-seven . . ." he trailed off with a wave of his hand to dismiss the count.

"Too much information." She mumbled as they pulled up to the shoddy complex, and she threw the car into park. She bolted out of the car and toward Cody's building, where she could see others from the Covenant already cleaning up the scene.

Once she made it into Cody's apartment, she saw Casey and Isaac on the floor. "My god, it looks like a bomb went off!"

"Yeah, no, no bomb, that'd just be this newborn hulk over here." Casey motioned down to Cody on the ground beneath him, where he was holding pressure on the big man's leg while Isaac held pressure on his arm. "We did the best we could, but it's been a *minute* since I passed a first aid class. You wanna . . . ?"

"Yeah." Lydia got down beside Casey and touched along the points of Cody's worst wounds, and within moments they started to knit and heal, stopping the bleeding instantly. As soon as his wounds started closing, Lydia needed a moment to grit through the onset of pain, since she bore the brunt of it as a healer of the Covenant. The cost wasn't paid entirely by her, but a large portion of it was borne by her.

Once she caught her breath she crawled over to Aimee, and she felt nauseous at the carving on her friend's arm. "Holy shit, Ames." She pressed her fingers lightly into Aimee's wrist and the flayed arm started healing up. "We're gonna need a stretcher for the big guy. His wounds are pretty extensive and I can't mend him completely here. Not in this shithole."

Once the bleeding was basically staunched for both of them, it was easier for Casey and Isaac to maneuver Cody onto a stretcher they assembled from the back of Lydia's car. Casey couldn't pick up even half the man, but Sin was on hand to help Isaac lift it and get Cody outside.

"Aimee? Aimee, can you hear me?" Casey was pacing the apartment, looking over the devastation and clearly trying to follow something, unsuccessfully.

Aimee groaned into consciousness, but she tried to sit up too quickly, and she cried out in pain for multiple reasons. Her voice was still ragged and hoarse. "Casey? Cody? Where is Cody?"

"He's alive, he's outside in the back of Lydia's car. You'll see him soon. I need to know, where is the other one?" Casey was darting around the apartment between comments to listen to her and keep looking at the same time. "Because this one, this one's right here," he pointed down to where Maggie's body had been smashed into the floor, "but I can't find the other one. There were two, right?"

"He threw him out." Aimee said as she gestured vaguely in the direction of the broken window.

Casey was already at the window, looking out over the trashed backside of the apartment complex for any sign of the man's body. "There's nobody back here." Casey ran quickly out the door and down the stairs, racing through the back of the complex faster than anyone's eyes could follow before coming back, breathing heavily. "I found where he landed, but he's not there."

Aimee looked groggy but she didn't know what else to say. "I don't know how anyone would have survived that."

"I certainly wouldn't have." Casey agreed, still looking around at the shattered apartment and wondering how in the world anyone outside the covenant was going to come in and not think a bomb had gone off in a random Vegas slum.

"He won't be a problem." Sin said quietly as he came back in the door with Isaac and the stretcher, in case Aimee needed it. "Others might, but he won't, at least for the time being." It only took a few of his extended steps to cross the room to get to Aimee, and he crouched down beside her with an odd, faint smile on his face. "Can you walk, Mrs. Saunders? Or would you prefer the use of the stretcher as well?"

"I think I can walk. It was my arm . . ." She looked at her arm and there was some faint scarring, but it wasn't a mangled mess like before. She was temporarily confused, since she didn't think anyone would pay the cost to heal her. "Who are you?" Her voice was still almost nonexistent, but she was trying not to worry about it.

"I'm called Sin these days." He offered her a hand up and then held onto her to make sure she was steady on her feet. "I'm an old friend of Darius and Sophia's. I was in the neighborhood and thought I'd come along to help out."

"You must be really old to be an old friend of theirs." She glanced back at Casey, but he gave her a reassuring nod to let her know that she was okay. "I'm really worried about Cody, and as you can see, I can't really talk . . . are you here to investigate for Darius or something? I didn't tell them anything."

"No, no, nothing like that. Investigation is not my skill set." The same odd smile quirked at his lips as he shook his head. "I'm only here to help. I think as a start, I'll handle the disposal of the woman's body, if that's agreeable. It won't do to have her found by the apartment managers or other authorities in this kind of state in Mr. Saunders' apartment."

She was kind of late in realizing that he had called her Mrs. Saunders until she heard him reference Cody, and her eyes widened a little more. "Wait, how did you know?" She looked down at the ring on her hand, but . . . "I've never met you. Have I?" Her ears were still ringing and her head was throbbing, but she was sure she would remember someone who looked like this guy.

"No, I don't believe you ever have." He put a hand on her shoulder, and the ringing in her head reduced somewhat, allowing the room to clarify slightly around her. "But congratulations all the same. The two of you will take good care of each other in days to come, I'm certain of it." His smile afterward was less mysterious and more . . . kind, though still not precisely an expression that could be called happy for its own sake.

He moved away from her before saying anything else, nodding down to Isaac and Casey. "Did you happen to find any car keys on the deceased?"

"Yeah, they're over here." Casey blinked to one side of the room and back with a violent jingle of a set of keys that had been placed on one of the few clear and undisturbed surfaces in the room. "I checked them in the lot, they go to a shitty silver four-door parked a block east."

"Thank you, Mr. Nielsen." Sin took the keys and proceeded into the bedroom, to begin stripping what was left of Cody's sheets in which to carry what was left of Maggie.

Aimee watched the mysterious stranger for a moment longer before she turned her attention back to Casey and Isaac. "Where did they take Cody? Zeke told me not to call 911, but I don't know where else we could go."

"He's in the car, come on. We'll get you two back to the compound and get you fixed up." Casey stayed close beside her to guide her out of the apartment, and stayed a step down from her in the rickety stairwell just to make sure she made it down safely.

Aimee held onto Casey's arm tentatively at first, but then a little tighter. "I didn't know if I would ever get to see you again. I wanted a chance to say goodbye, but you were asleep and they didn't give me any options. I'm glad I get to see you again, at least."

"It's good to see you too, Ames. I was . . . well, I've been asleep for most of this, honestly, but I'm glad you're alright. Darius and Sophia want to see you, once the two of you are patched up. Both of you." He escorted her to the passenger seat of Lydia's car, where she could see Cody laid out but stable-looking in the back seat, his chest rising and falling evenly.

"We'll stick around here and do what we can to clean up the place. The Porters are on their way over with the rest of the cleanup crew. We'll make sure the place gets reset and pack out your, um, your husband's belongings. We'll drop them at your house for the time being, if that's alright."

"My house? Is it even still mine? It was a crime scene, last I knew." Aimee definitely sounded bitter, but it wasn't Casey's fault. She got into the car and as soon as she saw Lydia, she gave her other best friend a small smile. It was bittersweet to see Casey and Lydia, knowing they were a part of something she was denied, and that she only had a short time to share with them. "We had a room at the Bellagio that I paid for. Maybe we can stay there until we're ready to leave."

Lydia glanced at Casey as he leaned in to make sure Aimee was all situated. "Just bring it all back to the complex, Case. I'll talk to Darius."

"Will do. Be safe. We'll see you soon. Don't get shot any more. It doesn't go with your complexion at all." Casey shut the door for her with a subdued smile.

Lydia looked over her friend before she pulled out and drove quietly through the city to get to the complex. She had a lot she wanted to say to Aimee, she wanted to apologize for not being there when her friend needed her, but in the end silence won out the entire drive.

Aimee checked on Cody obsessively as they drove through the city, although he appeared to be stable and he wasn't bleeding anymore. The silence stretched on as Covenant members helped her and Cody out of the car, and Aimee tailed behind Cody the whole time as they carried him to the apartment she previously shared with Lydia, although she supposed it was only Lydia's now. It was eerie to see her own belongings right where she left them before she was relegated to her house for lockdown, and Cody was even placed in her room on her bed, which was all still untouched.

Lydia busied herself with healing Cody, but she became visibly weakened the longer it took. Once she and Cody couldn't handle any more tampering, Lydia sat on the edge of Aimee's bed.

"He'll be okay. Everything is all fixed, except the things that he negotiated prolonged healing for. The weakness also seems to be a price he has to pay because he negotiated it. I can't really get around that." Lydia looked over at her friend and sighed. "I wish I would have been here. I'm sorry I wasn't, even though I didn't choose to be gone. Darius and Sophia made the wrong decision, turning you out. I argued with Darius about it as soon as I found out."

Aimee looked at her exhausted friend and scooted closer to give Lydia a hug. "We made it through. Although I do agree that they made the wrong decision. They don't seem the type to particularly care, though. They should know that attitude makes enemies and not friends."

"You think they would know." Lydia laughed softly before she convinced herself to get up. "I need to go take a nap, but you both will be okay. I'll get rid of that ugly scar on your arm when I wake up."

Aimee gave Lydia another hug before she watched her friend shuffle away tiredly into her own room. Once Lydia was gone, Aimee closed the door and crawled up onto her bed and behind Cody's large body. "I'm here. And we made it. Somehow."

Cody was barely conscious, and couldn't move except to put one arm behind him to hold her weakly against his back. "I . . . feel like I got hit by a truck. Your friend's healing packs a punch. Or maybe this is what I bargained for." He groaned, holding her tighter, or attempting to, and failing. "I could sleep for a week."

"Then you sleep for a week." She peppered him with kisses as she started crying again. "I love you. I'll be right here when you wake up."

* * * * *

Sin pulled Maggie's car off the side of the road twenty miles outside the city and put it in park, sighing once as he looked over at the body-bag behind him in the back seat.

"You didn't deserve to end like this." He sat there in the kind of silence only a desert could provide. "The gas chamber, the electric chair, maybe. Stoning would have worked too, but that's fallen out of fashion lately. Whatever the way, you didn't deserve this."

He got out of the car and pulled the body bag out onto the sandy ground, picking Maggie's body up effortlessly and placing her in the driver's seat. A gesture from him and most of the gore that had been a part of her face ended up on the inside of the windshield.

He took a step back from the car and sighed as he put his hands in his pockets, his multicolored hair swirling around his face in the cold evening breeze.

"You deserved much worse than this. But this is what you get."

He shrugged, and as his shoulders fell, the gas pedal went down inside the car, urging it into motion again. Fifty, sixty, seventy miles an hour over the desert floor, the car finally hit a hundred and twelve miles an hour before it went up and over a slight rise in the rocky ground. It came down nose-first on the other side, immediately crushing what was left of Maggie's body into an unrecognizable mass of blood and bone as the car caught fire.

The sound echoed out over the desert, but Sin knew no one had heard it. There was a perfectly straight line of tracks headed out from the highway to the crash site, and in twelve hours and twenty three minutes, the authorities would be along to identify Maggie as having fallen asleep at the wheel on her way to Vegas.

Open, closed, simple. Why couldn't every problem in the world be so simple to solve?

He stared at the small car fire for a while, burning angry orange and blue under the light of the half-moon in a clear sky, before he finally turned around and started walking back to the highway.

There would be someone there to give him a ride back into the city, and there would be plenty to do once he got back. He just wanted to walk alone in peace for a while, to give himself some time to process the constant flow of information through his mind. See where his path would lead from there.

He felt something in the world shimmer near him, and for the briefest of moments, he tensed for a fight, but then he recognized the presence that had appeared. He stopped walking altogether, closing his eyes with a sigh encompassing thousands of years of constant frustration.

"I thought you hated deserts." He said without looking behind him.

"You know, you're right. I do. But I enjoy seeing your face much more than I hate standing in a dry, hot, dirty place." The woman behind him came up to his side quickly, her long, black hair billowing in the wind ahead of the rest of her.

She was tall, though not quite his freakish height, and an impossible kind of beautiful. Her eyes shimmered black and gold like the Mark that glittered on the inside of her right wrist. "Especially the way your eyes roll back in your head and your face contorts when I tell you not to mess with other people's paths."

He laughed at that, but it was a sound as harsh as the desert around them. "Hiya, pot, I'm kettle. It's incredibly unpleasant to see you again." He stared down at her with eyes that were the match of hers, one of the few people in the world who could actually look down on her at all. "What do you want, Izzy? And more importantly, what are you doing in Vegas? You hate Americans."

"Oh, I want so, so many things." She twirled around as they walked, which she knew annoyed him further, but she enjoyed annoying him. "I used to want *you* once. I would cry for you, you know. You rarely responded to my distress, not quite like I respond to yours."

"The last time you responded to my distress, you lit a neighborhood on fire and killed fourteen innocent people." He glared over at her as he walked toward the highway, knowing better than to think he could just dismiss her, much as he wanted to sometimes. "And the last time you cried for me was when your lover in Johannesburg left you for another woman. You'll have to forgive me if that's not the kind of thing I come running to make better."

"We're still bound together." She glared at him as she thought about the very occasion that he referenced, and how much pain she had suffered then. Alone. "And you have no one to blame but yourself for that."

He stopped walking to return the look she gave him, but there was more sadness in his eyes than anger. "I've never blamed myself for that fact, Izzy. But you go on blaming me for it. I can accept that from you."

An impulse from thousands of years away still welled up inside him, to reach out and just hold the woman in front of him. To try and repair what had been broken between them for the vast majority of the centuries of their lives. But time and experience had shown him repeatedly that such a thing was worse than impossible. If he ever managed it, it was likely to destroy them both. "What are you really doing here?"

"It's part of my job to keep track of you." She said simply as she put more distance between herself and the man next to her. "Especially when you put yourself in danger for someone else. You don't know everything or see everything, like you think you do."

She tossed a pointed look back over her shoulder at the smoke starting to curl up into the night sky from the burning car. "Take care of this Hunter's partner and move on, Sin. If you linger here, you're going to end up in more pain than you bargained for." Which, she knew from experience, was a lot. "I'll stay and watch, if you decide to linger."

"In that case, I'll make sure to be elsewhere. Just to avoid the 'you standing around watching' part." The highway came into sight as they came over a low ridge, and he stopped, since he didn't want anyone to see the two of them together if he could avoid it. He also knew Izzy wanted nothing less than to be associated with him publicly.

He looked her in the eye directly, even though he knew better than to fully engage with the woman on anything. "I see more than you might think. I see where things are going, and I see what you're doing." He turned his back on the highway, looking at her evenly since he was standing at a distance down the slight hill. "You can walk away from it at any time. I would beg, but I know better."

"Begging would be amusing. Go ahead, if you like." She walked up to him after he stopped walking and kissed his cheek almost tenderly. "I'll find you when you least expect me."

"You always seem to." He put a hand up to the side of her face when she pulled away, millenia of complicated emotions in his eyes. The brief touch, though, was the extent of the affection that he returned. Without saying goodbye, he turned and walked away toward the highway, looking for a trucker who was likely to give him a lift as Izzy blessedly disappeared again with the same shimmer to the air that always accompanied her.

Three miles down the road, he found his guy. Doing overtime to try and make some extra money to pay for his wife's anniversary present in two months, and due to break down on the side of the road in a week. The man was going to have to wait for hours for someone to pick him up, and waste hours more getting his rig repaired. But there was someone on the way down that highway in a week that could pick him up and help save the driver's time and his job.

With a single thought, both situations were altered, and the trucker pulled over to the side of the road, popping his door open for Sin, the same way the driver in a week would pull over to help him in return. "You need a lift into town?"

Sin smiled as he jumped up into the passenger seat. "I do, actually. What a coincidence."

* * * * *

A trip to the morgue was fun for no one, even for assassins like the Hunters. Two people waited in the lobby while Barrett was pushed in a wheelchair back through the pristine hallways, the smell of death lingering in the air. A refined-looking doctor took over when they got to the examination room, and a body lay underneath a sheet, taunting Barrett as soon as he entered the room.

"There's not much to identify, really, but we need to be sure." The doctor stated softly as they approached the table. "There was identification, but you are the last listed emergency contact from old records, about a year ago. Margaret has no next of kin to contact."

"No, she doesn't. I'm it." He stared at the sheet for a moment in angry silence, then made a motion with the one hand he had left that still halfway worked. "Get me closer and let me see her."

The doctor pushed his wheelchair closer before she peeled back the sheet. Maggie's body was a mangled mess based on impact, but it hadn't actually burned too much. "The strange thing is that there wasn't much structural damage to the steering wheel of the car, but her skull tells another story. We're still not sure how her head took so much damage."

Barrett looked over what was left of his partner for a long time in silence, then moved the sheet covering her to look at one of her knees just to be sure. A great deal of her appearance could have been faked, but he knew her scars intimately enough to recognize them when he saw them.

"It's her." He confirmed without addressing the doctor's questions. It didn't matter how her skull had been turned to powder. She was just as dead. "It was always her intention to be cremated. Whatever you have to do to prep her for that, do it."

"Of course." The doctor answered just as politely all over again before she covered up the remains and walked across the room. "The car was swept, of course, but no indication of anything amiss. This was found in the car, it has her initials, so I'm assuming it belonged to her."

There was a bag with Maggie's knife inside, and she handed it to Barrett. "It was all of her personal effects that they could recover. Let me get you back to your friends." She took over his wheelchair again as soon as he had the knife in his lap, and she wheeled him back out to the lobby.

He didn't touch the knife at first, but on the long ride back through the halls, his hand slowly migrated to it as if of its own accord. The doctors had already laid his own condition out for him clearly. He would never walk again, his right arm would probably never regain full functionality, and one of his lungs had been badly punctured by one of his own shattered ribs, forcing them to remove a portion of it. He was half of himself, and Maggie was gone.

Not only that, he knew what was written on the faces of the two who had been sent to pick him up. They were there to take over what he and Maggie had started, that much was obvious, but they were also there to see that he was put on a plane back to Amsterdam, with an escort to make sure he got there.

He was going away for a long time, and there was no part of him strong enough to fight the consequences of his actions.

All the same, the fingers of his left hand closed around the knife until his knuckles ached.

He didn't know how. He didn't know how long it would take. Maybe the rest of his life.

But someday, he would come back to Vegas. The job wasn't finished.

EPILOGUE

Cody crossed the parking lot, shaking out his hands as he approached the car. "You know there's a jack in the Evans's garage, right?"

"Yeah, but you were just walking by, and this'll only take a minute." Hank, the covenant groundskeeper, was also a sometime-mechanic when things went wrong, and had a set of tools at the ready to quickly change out a tire that had blown out.

"Fine, fine." Cody stepped down off the curb and reached under the car to grab the frame, concentrating briefly to lift the car up with one hand until the wheel in question was well off the ground. "Make it quick, alright? This ain't free."

"Alright, alright! Just hold it still." Hank made quick work of the tire change, tightening up the bolts on it like he was auditioning for a pit crew.

Cody looked away at the apartment nearby as Hank worked, holding the car absently as he waved at Aimee with his free hand. "Hey, sleepyhead, is it that time? I forgot what time our appointment was."

"Right before lunch, and we have plans afterwards!" Aimee was in cutoff jeans and a halter top, with her ruby hair in two braids. Everything about the woman would grab anyone's attention, although most of the Covenant was used to her by now. Parents of teenagers still grumbled from time to time, but Aimee and Cody were well-loved and accepted. At least she fucking hoped so, this time.

"Plans? What plans do we have afterward?" Clearly, whatever other talents Cody had, a solid memory was not one of them.

"If you can't remember, I'm not telling you." Aimee jogged her way to him and stood by as he showed off his strength. "Don't burn out on me this early, stud."

"I spent most of last week down at half capacity. I'll be fine for a long while yet. Are you about done?" He seemed to remember he was holding up a car, and turned his attention from his extraordinarily sexy wife back to the covenant handyman.

"Almost there, just one more . . . there. All good. You can go ahead and put it down now."

As soon as Cody put down the car, Aimee jumped onto his back and held onto him like her life depended on it. "We're going out to the house, remember?" They decided to buy land and have a house built, completely separate from the Covenant . . . just in case. "They finished the floors yesterday. We can start moving in, but I want to go see. We haven't seen it in weeks."

"Oh, I forgot they got the floors done. I thought we were picking out paint or something." He had enjoyed the process of designing the house with her, and thought he might try his hand at some of it on his own later on, but he had to admit, the details of the decorating process had gotten away from him. "I'm not working until tomorrow afternoon, so we can take some stuff over there and spend the night, unless the whole place smells like glue or something."

"Yes! I want to do that." Aimee grinned and kissed his cheek and neck as he carried her to Darius' office in the complex. "I'll pack a picnic and an air mattress."

"Whatever air mattress you grab, make sure to talk to it first and make sure it has a death wish." He grinned as he carried her, shifting her up higher on his back as he climbed the steps to the central building of the compound.

They had waited six months for the summons they received that morning, but now that it had finally arrived, Cody wasn't sure how he felt about it. He had met with Darius and Sophia only a few times, and every interaction had left him feeling more terrified of them than the last.

Even so, the rest of the covenant was full of good people, and Cody was fond of most of their neighbors. All of them were just trying to live their lives as simply and calmly as possible, while carrying around magic everywhere they went. It wasn't an easy balance to strike. "We're sure about this, right?"

"I think so." Aimee wrapped her arms leisurely around his thick neck. "We can't stay in Vegas if we don't join. And I don't want to leave. Casey and Lydia are basically my family." It wasn't long after Cody's recovery that Aimee divulged as much information about her past that her life-altering pact had allowed, and Cody knew she had no family other than the family she made.

He knew truths about her that she could never explain to him before, and though there was a lot she could never tell anyone, she hoped he was satisfied in knowing that she had given him all that she could. Her past didn't matter to her anymore. He mattered to her more than anyone or anything. "But if you want to go somewhere else and sell our beautiful new house, I'd do it and follow you."

"We put a lot into that house." He agreed, ducking so that she wouldn't hit her head on the top of an archway. "And no, I don't want to leave Vegas. Not permanently, anyway. I still need to take you down to Tijuana sometime, that's still very much on."

He swung her around to set her down once they got closer to the main gathering hall of the covenant, and the stairs leading up to their leaders' apartments up above.

"Here goes nothing, then. Not just living with the mob anymore, but actually kissing the ring."

"I think the ring is a tattoo on your thigh." She smirked, since she was trying to be confident about the conversation ahead of them. "Are there nude beaches in Tijuana?"

"Official ones? No. Unofficial ones? We'll go and fucking make one for ourselves." He offered her his arm as if in escort on the way up the stairs, keeping his attention on her instead of the way ahead.

Aimee knocked, expecting the wait that always accompanied a meeting with Darius. He was never just . . . readily available. "Lookie here. It's Jacob."

Jacob was indeed ready on the door, and gave them one of his brief bows as he motioned them inside. "He is concluding a call at the moment, but he asked that I see you settled. I am just about to see to your drinks. Please." He shut the door behind them and headed over to the bar to begin mixing.

It had taken Aimee a few more visits to Darius's flat before learning to trust Jacob's selection of drinks, but it was trust well earned. He generally didn't take orders, but every drink he brought was satisfying in some way she hadn't known to ask for. Cody had quickly learned just not to ask questions.

"Picking our brains requires alcohol." She explained as she held firmly to her husband's hand. "It's not fun, really."

"I didn't really expect it to be, honestly." Cody didn't exactly look nervous, but there was nothing about Darius's unit that in any way set him at ease. Every instinct he had about the two leaders of their covenant told him that they were dangerous people. Possibly the most dangerous people he had ever met, and yet they surrounded themselves with, and seemed to genuinely care for, good and hard-working people. It was a contradiction that Cody didn't pretend to understand. "Anyway, it doesn't matter. I don't think there's much in my brain that's worth picking."

Aimee yanked him down into a searing kiss. "I don't

know, I like it every time I go picking into your brain. You have such dirty thoughts."

"Well hopefully he's not gonna go looking for *those*. I don't have any of those when it comes to him. So if that's the criteria for entry, we may have to go looking for some other real estate regardless." He grinned as Jacob delivered their drinks, unobtrusive as ever.

She took her drink from Jacob and took a sip before she looked away from Cody to smile at Jacob. "Compliments to the bartender as usual, Jacob." She tipped her drink toward him when she heard Darius' office door open.

"Forgive my tardiness, I was requesting an update on the status of the surviving Hunter." He closed the office door behind him and went to take his seat just as Jacob set his own drink down near him, without being acknowledged or seeming to expect acknowledgement from Darius. "His status remains unchanged. He appears to have been remanded to a long term care facility just outside of Amsterdam."

"It'd be simpler if his status was an unmarked grave somewhere, but I'll take it." Cody sipped at his drink without looking particularly comforted by the news. "You said before they're just gonna send more."

"They have sent several in the last six months since the attack, but none who have come close enough to any covenant holdings to make us nervous. The individuals you encountered were particularly . . . zealous, in a way that is atypical for their order. They are generally more methodical until they are certain, which makes them much more dangerous." Darius waved a hand. "But that is not today's concern. I'm glad to see both of you still here, rather than getting notice that you've chosen to pack your bags and find another place to put down roots."

"I told you once and I'll tell you again, this city is my home. Casey and Lydia are family to me. It was you who tried to kick me out, not the other way around." Aimee apparently wasn't completely over the fact that she'd been cut out, but she wasn't going to leave either.

"We had our concerns. I hope in time you are able to forgive us for the choice we made given our knowledge at the time. You will always be- at least partly- an unknown. But we can live with that, so long as you can live by our way of life here." Darius had never exactly apologized for what they had done, and it was clear he didn't think they had made a mistake. They had, however, cut down the probationary period in Cody's case to only half a year to help make up for the discrepancy and the hardship they had suffered as a result of being left out to dry.

"I've told you as much as I can. The limitations of my own pact make it impossible to tell you anything more." Aimee defended as she finished off her drink with the very arm that had been tortured when she was questioned by a psychopath. "You can see for yourself that my loyalty to this covenant was already tested when a Hunter carved her name into my skin. I'm not sure what else I can do."

"Loyalty is a lifetime in the proving. But that saying applies as much to me as it does to you." Darius admitted with a solemn nod. "We have that ahead of us yet, all of us. Which is why we are here today." He leaned forward over his knees with his hands open briefly toward them both.

"The limitations of your pact may prevent you from saying anything else regarding your past, Aimee, but in our case, it is prudence rather than a pact that keeps me or my sister from speaking in too much detail regarding our own past. But to be joined in this covenant, we find it practical that you know more about us, where we come from, and where our loyalties lie. If you can tolerate those arrangements and those facts of our purpose here, then we will be all too glad to admit you both to full fellowship."

"Okay . . ." Aimee responded cautiously, since she wasn't sure what exactly that would entail. "What does that mean? What do we need to do?"

Darius shook his head, and just looked between the two of them, the gold and shadows of the Voice's power tickling at the back of their minds as they found themselves caught up in the presence along with Darius's own mind.

Familiar scenes flowed first, images of the apartment complex and their secure floor at the Bellagio, ideas of the measures they had taken to secure their homes and a few other small pieces of the larger city against any kind of tampering or intrusion.

Unfamiliar places quickly followed, some of them in lush climates, some of them in snow, some of them on waterfronts. In each of them, there were communities built, safe havens overseen by others who bore the Mark, keeping a watchful eye on their environs. Some lived in luxury, some in relative simplicity. Some were separated from the world, some in the thick of it. As the images passed through their minds, the people in them changed, like watching fashions rewind through time, lines picked and chosen from passages of history to form a collage of interconnected life that was centuries in the making.

"Sophia and I have been alive for a very long time." Darius began, his tone just as understated as ever with such a revelation. "In that time, we have always endeavored to serve the Marked, to form relationships all across the world. We have fought wars, we have broken laws, and we have broken people. We would, and will, do the same again, if it becomes necessary, to protect our people."

Images of battlefields shone through both their minds, flat, desert expanses of blood and shattered life as far as the eye could see. They could see Darius, Sophia, and Jacob, all covered in blood and gore, wearing ancient armor with bloodied weapons discarded nearby. There were dozens of others around them, all recovering from the slaughter. Aimee and Cody could see in their eyes the echoes of their own violence as they caught their breath. Victory was only ever a reprieve, not a permanent state of affairs.

They're fucking old. Aimee said directly to Cody as she looked at Darius wide-eyed. "Is it . . . like a religion to you or something?"

"That is . . . one way of putting it." Darius agreed, letting the images fade for the time being. "Religion to people of our era was a very different matter than it is in this one. Our gods were rarely just distant concepts to us. They were present, and available. Often they were more like demons to be propitiated and satisfied than gods to be revered. But that was then. These days, we take care of people. And we try to help people live as close to the life they want as will not destroy them, or the ones they love."

"I definitely consider the Voice more demon than anything else." She chewed on her lip and stared at Darius a little closer. "The pact that changed my life was my biggest regret for so long." Aimee looked over at Cody before she continued. "Now I can say that I'm happy, even though the road to here was difficult and painful. Although I will probably never trust the Voice the way a lot of people do."

"Nothing about our covenant practices requires you to. Or to ever deal with the Voice again, if you choose not to. Some have come to us because they're looking for training on how to best utilize it, some because they just want a haven where they can help without being required to give more of themselves. If you, either of you, never make another pact with the Voice again, that is your right. We don't believe in forcing anyone to give of themselves against their will, in any respect." Darius' tone and voice were even, clearly well-practiced at the kind of pitch they were talking about.

"So what *do* you require? There has to be a price other than working at the properties owned by the covenant." Aimee wanted to get to the bottom of everything, good, bad, or ugly.

"Being a part of this covenant means that everyone's lives are bound together, as a single body. If one of us is harmed, all of us feel it, but all of us are bound up together to heal whatever happens. It is no small thing to be willing to make yourself a part of something like that, to protect strangers or people in the covenant you may not even like.

But it is the way we keep our people safe."

Darius took a small knife from his pocket and nicked the back of his arm so that they could see the injury. He neither flinched nor hesitated as he drew his own blood, but they could both see a small twitch of Jacob's own arm across the room. As the blood gathered on his skin, they could already see the cut healing, the wound knitting itself closed before their eyes.

"That's . . . wow." Aimee looked back and forth between Darius and Jacob before she said anything else. "I knew Lydia was a healer, but I wasn't sure how that worked or how she facilitated it without paying an insane price. I know the times Cody and I have helped each other were steep." Aimee paused. "Wait, what does that mean for something like childbirth or children? Cody and I definitely want to have kids. Someday."

"Lydia manages some of the ebb and flow of that pact more directly than most in the covenant aside from Sophia and myself." He nodded at her question, almost smiling. "Days on which someone in the covenant is giving birth are . . . interesting. And often rather uncomfortable. But again, Lydia helps to manage those. It's not her area of specialty, but she does her best to be on hand to help whenever someone in the covenant goes into labor."

"Lydia has a big role, it seems." She thought about her friend and reached out for Cody's hand. "I don't have any problems with any information you've shared or requirements you've stated."

Cody squeezed her hand, but he was looking less confident about the entire arrangement. "Where Aimee goes, I go." He stated unequivocally before looking back up at Darius. "But I'm not . . . I realize I fight for a living, and I'm good at it, but when I started doing that, I did it as a way to make money. The way your life looks . . . you've fought wars. I just want to make sure you're not still fighting one, or expecting us to fight one for you."

Darius was quiet a while after that question, as he

considered how to answer for once. "You aren't signing up to fight in any wars by joining this covenant, though I will, if necessary, ask you to fight to protect the others who are a part of it. Especially because you have a background in it already. The larger war to fight, though, will only involve you if you choose to involve yourself."

Aimee hesitated as well after considering Cody's question. "Can we leave this if we want to? Or once we're bound, we're bound?"

"Nothing will bind you here against your will. If you wish to leave, I am told the headache that comes after is fairly brutal, but you can do so whenever you choose. To re-bind someone to the covenant takes either me or Sophia. Though we enforce the same terms if you choose to leave." Darius's tone clearly wouldn't bend on that particular subject.

"Live by the rules or get out of Vegas, right. We remember those." Cody did his best to keep the anger out of his voice, since it had been six months, and they had gotten as close to an apology from Darius as the man had likely ever given.

He looked back at Aimee with a small nod as he squeezed her hand. *They certainly don't fuck around. This is a good thing to be a part of, for as long as it suits us. If things get weird, they get weird and we make plans somewhere else.*

Okay. I say we do it, then. She looked back at Darius and gave a nod. "Okay. I agree for my part, though I won't speak for Cody."

"Just like she said. I'm in. Not to fight a war, but I'm not against fighting when it's needed." Cody agreed, letting out a sigh afterward with the acceptance.

"I'm very glad to hear that from you both." Darius seemed relieved on his own, and slid forward in his chair, reaching out to take both their arms. The world took on undertones of gold and moving shadows that no one beyond the Marked would have been able to see, as if the lights and the darkness were moving to bind between the three of them, reaching out across the city to grasp the hundreds of others who lived their lives bound to the same covenant.

Almost immediately, Cody could feel some of the small aches of the morning, the slight lingering soreness in his arm and hands from lifting the car especially, lift from him by degrees as if it was being washed out of his system. It was a disorienting feeling, a slight headache coming and going almost before he noticed the twinge of pain that came with it. Had someone somewhere gotten a migraine and then lost it again just that fast? Cody couldn't bring himself to ask. "That . . . is new."

Aimee felt well-rested and energized, though she didn't have any lingering pains to worry about. She held tighter to Cody and took a deep breath once it all passed. "Definitely new. We can hear each other's thoughts, but that doesn't mean other people can hear us talking to each other, right? We take sexy talk to another level."

"Telepathy pacts tend to have that effect, especially on newlyweds." Darius's mouth curled up just slightly. "No, there are no bonds in this covenant's pact regarding sharing thoughts. I've seen very few true communes in my travels, and all of the ones I have seen that became functional are . . . disturbing, even to me. Your thoughts are your own."

Aimee visibly relaxed and held tight to Cody. "Is there anything else? Or are we official now?"

"You are official now." Darius rose to his feet slowly, as if he had to make a conscious effort at any moment to keep his movements from appearing aggressive. "We recommend that you stay more or less at home for the first week, until you've become accustomed to all the little twinges and scrapes that often come with the pact. They can sometimes be distracting and difficult to explain away easily if you're out in public the first few times you experience them."

Cody stood along with Aimee, scratching at his neck at the presence of someone's sore throat that came and went as quickly as he noticed it. "Darn. We'll just have to go into isolation for a while. What a terrible, terrible thing." His deadpan sarcasm very nearly got an eye roll from their dignified leader, but not quite.

Aimee was all too happy to get going, especially for their planned picnic and her planned seduction of her husband in their new house. "We're driving to our new house. We'll gladly stay out of sight for a week."

"Be safe, then, and welcome, formally. Have Zeke set an appointment for next Thursday and we'll discuss what to do with the two of you from here." Darius gave them both a nod on their way out the door, held by Jacob as always.

Once the door closed behind them, Aimee pulled Cody down into a rough kiss and kept kissing him until she was breathless. "What do you think? How do you feel?"

"I feel pretty good, actually. I can see what he means, though, there's a lot of random little . . . things. Like the neck just now? Did somebody just sleep on it wrong? And the knee? I don't know, there's too many to even keep up with, but they only last for a blink and they're gone."

Cody had made no secret of his own aversion to dealing with the Voice. He'd made no more pacts with it since the day he was Marked, aside from one to reciprocate her own ability to open their thoughts to each other, and one between the two of them to share their own injuries more freely. He didn't see the need. He had Aimee, and therefore he had everything he could have ever wanted. "What about you? Are you feeling alright? He showed us a lot."

"It will definitely take some getting used to." She looked up into Cody's eyes with a smile, though. "I'm glad to be out of limbo, honestly. I have you. We have a home." Aimee pulled him down into another searing kiss. *Everything I lost led me here. To you. I love you, Cody.*

No more losing things. He moved to put her back against the wall across from Darius's rooms, celebrating with her in a tease of what was to come for the rest of their week ahead. *I love you too. Let's get out of here. I sort of imagine our ancient bosses would take exception if I were to fuck you on their doorstep.*

They would be lucky to see such a sexy show. She teased as he held her up, his hands on her ass, and her legs around his waist. *Let's go. Our future awaits.*

ABOUT THE AUTHOR

D. Brumbley is a husband/wife duo from Kansas City who spend most of their time in each other's heads. In suburbia the duo lives in a simple house with a dog and two feisty kiddos. One half of the duo loves football, baseball, libraries, and romance. The other half of the duo likes D&D, Fantasy novels, Marvel Comics, and cheesecake. A country girl and an east coast boy met online, became best friends, fell in love, and somewhere along the way decided that telling stories together would be fun.

Best. Decision. Ever.